Alexander John Arbuthnot

Major-General Sir Thomas Munro

Bart., K.C.B., Governor of Madras, a memoir

Alexander John Arbuthnot

Major-General Sir Thomas Munro
Bart., K.C.B., Governor of Madras, a memoir

ISBN/EAN: 9783337402372

Printed in Europe, USA, Canada, Australia, Japan

Cover: Foto ©Andreas Hilbeck / pixelio.de

More available books at **www.hansebooks.com**

MAJOR-GENERAL

SIR THOMAS MUNRO

BART., K.C.B.

GOVERNOR OF MADRAS

A MEMOIR

BY

SIR ALEXANDER J. ARBUTHNOT, K.C.S.I.

LONDON

KEGAN PAUL, TRENCH & CO., 1, PATERNOSTER SQUARE

1889

PREFACE.

THE following pages are a reprint, with but few alterations, of the Memoir which was prefixed to the compilation of Sir Thomas Munro's Minutes, edited by me in 1881. It has been more than once suggested that the Memoir should be published in a separate volume for the use of those readers who would be interested in the career and opinions of the distinguished Soldier-Statesman of whom the Memoir treats, but might not care to peruse at length the official writings which are contained in the larger work. In this Memoir, as I said in the preface to the larger work, I have drawn largely, not only upon the Minutes and other official papers, but also upon the private letters published by the late Mr. Gleig in his Life of Munro; for the Minutes, without the aid of the private letters, would furnish a very inadequate account of Munro's opinions, or of the extent to which he influenced the views of his official superiors on the great political and military questions, with which, in the time of Lord Cornwallis, of Lord Wellesley, and of Lord Hastings, the Government of India had to deal, inasmuch as up to 1820, when Munro became Governor of Madras, his situation was a comparatively subordinate one, and it was only by means of private correspondence that he was in a position to urge his views on matters beyond the scope of his official duties. Under this category must be included everything that he wrote on the policy to be pursued towards Tippoo and the Mahrattas, on the question of subsidiary forces, and generally on the political prospects and requirements of British rule in India up to the date of its consolidation by the war with the Mahrattas in 1817 and 1818.

Notwithstanding the vast changes which have taken place in India during the sixty-two years which have elapsed since Munro died, it cannot be said that his views and opinions as to the principles which should be observed in the administration of our great dependency are in any way obsolete. On the contrary, it may be affirmed with perfect truth that at the present time there is, if anything, a greater need, than there has been at any previous period, for keeping in view the policy enjoined by Munro, especially on the important question of the treatment of our native Indian fellow-subjects. To all who read this Memoir it will be apparent how liberal, and how greatly in advance of the views commonly entertained, not only by his contemporaries, but by many of those who came after him, are the opinions which Munro held as to the degree in which the natives of India should be associated with their English rulers in the government of their country. At the same time, it will be equally clear that Munro would have been the last man to sanction any measure, however popular, and however much in accordance with the prevailing sentiment of the day, which could possibly tend to impair British supremacy. His famous dictum, that 'the tenure with which we hold our power never 'has been, and never can be, the liberties of the people,' is alone sufficient to prove how stoutly he would have combated some of the measures which, either for the purposes of party politics, or in deference to ignorant and foolish sentiment, have been, and are being, pressed by English statesmen and by some Anglo-Indian administrators.

I have quoted on page 153 the language used by the Duke of Argyll in connection with the Act of 1870. Not less worthy of being cited in support of Munro's opinions is the following remarkable passage, which occurs in a paper written by the late Lord Lawrence shortly after the suppression of the Mutiny :—

'Placed as we are, widely separated from the consti-
'tutional Governments of England or America, our Govern-
'ment is established, as all Governments should be, for the
'good of the people; but while in their case the popular
'will is generally taken as the criterion of the public good,
'that is not always the case in India. We are not elected
'or placed in power by the people. We are here by our
'moral superiority, by the force of circumstances, and by
'the will of Providence. These alone constitute our
'Charter of Government in India, and in doing the best
'we can for the people, we are bound by our conscience,
'not by theirs.'

A. J. ARBUTHNOT.

CONTENTS.

CHAPTER   PAGE

I.   BOYHOOD AND EARLY YEARS IN INDIA   ... 1

II.   THE BARAMAHAL   21

III.   SERINGAPATAM AND CANARA   41

IV.   THE CEDED DISTRICTS   ... 69

V.   SOJOURN IN ENGLAND   95

VI.   SPECIAL COMMISSION AND MILITARY COMMAND   110

VII.   GOVERNMENT OF MADRAS—DEATH 136

SIR THOMAS MUNRO.

CHAPTER I.

BOYHOOD AND EARLY YEARS IN INDIA.

THOMAS MUNRO was born at Glasgow on the 27th of May, 1761. His father, Mr. Alexander Munro, was a Glasgow merchant trading with Virginia. Thomas Munro attended the Grammar School at Glasgow, and at the age of thirteen entered the College and University of that city. He was considered at school not particularly studious, but decidedly clever, always maintaining a high place in his classes, though he studied but little out of school hours. At College he developed a taste for reading, which he appears to have retained to the end of his life. His favourite studies were history, especially military history, mathematics, and chemistry. While still a mere lad, he commenced the study of political economy. He was at the same time a keen reader of poetry and romance, and had a turn for languages which stood him in good stead in after-life. At the age of sixteen, with the help only of a grammar and dictionary, he acquired a sufficient knowledge of the Spanish language to enable him to read 'Don Quixote' in the original. He had also made some progress in French and Italian. He was an adept at all athletic sports—a good swimmer and a skilful boxer. With reference to the latter

B

accomplishment, it was said of him by one of his school-
fellows, that ' he beat every boy in the school he fought,
' but he never sought a quarrel and was never in the
' smallest degree insolent or domineering; on the contrary,
' he was remarkably good-natured and peaceable, and his
' superiority in fighting became known only in consequence
' of his resisting unprovoked attacks of quarrelsome boys of
' superior age and strength, and beating them by his cool-
' ness, his courage, and his unequalled endurance. He was
' the protector of the weak against the strong, and at the
' same time he was so inoffensive that he had no enemies.'

With such qualities Munro was naturally a popular
boy; but even in boyhood a certain degree of prudence
and reserve, which seem to have characterized his disposition throughout his life, somewhat narrowed the circle of
his school friendships. Among his most intimate friends
at that period were the two Moores—Sir John, who was
killed at Corunna, and Sir Graham, a naval officer, with
whom he kept up a correspondence to the end of his life.
Munro's views on the subject of school friendships were
such as are seldom expressed, although, perhaps, more
often entertained than is commonly supposed. Writing
on the subject to one of his brothers some years after he
went to India, he remarked :

Our attachment to early acquaintances is as frequently
owing to chance placing us together,—to being engaged in
the same studies or amusements as to worth or merit of
any kind. Such friends are not selected; and therefore
men, as they advance in years, drop them for others they
think better of; and if they retain an affection for any of
them, it is perhaps only for one or two who may possess
those qualities which they would wish chosen friends to
possess, though it may have been circumstances very
different from those qualities that formed the first attachment. If among your school friends there are many who
are worthy of a warm friendship, you have been more

fortunate than I; for though I was happy with my companions at home, when I pass them in review, and recollect their habits, tempers, and dispositions, I can hardly see more than one or two whose loss I can with reason regret. Whatever you may think now, you may be assured that those who have now the first place in your esteem, will give way to objects more deserving, because chosen when your discernment was more mature. It must be confessed that there is a satisfaction in the company of men engaged in the same pursuits as ourselves; but it does not follow that they alone are deserving of our friendship, and that there is no happiness in the society of other men. I like an Orientalist, a politician, a man that walks and swims or plays fives, because I like all these things myself; but I at the same time have, perhaps, a greater friendship for a man who cares for none of these amusements.

At the age of sixteen Munro left College and entered the counting-house of Messrs. Somerville and Gordon, West India merchants at Glasgow, for the purpose of being trained for the mercantile profession. He remained in this employment for two years, when, his father's affairs having become involved, in consequence of the American War, it was found that it would be impossible to establish Thomas Munro in business, and an appointment was accordingly procured for him in the maritime service of the East India Company, which was shortly afterwards exchanged for a cadetship of infantry at the Presidency of Madras. Munro sailed for India in the same ship (the *Walpole*) to which he had been posted as a midshipman previous to his nomination to a military cadetship, and arrived at Madras on the 15th of January, 1780.

The period at which Munro reached India was one of the most critical periods in the history of British rule in that country. On the western side of the peninsula the English had been engaged for five years in a war with the Mahratta chiefs of Poona, Gwalior, and Indore. Towards the close of the previous year a confederacy had been formed between the chiefs in question, the Rájá of Berár, the Nizam of Hyderabad, and Hyder Ali Khán, the ruler of Mysore, the avowed object of which was the expulsion of the English from India. The aspect of affairs at Madras was most critical. The especial danger to that Presidency lay in the direction of Mysore, whose able and warlike chief was already engaged in preparations for a second invasion of the Carnatic. Hyder Ali's first inroad into that country, just eleven years before, when he had carried fire and sword through the districts immediately adjoining Madras, and had dictated a treaty under the walls of Fort St. George, was still fresh in the memories of the English residents. Nor was the condition of the British adminis-tration in any part of India such as to justify confidence in its power to overcome the dangers which threatened it. At Calcutta the Supreme Government was convulsed by divisions among its members, which for a time paralyzed the efforts of the able statesman who presided over it. At Madras, where, only a few years before, the Governor * had been violently deposed from his office and placed in confinement by a majority of his Council, the local Govern-ment was incapable of adequately realizing or effectively dealing with the crisis in which it was placed. The Madras authorities had received ample warning of Hyder Ali's hostile intentions, and had some months previously communicated their apprehensions to the Government of Bengal; but as the time drew near for those intentions to be carried into execution, they seem to have lost all thought of the necessity for preparation, and to have been only awakened to a sense of their real position when Hyder's army was within a few days' march of Madras. In the course of the months of January and February, 1780, troops which could ill be spared from the defence of the Carnatic, were sent to Bombay to the assistance of General

* Lord Pigot.

Goddard, and in the latter month the Governor* of Madras, who was about to leave India, placed on record a Minute expressing his satisfaction at 'the perfect tran-'quillity of the Carnatic' and of the Company's northern possessions, and his expectation that, in consequence of 'the arrival of the fleet with the King's troops,' that part of India would 'remain quiet.' Even as late as the 17th of July the new Governor and the Commander-in-chief declared that there was no danger of an immediate invasion. Four days later, Hyder entered the Carnatic.

At Bombay the local administration appears to have been free from internal divisions; but it had given signal proof of incapacity in its management of the Mahratta War, which, but for the energy of Hastings and the strategic ability of General Goddard,† must have ended in disaster.

* Sir Thomas Rumbold.

† Just a year before Munro reached India, General Goddard had made a march which, until a few years ago, was unexampled in the annals of Indian warfare. In the early part of the first Mahratta War, Hastings despatched across the continent of India a small force of 4000 men, of whom only 600 were Europeans, to the aid of the Government of Bombay. It was a bold undertaking, for up to that time no British force had ever crossed that part of the Indian continent. The command was entrusted in the first instance to Colonel Leslie, an officer of good reputation, but who was in bad health and made such slow progress, that Hastings deemed it neces-sary to supersede him, and to appoint General (then Colonel) Goddard to the command. Goddard marched from Burhanpur to Surat, a distance of 300 miles, in 19 days, or at the rate of about 15¾ miles a day, eluding by the expedition of his movements a force of 20,000 horse, which the Mahrattas sent to intercept him. The march was through a country then utterly unknown, and of which no maps existed. It was denounced by Mr. Dundas, the India minister of the day, as 'one of the frantic military exploits of Hastings.' It is natural, at the present time, to compare with General Goddard's achievement the brilliant feat performed by Sir Frederick Roberts, in his march from Cabul to Candahar, which, when it was under-taken, was denounced in some quarters in language not very dis-similar to that used a century ago regarding Goddard's march. The rapidity of Roberts's march was somewhat less than that of Goddard's, the distance marched by the former having been 322 miles and the

The British possessions in India, except in Bengal, were at that time extremely limited. In the south, the East India Company owned the fort and town of Madras, the adjoining district (known in those days as the Jagír, and now styled the district of Chingleput), the town and fort of Cuddalore and some of the adjoining territory, the port of Dévikota and certain villages in Tanjore, and four out of the five sirkárs on the eastern coast, now known as the Northern Sirkárs, for which, however, they were bound to pay an annual tribute of five lakhs of rupees (£50,000) to the Nizam. The rest of the Carnatic, in-cluding the districts of Nellore, North Arcot, the greater part of South Arcot, and Trichinopoly, still belonged to the Nawáb of the Carnatic. Of the remainder of what now constitutes the Madras Presidency, the greater part of Tanjore was still held by its Mahratta chief; Cuddapah, Salem, Coimbatore, Madura, Tinnevelly, Malabar and Canara, Karnúl, and a portion of Ballári had been brought under the rule of Hyder, while the remainder of Ballári and Guntúr belonged to the Nizam. In Bengal, though the youngest of the British settlements, the Company, owing to the genius and vigour of Clive, had become possessed of a far more extensive, and at the same time extremely compact, territory, comprising the whole of the

time occupied, including two halts, 23 days, or a rate of 14 miles a day, against Goddard's 15¾ miles; but the country through which Roberts passed, though better known, having been recently traversed by Sir Donald Stewart's division, was far more difficult and more trying to the troops than that traversed by Goddard in 1779. In each case the object of the march was to retrieve a disaster to the British arms, and in each case that object was accomplished with brilliant success.

Lord Lake's famous march in 1804 in pursuit of Holkar's cavalry, when he traversed 350 miles in 14 days, cannot be compared with either of the above achievements, as Lord Lake's force was composed entirely of cavalry and mounted artillery. The same may be said of the most rapid marches in the Mutiny, which, when of any con-siderable length, were made with mounted troops.

fertile districts of Bengal proper, south of the Brahma-
putra, Behar, and a part of Orissa. Bombay was still
little more than a commercial factory, holding no territorial possessions, except the island of Bombay, the
adjoining port of Bassein, and the island of Salsette.

In addition to the formidable confederacy of native
chiefs, which at the time of which we write actually
threatened the British power in India, there was every
prospect of that confederacy being speedily strengthened
by aid from France, which had declared war against
England in 1778, and which subsequently afforded material
assistance, both by land and by sea, to Hyder Ali and to
his son and successor Tippoo Sultán.

Nor were the difficulties and weaknesses of the position
in India counterbalanced by the strength of the Home Administration. Lord North's weak and unfortunate Government was still in office, tottering towards its fall. A
strong party in the Court of Directors was opposed to the
Governor-General, and supported the factious antagonism
arrayed against him in his Council; and there can be
little doubt that had the confederacy of native chiefs
been more united in their operations and in their aims, or
had a weaker man than Warren Hastings filled at this
time the position of Governor-General, the extension and
consolidation of British rule in India, which only a few
years later had become an established fact, would have
been one of the many "might have beens," which abound
in the history of nations, as well as in the lives of individuals.

Such was the state of public affairs when Thomas Munro,
then a lad nearly nineteen, landed at Madras. He remained for six months at the Presidency town, where he
did duty with the cadet company, learnt his drill, and
studied the native languages. Immediately on his arrival
he was robbed by a native servant of some of his money

and the greater part of his wardrobe, which he found it
no easy matter to replace; for in those days the pay of a
cadet of infantry was only eight pagodas, or about £3 a
month. Among the residents of Madras to whom he was
introduced, his chief friends appear to have been Mr. David
Haliburton, a civil servant, who was afterwards a member
of the Board of Revenue and Persian translator to Government, and an eccentric merchant of the name of Ross, at
whose house he made the acquaintance of a still more
eccentric man of science, of the name of Kœnig, a native
of Livonia, whose English Munro describes in his letters
as a mixture of Latin, Portuguese, and French, but who
seems to have been much attracted by the young cadet's
proficiency in chemistry. After having had a narrow
escape of being appointed, at his own request, to the
unfortunate detachment under Colonel Baillie, which on
the 10th of September was beaten by and surrendered to
Hyder, Munro was sent in July with the regiment to which
he was attached, first to Poonamallee and afterwards to
St. Thomas' Mount, whence, on the 20th of August, he
marched with the army under the command of his name-
sake, Lieutenant-General Sir Hector Munro,* to meet the
invading army of Mysore. Munro appears to have been
present at all the operations under Sir Hector Munro and
Sir Eyre Coote in 1780, 1781, 1782, and 1783, when,
peace having been made with France, and Tippoo—who,
on the death of Hyder Ali in 1782, had succeeded his father
on the throne of Mysore—having moved the Mysorean
army to the western coast, hostilities ceased in the Carnatic.
These operations included the retreat of Sir Hector Munro
from Conjeveram to Madras after the defeat of Colonel
Baillie's force, the relief of Wandiwash, the battle of Porto
Novo, the battle of Sholinghar, the taking of Chittoor,

---

* Sir Hector Munro does not appear to have been related to the
subject of this memoir.

the battle and siege of Cuddalore, and several other engagements. In November, 1781, when still an ensign of less than two years' service, Munro was appointed quartermaster of a brigade, and at the attack on the French lines and battle of Cuddalore on the 13th of June, 1783, he acted as aide-de-camp to the officer who commanded the centre attack. From 1783 to 1788 Munro was employed on garrison duty at various stations. During this period he served with no less than five regiments, viz. the 1st, 16th, 21st, and 30th Native Infantry and a regiment of European Infantry, the number of which is not given, but to which he appears to have been posted on his promotion to the rank of lieutenant in 1786. In August, 1788, he was appointed an assistant in the Intelligence Department under Captain Read, and was attached to the head-quarters of a force sent to take possession of the district of Guntúr, which in that year was ceded by the Nizam to the Company. He continued to be employed in the Intelligence Department until October, 1790, when, war having broken out afresh with Tippoo, he rejoined his regiment, the 21st Native Infantry, and served with the army under Colonel Maxwell, which invaded the Baramahal. He subsequently shared in the pursuit of Tippoo by Lieutentant-General Meadows through the Tapur pass on the 18th of November, 1790, and afterwards, in 1791 and 1792, in most of the operations under Lord Cornwallis, including the siege and capture of Bangalore. In March, 1792, he accompanied the detachment in charge of the two sons of Tippoo, who were sent as hostages to Madras, and in the following month he was appointed one of the three military assistants, deputed to conduct the civil administration of the Baramahal under Captain (afterwards Lieutenant-Colonel) Alexander Read.

During the whole of this period, as indeed throughout his life, Munro kept up a constant correspondence, principally with the members of his own family. His letters, even in the earliest years of his Indian service, especially those addressed to his father, to whom he usually wrote on the military operations, if they do not manifest brilliant literary ability, are remarkable productions to have come from the pen of so youthful a writer. Clear in expression, copious in their details, and free from all affectation of style, they contain what have been considered by competent judges as the most trustworthy narratives that have been written of the operations to which they referred. Dr. Wilson, in his annotations to Mills' 'History of British India,' more than once cites Munro's letters as embodying the most accurate accounts available of some of the engagements with Hyder, incidents in which had become the subject of controversy. These letters are for the most part simple narratives of facts which came under the writer's observation, and are but seldom interspersed with comment or criticism; and when comments do occur, they are very often merely recapitulations of the remarks and arguments which have been used by others regarding the tactics or policy of the generals. Thus, referring to the defeat of Colonel Baillie's force, Munro wrote:

The loss of Colonel Baillie's army is the severest blow the English ever sustained in India. Some persons pretend to vindicate Munro; * but by far the greater part impute to his imprudent conduct the destruction of the detachment. Why, say they, did he linger so long within a few miles of Baillie without attempting to join him? Why, instead of sending the Grenadiers, did he not go with the whole army? And why, when he saw Hyder march, did he not follow him instantly, instead of waiting till the morning? On the other hand, it is said that it was reasonable for him to conjecture that, as Baillie had been able without any assistance to repulse the enemy, he would be still more able to do so again after being so

---

* Sir Hector Munro is here referred to.

powerfully reinforced; and that by sending a detachment, had it succeeded, he would have lost less time than by going with the whole army.

Occasionally, however, remarks are made which show that the writer had very definite views of his own. Thus, in reference to the same disaster, he remarks :

The General, by paying spies too sparingly, received very little and often false intelligence : he neither rewarded those who told the truth, nor did he punish those who deceived him. One day upon the march a harkára * came up and delivered him a letter from Colonel Baillie. He read it; he seemed pleased with the contents, and he ordered his dubash to give the messenger two pagodas (sixteen shillings). The man smiled. It was a poor reward for having received two wounds and risked his life in bringing him the intelligence. On our way to join the detachment, three men who were found sitting near the road were brought to the General. He told them if they would carry him to Baillie he would reward them ; but if they should misguide him, he would instantly put them to death. They walked at the head of the army with halters about their necks, and they conducted us to the side of a lake where the road terminated. The General followed them, notwithstanding that it was obvious to every one that they were carrying us away from the scene of action, as we heard the firing and saw the smoke of the cannon nearly four miles distant in a different direction. These men were suffered to escape.

In a later letter referring to the operations against the French before Cuddalore in 1783, the command of which, owing to the illness and departure of Sir Eyre Coote, had devolved upon General Stuart, a very incompetent officer, Munro wrote :

The flank attack did not move till the front one was repulsed. Had it advanced at the same time, two regi-

* *Harkára*—a messenger.

ments that were at the redoubt would have been cut off. There seemed to be no connection in our movements, every one was at a loss what to do, and nothing saved our army from a total defeat, but the French being, like ourselves, without a general.

The letters contain no mention whatever of his own part in these actions, many of which were hotly contested, and attended with heavy losses. In one of them the loss on the British side in killed and wounded was nearly sixty officers, seven hundred European soldiers, and two hundred and fifty sepoys. In another the loss was five hundred men. But although Munro makes no mention of his own services, it is evident, from his having been selected in his second year of service for the appointment of quartermaster of a brigade, that he gained the favourable opinion of his military superiors at a very early date, and it is to be gathered from a remark in one of his letters, to the effect that his situation (he was writing in November, 1785) was not such as it would have been, had Sir Eyre Coote lived, that he had attracted the favourable notice of that distinguished general.

During the five or six years which followed the conclusion of the war, and which he spent in the comparative leisure of regimental duty in garrison, Munro appears to have devoted a good deal of his spare time to the study of the Persian and Hindustáni languages, in both of which he acquired considerable proficiency, and to which he subsequently added a good practical knowledge of the Telugu and Canarese languages—the languages of the districts, in the civil administration of which he was afterwards employed. It was probably to his attainments in the Oriental languages, combined with his general ability, that he owed his appointment to the Intelligence Department under Captain Read, which was followed two years later by his selection for civil employment under the same officer. But

Munro's claims to advancement were by no means confined to proficiency in the native languages—a qualification which, valuable as it is when combined with others, has in India too often led to the promotion of studious men, with a turn for languages, to situations for which in other respects they were quite unfit. Munro was, from the first, a careful and sagacious observer of the events passing around him, both in Southern India and in other parts of the country; and at a very early period had formed clear and definite views as to the policy most likely to be conducive to the maintenance and extension of the British power. In opposition to the opinion which, at that time, generally found favour with the authorities, both in England and in India, he recognized the paramount importance of subverting the powerful and dangerous empire which Hyder Ali had founded in Mysore. He wrote in 1790:

It has long been admitted as an axiom in politics by the directors of our affairs both at home and in this country, that Tippoo ought to be preserved as a barrier between us and the Mahrattas. This notion seems to have been first adopted without much knowledge of the subject, and to have been followed without much consideration. It is to support a powerful and ambitious enemy to defend us from a weak one. From the neighbourhood of the one we have everything to apprehend; from that of the other, nothing. This will be clearly understood by reflecting for a moment on the conditions of the two Governments. The one, the most simple and despotic monarchy in the world, in which every department, civil and military, possesses the regularity and system communicated to it by the genius of Hyder, and in which all pretensions derived from high birth being discourged, all independent chiefs and zemindárs subjected or extirpated, justice severely and impartially administered to every class of the people, a numerous and well-disciplined army kept up, and almost every employment of trust or consequence conferred on men raised from obscurity, gives to the Government a vigour hitherto unexampled in India. The other, composed of a confederacy of independent chiefs, possessing extensive dominions and numerous armies, now acting in concert, now jealous of each other and acting only for their own advantage, and at all times liable to be detached from the public cause by the most distant prospect of private gain, can never be a very dangerous enemy to the English.

The first is a government of conquest; the last, merely of plunder and depredation. The character of vigour has been so strongly impressed on the Mysore Government by the abilities of its founders, that it may retain it even under the reign of a weak prince or a minor. But the strength of the supreme Mahratta Government is continually varying according to the disposition of its different members, who sometimes strengthen it by union and sometimes weaken it by defection, or by dividing their territories among their children.

The nation likewise maintains no standing army, adopts none of the European modes of discipline, and is impelled by no religious tenets to attempt the extirpation of men of a different belief. But Tippoo supports an army of 110,000 men, a large body of which is composed of slaves, called Chelas, trained on the plan of the Turkish janizaries, and follows with the greatest eagerness every principle of European tactics. He has even gone so far as to publish a book for the use of his officers, a copy of which is now in my possession, containing, besides the evolutions and manœuvres usually practised in Europe, some of his own invention, together with directions for marching, encamping, and fighting; and he is, with all his extraordinary talents, a furious zealot for a faith which founds eternal happiness on the destruction of other sects.

Nor was the young soldier's attention limited exclusively to the affairs of India. He carefully and anxiously observed the startling revolution which was taking place in France, and noted its possible effects on the future of England and of British rule in India. His first impressions were very

similar to those held alike by Pitt and Fox at the commencement of the Revolution, but he did not share their
anticipations that a more popular form of Government in
France would improve the relations between that country
and England. Writing to his friend Mr. Foulis on the
2nd of April, 1790, he described 'the restoration of French
'liberty as an event, which, as a friend to the prosperity and
'glory of Great Britain, he could not behold with indiffer-
'ence.' In his opinion, that nation, already too powerful,
wanted nothing but a better form of government to render
her the arbiter of Europe. He wrote:

You and I may live to see the day when the fairest
provinces of India, reversing Mr. Gibbon's boast, shall not
be subject to a Company of merchants of a remote island
in the Northern Ocean; but when perhaps those merchants
and their countrymen, being confined by the superior
power of their rival to the narrow limits of their native
isle, shall sink into the insignificance from which they
were raised by their empire of the sea. With the freedom
of our government we may retain our orators, our poets
and historians; but our domestic transactions will afford
few splendid materials for the exercise of genius or fancy,
and with the loss of empire, we must relinquish, however
reluctantly, the idea so long and so fondly cherished by us
all, of our holding the balance of power. In looking
forward to the rising grandeur of France, I am not influenced by any groundless despondency, but I judge of
the future from the past: and when I consider that after
the Revolution she opposed for some time successfully
the united naval Powers of England and Holland; that
she did the same under Queen Anne and under George II.
until '59; and that, notwithstanding the almost total
annihilation of her marine in that war, in the east of
Europe, America, and the West Indies, she never shunned
and sometimes sought our fleets, and met us in this country
(the East Indies), if not with superior force, at least with
superior fortune and perhaps bravery; that she made all
those exertions when she was left to the mercy of capricious

women, who made and unmade ministers, generals, and
admirals almost every month; and when commerce, and
even the naval profession, met with no encouragement;—
I cannot but fear that when she shall direct her attention
to the sea, she may wrest from Britain her empire of that
element and strip her of all her foreign possessions. When
two countries have made nearly the same progress in the
arts of peace and war, and when there is no material
difference in the condition of their governments, that
which possesses the greatest population and the most
numerous resources from the fertility of her soil, must, in
the end, prevail over her rival.

Groundless as the apprehensions which are embodied in
the foregoing observations have happily proved, it must
not be forgotten that the superiority of Great Britain over
a France set free from the shackles which had hitherto
impeded her progress, had yet to be established; that the
battles of the Nile and Trafalgar had still to be fought;
and that the future victor at Assye and at Waterloo, whom
Munro was destined to meet nine years later under the
walls of Seringapatam, was still a young regimental officer,
unknown to the world at large. Nor was Munro singular
at that time in his dread of the power of France. The
previous struggle between the English and the French in
India had been long and severe, and there was nothing
that Warren Hastings had regarded with greater apprehension than a renewal of that struggle.

Munro's mode of life at this time is thus described by
him in a letter to his sister:

Seven was our breakfast hour, immediately after which
I walked out, generally alone; and though ten was my
usual hour for returning, I often wandered about the
fields till one; but when I adhered to the rules laid down
for myself, I came home at ten and read Persian till one,
when I dressed and went to dinner—came back before
three and sometimes slept half an hour, sometimes not,

and then wrote and talked Persian and Moors * till sunset, when I went to the parade, from whence I set out with a party to visit the ladies or to play cards at the commanding officer's. This engaged me till nine, when I went to supper, or more frequently returned home without it, and read politics and nonsense until bedtime, which, according to the entertainment which I met with, happened some time between eleven and two. I should have mentioned fives as an amusement that occupied a great deal of my time. I seldom missed above two days in a week at this game, and always played two or three hours at a time, which were taken from my walks and Persian studies. Men are much more boyish in this country than in Europe, and in spite of the sun take, I believe, more exercise, and are, however strange it may appear, better able to undergo fatigue, unless on some remarkably hot days. I never could make half the violent exertions at home that I have made here. My daily walks were usually from four to twelve miles, which I thought a good journey in Scotland. You see children of five or six years of age following the camp, and marching fifteen or sixteen miles a day with the same ease as their fathers.

The life of a subaltern in India is not a very luxurious one, even at the present time; but in those days, when the pay was very much smaller than it is now, it was a life of poverty and of hardship. Munro says in one of his letters, written after he had been nine years in the country, that he 'never experienced hunger or thirst, fatigue or 'poverty,' until he came to India; but that since then he had frequently met with the first three, and the last had been his constant companion. He was three years in India before he was 'master of any other pillow than a 'book or a cartridge-pouch;' his bed was a 'piece of 'canvas stuck on four cross sticks,' and the greater part of

* *Moors* was in those days the name commonly applied to the Hindustáni language, or the language of the Muhammadans or *Moor-men*, as the Muhammadans in Southern India are often called. In Madras Hindustáni is seldom spoken by the Hindus.

C

his journeys he had to make on foot; the only horse he
possessed being so old that he was always obliged to walk
two-thirds of the way. In such circumstances it is very
much to his credit that he practised sufficient self-denial
to enable him to send material help to his father out of
his scanty income.

Munro's letters during the third war with Mysore,
which, under the immediate direction of Lord Cornwallis,
then Governor-General of Bengal,* ended with the Treaty
of Seringapatam in 1792, are extremely interesting;
especially his account of the storming of Tippoo's lines
near Seringapatam on the night of the 6th of February of
that year, which practically brought the war to a close.†
Munro entertained a high opinion of Lord Cornwallis's
capacity as a general; but, adhering to the views he had
all along held as to the necessity of completely subverting
the power of Tippoo, he was much disappointed at the
liberality of the terms conceded to the Mysore ruler,
who was allowed to retain half his dominions. He
wrote:

I am still of the old doctrine that the best method of
making all princes keep the peace, not excepting even
Tippoo, is to make it dangerous for them to disturb your
quiet. This can be done by a good army. We have one;
but as we have not money to pay it, we ought to have
taken advantage of our successes for this purpose, and
after reducing Seringapatam, have retained it and all the
countries to the southward and westward of the Cavery.
By doing this we could have maintained a good body of
cavalry, and so far from being left with a weak and

* It was not until 1833 that the Governor-General received the
official designation of Governor-General of India.

† Munro was not present on this occasion, having been employed
at the time at Bangalore with a detachment engaged in forwarding
supplies to the army before Seringapatam; but he made careful
inquiries about the details of the assaults, and wrote a clear and able
account of it.

extended frontier, the usual attendant of conquests, we should, from the nature of the country, have acquired one more compact and more strong than we have at present. If peace is so desirable an object, it would be wiser to have retained the power of preserving it in our own hands, than to have left it to the caprice of Tippoo, who, though he has lost half his revenue, has by no means lost half his power. He requires no combination, like us, of an able military governor, peace in Europe, and allies in this country, to enable him to prosecute war successfully. He only wants to attack them singly, when he will be more than a match for any of them; and it will be strange if he does not find an opportunity when the confederates may not find it convenient to support the general cause.

Another question upon which Munro's views were not less decided, was one regarding which difference of opinion has prevailed thoughout the period of the British connection with India, and still prevails—the question of the extension of territory. His opinion was that the territorial possessions of the East India Company must be extended, if the Company was to continue to exist as a territorial power at all. He said :

Men read books, and because they find that all warlike nations have had their downfall, they declaim against conquest as not only dangerous but unprofitable, from a supposition that the increase of territory must always be followed by a proportionate increase of expense. This may be true when a nation is surrounded by warlike neighbours, which, while it gains by a province on one side, loses as much on the other; but there are times and situations when conquest not only brings a revenue greatly beyond its expenses, but brings also additional security. The kings of England knew this when they attempted the reduction of Scotland. There is, however, another example which would apply better to our position in the Carnatic. When Spain was, in the last century, engaged in a war with France and Portugal, would not the possession of the latter country have added much to her strength and security by removing every possibility of an attack except from the frontiers of France? By subduing the country below the Gháts, from Pálghátcheri to Ambúr, we have nothing to fear. The sea is behind us, and in front we gain a stronger barrier than we now have, which would enable us to defend the country with the present military establishment; but as this, with the civil expenses, would be nearly equal to the whole revenue of the country, let us advance to the Krishna, and we shall triple our revenue without having occasion to add much to our military force, because our barrier will then be both stronger and shorter than it is now. I do not mean that we should at once attempt to extend ourselves so far, for it is at present beyond our power; but we should keep the object in view, though the accomplishment of it should require a long series of years. There is no necessity for precipitation; the dissensions and revolutions of the native governments will point out to us the time when it is proper for us to become actors. Nothing can be more absurd than our regarding any of the native governments as powers which are to last for ages. It would not be surprising if all of them were to cease to exist in the course of twenty or thirty years.

CHAPTER II.

THE peace concluded with Tippoo in 1792 brought Munro's military employment to a close for some years, and indeed, with the exception of two brief periods—the first during the war which seven years later, terminated with the defeat and death of Tippoo and the extinction of his dynasty, and the second during the Pindári War of 1817 and 1818, when Munro, with the rank of brigadier-general, proved, during a short but brilliant campaign in the Deccan and Southern Mahratta country, his high qualifications as a military commander—the remainder of his life was destined to be spent in the discharge of duties of a civil character. Under the Treaty of Seringapatam Tippoo ceded to the East India Company and their allies, the Mahratta chiefs and the Nizam, a moiety of his dominions. The share of the Company consisted of the district of Malabar on the western coast, which at first was placed under the Government at Bombay; the greater part of the present district of Salem, then designated the Baramahal; and the province of Dindigal, which forms a part of the present district of Madura. The Baramahal and Dindigal were placed under the Government of Madras; but, owing to the deficiency in that Presidency of civil servants possessing a competent knowledge of the native languages, and to the unsatisfactory manner in which the revenue administration of the older possessions

of the Company under the Madras Presidency had been
conducted, Lord Cornwallis resolved to employ military
officers for a time in the management of the Baramahal.
The chief place, with the designation of Superintendent
of Revenue in the Baramahal, was given to Captain
Alexander Read, under whom Munro had recently served
in the Intelligence Department; Munro and two other
young officers of the Madras army, Lieutenants McLeod
and Graham, being appointed his assistants. These
appointments were made direct by the Governor-General,
and were at first intended to last only for a year, at the
end of which time Collectors were to be 'appointed by
'Government for the said concerns from the list of civil
'servants.' The arrangement, however, continued in
force until the renewal of military operations in 1799,
when Read and Munro both left the Baramahal. It seems
that, owing to a misunderstanding on the part of Read,
caused by Munro having declined in the previous year to
leave his regiment while the war was going on, for the
purpose of rejoining the Intelligence Department, Munro's
appointment to the Baramahal Commission was very near
not being made. Read, indeed, had applied for the
appointment of another officer; but his application was
not complied with by the Governor-General, and on
Munro intimating to Read that he was willing to serve in
the revenue line, he was at once appointed. The temporary
misunderstanding did not in any way affect the subsequent
relations of the two men, which were invariably most
cordial. Munro's letters show that he entertained a very
high opinion of Read, whom he described as 'a man
'whose conduct is invariably regulated by private honour
'and public interest, and in whom the enthusiasm in the
'pursuit of national objects which seizes other men by fits
'and starts, is constant and uniform.' 'These qualities,
'joined to an intimate knowledge of the language and

'manners of the people,' eminently qualified Read for the station which, in the opinion of his assistant, 'he filled 'with so much credit to himself and benefit to the public.' Of the estimation in which Read held Munro, the best evidence is afforded by the fact that after they had been seven years together in the Baramahal, Read, on being appointed to the command of a body of troops detached to collect supplies for General Harris's army, took Munro with him as his secretary.

The duties entrusted to Read and his assistants were very comprehensive, involving no less than the whole administration, revenue, police, and judicial, of that portion of the ceded territory which was assigned to them, comprising a tract of country one hundred and forty miles in length with an average width of sixty miles ; but their first and most important business was to settle the revenue, and especially the land revenue, which was then, as now, the most important branch of the Indian revenue. In the discharge of this duty they had little or no assistance from the arrangements which had been made in settling the land revenue in other parts of India. In Bengal the revenue settlements had been the least able of Hastings' measures, had been a source of constant controversy with his opponents in the Council, and had met with emphatic disapproval from the Court of Directors. In Madras the inefficiency of the revenue management of the Northern Sirkárs and of the Jágír, had, as we have seen, induced the Governor-General to look beyond the civil service when selecting officers for the Baramahal. In the Sirkárs a considerable portion of the land was in the hands of zemindárs, who collected the revenue from the ryots or cultivators, paying a fixed sum to the Government. The zemindárs, for the most part, employed renters or farmers of the revenue, who made the collections from the ryots, and oppressed them grievously by unauthorized exactions.

Renters were likewise employed by the Company's officers to collect the revenue of land not under zemindárs, a whole sirkár being sometimes let to one renter. The persons thus employed were usually strangers to the country, hangers-on of the chiefs or members of the Provincial Councils, three of which Councils, stationed at Ganjam, Vizagapatam, and Masulipatam, were vested with the superintendence of the affairs of the Sirkárs. The renters employed by these Councils appear to have abused their powers even more grossly than those under the zemindárs. In the Jágír also, the renting system had been adopted, with very similar results to the ryots and with serious loss to the Government; and in this case the mal-administration was intensified by the intervention of a class of persons called "dubashes," some of them domestic servants of the European residents at Madras, who, after the invasion of the Carnatic by Hyder in 1780, purchased rights in the land at absurdly low rates, and exercised a most mischievous influence in the district.

Added to these defects of method in administering the revenues, the standard of official morality recognized by those employed to administer them, was extremely low. The salaries allowed to the members of the Provincial Councils, and subsequently to the Collectors, to whom, on the abolition of the Councils, the revenue administration was entrusted, were so small, that it had become the universal practice to augment them by unauthorized receipts, which these officers, from the nature of their duties, had ample facilities and great temptations for obtaining. The evil had attracted the attention of Clive during his second government of Bengal, and, although himself a prominent offender in his earlier administration, he had adopted vigorous measures for its repression; but the arrangements which he made for removing, by the grant of suitable salaries, the temptations to which the servants' of the Company were exposed, not having been sanctioned by the Court of Directors, the previous malpractices had revived, and had not been extirpated until they were grappled with by Lord Cornwallis, who, in the same year in which the Baramahal was ceded by Tippoo, addressed the Court of Directors on the subject in the following terms :—

I consider it a duty to you and my country to declare that the best rules and regulations that can be framed, either by yourselves or by the governments in India, will prove totally nugatory and useless, unless you adopt, as a decided and fixed principle, that liberal salaries shall be annexed to every office of trust and responsibility at all the Presidencies; that all perquisites shall be abolished; and that the most vigorous checks shall be established to prevent your servants from attempting to acquire fortunes by means that are often practised, though never publicly avowed, but for the pursuit of which many of them find an almost unanswerable apology by representing the impossibility of their even existing upon their narrow and wretched public allowances. The system that has been so long and so fatally pursued in this country, of granting trifling salaries to men employed in high trust, and who are surrounded by great temptations, and of leaving them to look for their subsistence and future hope of retirement to perquisites and unavowed emoluments, is as cruelly destructive of the morals of individuals, as it is ruinous to the interests of the Company.

Warned by the unsatisfactory results of the systems tried in their older possessions, the Madras Government, on receiving charge of the Baramahal, resolved to adopt a different plan. A few years previously, there had been established at Madras a Board of Revenue, whose business it was to superintend the administration of the revenue in all its branches, and to advise the Government on all matters connected with it. The instructions issued by this Board to Read provided for the settlement being

made with the ryots individually—an arrangement which
was much facilitated by the fact that in the greater part
of the Baramahal there were no zemindárs. The condition
of the country, when Read took charge of it, was far from
prosperous. Notwithstanding what Munro had written
in one of the letters quoted in the last chapter, regarding
Tippoo's capacity as a ruler, he had not been long in the
Baramahal before he discovered that the administration
of that province, both under Hyder and under Tippoo,
had been oppressive in the extreme. Their system was
similar to that followed by most of the native governments, and copied, as we have seen, by the Company's
Government in the Northern Sirkárs and in the Jágír,
of letting out the country to renters, who pillaged the
people by unauthorized exactions, but who in this case
were constantly subject to have their illicit gains, or a
great part of them, extorted from them by the Sultan,
and were thus driven to recoup themselves by further exactions. This oppressive system had reduced the country,
when delivered over to the Company, to such a state that
'a rich farmer was nowhere to be found.' 'Not one
'among them, perhaps, was worth one hundred pagodas,
'exclusive of his farming stock.' Scarcely one of them
rented lands to the amount of fifty pagodas a year. One-
half of all the farms were not above ten pagodas each,
and if there anywhere appeared a farm of eighty or one
hundred pagodas, though 'nominally held by one person,
'it was in fact occupied by three or four families of brothers
'or relatives.' Many of the ryots had 'not even a single
'bullock,' but borrowed or hired 'a pair for a short time
during the ploughing season.'

The first thing that Read did was to divide the province
into three divisions, and to assign a division to each of
his assistants, confining himself to the superintendence of
their work, and to considering the measures best adapted

to secure the welfare of the people and a sufficient revenue
to the State. For the first year temporary arrangements
were made for the collection of the revenue with the aid
of such village accounts as were forthcoming, and then
a survey and assessment of each division was set on foot.

At first the intention was that the land should be let
on lease for five years, and orders to this effect were
sent from Madras. This was partially carried out, but
long before the five years had expired, the lease system
had collapsed, and was superseded by that which, with
some modifications and amendments, was afterwards extended over the greater part of the Madras Presidency,
and is commonly known as the ryotwár system. Regarding this system there has been, and still is, a good deal of
misapprehension, even in official quarters. It is generally
known that, under the ryotwár system, the revenue is
collected by the Government officers direct from the ryots ;
but because it is necessary, for a reason which will be
stated presently, to make an annual inquiry as to the extent of each ryot's holding, it is often erroneously supposed
that there is an annual revision of the rate of assessment,
and that the landholders have no guarantee that that
rate will not be raised from year to year. The fact is
that there is no annual settlement of the rate of assessment. All that is inquired into is the extent of each
ryot's holding, and this is rendered necessary by the
option which, under the ryotwár system, is conceded to
the ryot to give up, or diminish, or extend his holding
from year to year. Every registered holder of land is
recognized as its proprietor, and pays the revenue assessed
upon his holding direct to Government. He is at liberty
to sublet his property, or to transfer it by gift, sale, or
mortgage. He cannot be ejected by Government so long
as he pays the fixed assessment, and he has the option of
annually increasing his holding, provided that there is

waste or other land available, or of diminishing it or entirely abandoning it. In Madras, as in other parts of India where the revenue demand has not been permanently settled, the rate of assessment has been fixed for thirty years. In unfavourable seasons remissions of assessment are granted for entire or partial loss of produce. The assessment is fixed in money, and does not vary from year to year, except in those cases where water is drawn from a Government source of irrigation to convert dry land into wet, or one-crop into two-crop land, when an extra rent is paid to Government for the water so appropriated, nor is any addition made to the assessment for improvements effected at the ryot's own expense. The ryot under this system is virtually a proprietor with a simple and perfect title, and has all the benefits of a perpetual lease without its responsibility, inasmuch as he can at any time throw up his land, or a portion of it, but cannot be ejected as long as he pays his dues. He receives assistance in bad seasons, and is not held responsible for the payments of his neighbours.*

This is the system which, originated in its main features by Read in the Baramahal, and extended in after-years by the powerful advocacy of Munro, has long prevailed in the greater part of the Madras Presidency and in the adjoining Presidency of Bombay; but it was not until after the lapse of many years that it was set free from certain serious defects which, contrary to the wise views of its founders, though strictly in accordance with native ideas, were allowed to hamper its working for many years. Of these, one of the most important was the rate of assessment, which in many parts of the country constituted an unduly heavy burthen upon the ryots, and seriously re-

* The above is nearly *verbatim* the description given of the ryotwár system in the Administration Report of the Madras Presidency for 1855-56.

tarded the prosperity of the country. Both Read and
Munro appear to have been very sensible of the importance of moderate assessments. 'The great point in
'making a settlement,' wrote Munro, 'is the rate of
'assessment. All other regulations connected with it are
'of very inferior importance.' Another was the taxation
of improvements effected by the ryots themselves, as, for
instance, the imposition of a higher assessment upon
land watered from a well constructed by a ryot at his
own expense. Another was a rule which made the rate
of assessment depend upon the description of the crop,
exacting a higher rate in the case of the more valuable
descriptions of produce. On both these points Munro,
at a very early period in his revenue service, recorded
opinions characterized by a statesmanlike sagacity very
much in advance of his time. He wrote :

Nothing would more tend to secure a country from
famine than numerous wells. They are so little affected
by the seasons, that their crops seldom fail ; they require
no expensive repairs ; they do not fill up, nor are they
liable to be swept away by floods, or to be destroyed by
an enemy, like tanks ; but they enable the cultivator to
resume his labour, without even waiting for rain, the
moment the danger is over. Private tanks, as they would
be so small, and scattered over every part of the country,
would be less subject, than those of Government, to the
accidental loss of their produce, and would therefore be a
better security against scarcity. Had it ever been the
practice under Indian governments, instead of building
tanks themselves, to have let the ryots do it, without
raising their rents, there would now have been infinitely
more wet lands than there are ; an equal or greater
revenue from them, and without any expense to the public.
If the old system of imposing an additional rent on every
improvement be persevered in, the people will remain for
ever poor and revenue uncertain.

Again :

To raise less grain, and a greater quantity of the more valuable productions of the soil, seems to be the most likely method of rendering it a more profitable commodity to the farmer than it is at present; but as the cultivation of these productions is more expensive than that of grain, and as few of the farmers have much stock, every impost, every restraint, that might the least discourage them from engaging in such undertakings, ought to be done away with. All the late duties, therefore, on betel, tobacco, and other garden productions, are extremely impolitic, and can only tend to perpetuate the poverty under which the farmers have hitherto laboured.

Munro was at first in favour of a system of leases, on the ground that the liberty of giving up or varying their holdings from year to year might tempt the ryots to abandon the cultivation of land which had been rendered to a certain extent productive, for the sake of obtaining waste land, of which there was an abundance, on favourable terms, and that, as the cultivation of waste land required more labour than that of land already brought under the plough, the produce of the country, and with it the public revenue, would be diminished; but he does not appear at any time to have attached much importance to this view, and subsequently he came round to the opinion which seems to have been held by Read at an early period, that any attempt to establish a system of leases in the then condition of the Baramahal would be, to say the least, premature. Writing to his father on the subject in 1798, he says :

I do not myself approve of attempting to establish a general lease at once over the whole country. There are many arguments against such a measure, founded on the poverty, the ignorance, and the manners of the people, which it would be tedious to detail. I rather wish to continue the plan now followed, which consists in letting every farmer please himself : he may take as much or as little land as he pleases every year; he may reject his old

fields and take new ; he may keep a part of the whole for
one year or twenty, as he finds it most convenient; and as
every field has a rate of assessment which never varies, he
knows perfectly what he has to trust to, and that his rent
can never rise or fall but exactly in proportion to the
extent of land he occupies. All that is required of him is,
that he shall give notice, between the 12th of April and
the 12th of July, of whatever land he means to relinquish,
in order that it may be given in these months, which are
the principal seasons of cultivation, to any other man who
wants it. If he fails in this, he is obliged to pay the rent
for the ensuing year. By persevering in this system the
farmers would soon know how much land they could
manage ; they would cease to abandon whatever fields
they had in any degree improved; and this practice,
which would answer every purpose of a lease, would
gradually extend over the whole country. If we
endeavour to establish the lease anywhere at once, it could
not be permanent; for ignorance and inexperience, both
on our side and on that of the farmers, would lead many
of them into engagements which they would not be afterwards able to fulfil.

Another point on which Munro at one time advocated a
rule which has long ceased to form one of the regulations
of the ryotwár system, was that of enforcing upon the
ryots of a village a joint responsibility for the failures of
individual ryots. This rule was in conformity with the
long-established practice obtaining under native governments. Read doubted its justice. Munro held that it
was not unjust, and that, without such a rule, there could
be no certainty of collecting the revenue. He argued that
'if it was not unjust to raise a land-rent * to answer the

---

* Munro, frequently in his earlier papers, and occasionally in his
later ones, uses the term 'rent,' when 'revenue' or 'assessment'
would seem to be the more appropriate term. Indeed, in one of his
Minutes he goes so far as to apply the term 'house-rent' to a tax
on houses in force in the districts of Cuddapah and Ballári. In using
this language he apparently had in view the fact that in India the
Government has invariably been recognized as in a certain sense

'demands of Government, or even to increase this rent on
'particular emergencies,' it could 'not be regarded as more
'unjust to collect the deficiencies of the fixed revenue by a
'second assessment.' 'The increase of revenue and the levy
'of the deficiency are both taxes of the same nature to the
'inhabitants. They are somewhat more than they expected
'to have been called upon for; but as they are raised by a
'measure which has no partiality in its operation, but is
'the same to all men, they may be disagreeable, they may
'be even oppressive, but they cannot be deemed unjust.'

I have said that Munro was a staunch advocate of
moderate assessments. He was equally in favour of fixity
in the rate of assessment, so far as this could be conceded
with a due regard to the necessities of the State. Indeed,
he has sometimes been cited as a supporter of permanent
assessments, but there is more than one passage in his
Minutes which shows that when referring to assessments
of the land revenue, he used the term ' fixed ' in a qualified
sense, and that he was not in favour of such a permanent
settlement as would preclude the Government from raising
the assessment in money under any circumstances what-

the lord of the soil, or, to state the matter more precisely, that by
the ancient law of the country the ruling power is entitled to a proportion of the annual produce of the land, or to the equivalent of that
proportion in money. In one of his Minutes, written when Governor
of Madras, Munro defines the relative positions of the ryot and the
Government in these words: 'The ryot is certainly not like the
'landlord in England, but neither is he like the English tenant. If
'the name of landlord belongs to any one in India, it is to the ryot.
'He divides with Government all the rights of the land. Whatever is
'not reserved by Government, belongs to him. He is not a tenant at
'will or for a term of years. He is not removable because another
'offers more. The case, it is true, sometimes happens, but it is always
'regarded as one of injustice. He holds his land, or putkutt, by in-
'heritance, as long as he pays the public assessment upon it. That
'assessment has, under the native princes, always fluctuated and
'been a great bar to improvement. It is our object to limit the
'demand upon his land, to secure him in the possession of it, and thus
'to render it valuable property.'

ever ; such, for instance, as precludes an enhancement of
the money assessment in the zemindári districts of the
Lower Provinces of Bengal. The rise which has taken
place of late years in India in the value of produce, as
estimated in silver, was not one of the contingencies
thought of when Munro's Minutes were written ; but
there can be little doubt, if we may judge from the general
tenor of his writings, that while strongly opposed to any
policy which might diminish security of tenure or check
the application of capital to the land, Munro would have
been in favour of a revision of the money assessment when,
owing to a depreciation in the value of the currency,
or to any other cause, the assessment ceased to be a fair
equivalent of the share of the produce to which, by
long prescription, the State was entitled, or which was
demanded by its financial requirements.

Munro's life in the Baramahal was a life of incessant
labour. He described the system of revenue management
as one of 'plain hard labour,' alleging that whatever
success had attended it, was to be 'ascribed to this talent
'alone,' and that it must be 'unremittingly exerted, not so
'much to make collections, as to prevent them by detecting
'the authors of private assessments. We have only to guard
'the ryots from oppression and they will create the revenue
'for us.' He wrote :

I go from village to village in my tent settling the
rents of the inhabitants, and this is so teazing and tedious
a business that it leaves room for nothing else ; for I have
no hour in the day that I can call my own. At this
moment, while I am writing, there are a dozen people
talking around me. It is now twelve o'clock, and they
have been going and coming in parties ever since seven in
the morning, when I began this letter. One man has a
long story of a debt of thirty years' standing, contracted
by his father ; another tells me that his brother made
away with his property when he was absent during the

D

war; and a third tells me that he cannot afford to pay his
usual rent, because his wife is dead, who used to do more
work than his best bullock. I am obliged to listen to all
these relations, and as every man has a knack at description, like Sancho, I think myself fortunate when I get
through any one of them in half an hour. It is in vain
that I sometimes recommend them to begin at the end of
the story. They persist in their own way of making me
full master of all the particulars; and I must, after
making my objections and hearing their replies, dictate
answers in the same style to them all, so that I cannot be
sure that this letter will be ready to go by the next ship.

But, incessant and laborious as his duties were, there
was much in Munro's life in the Baramahal that he found
extremely enjoyable. The country is picturesque and the
climate agreeable during several months of the year. He
was not a sportsman, but he was fond of all other country
pursuits. He was an indefatigable walker, and had a
keen appreciation of beautiful scenery. At Dharmapúri,
the head-quarter station of one of the districts under his
charge, he made a garden, which was a great source of
interest and amusement to him, and to the loss of which
he refers pathetically in one of his letters after he had left
the Baramahal.* The proximity of that country to the
Carnatic, where most of his old friends were stationed,

* 'It is a romantic country, and every tree and mountain has
'some charm which attaches me to them. I began a few years ago to
'make a garden near Dharmapúri, sheltered on one side by a lofty
'range of mountains, and on the other by an aged grove of mangoes.
'I made a tank in it about a hundred feet square, lined with stone
'steps; and the spring is so plentiful, that besides watering abundantly
'every herb and tree, there is always a depth of ten or twelve feet of
'clear water for bathing. I have numbers of young orange, mango,
'and other fruit trees in a very thriving state. I had a great crop of
'grapes this year; and my pine beds are now full of fruit. When I
'happened to be at Dharmapúri I always spent at least an hour every
'day at this spot; and to quit it now goes as much to my heart as for-
'saking my old friends' (Letter to his sister, dated Darya Daulat
Garden, Seringapatam, 30th June, 1799).

was also a great attraction to him, as giving him opportunities of meeting them from time to time.

During all these years Munro continued with unabated
vigour his correspondence with his family and friends.
Indeed, some of the most interesting of his private letters
are among those which he wrote from the Baramahal. In
those days the overland route had not come into use, and
letters from India took some six months, on the average,
in reaching England. The opportunities for sending them
were also, of course, far less numerous than they are now.
As a general rule, therefore, the letters from India were
longer than the overland letters of the present day. Indeed, the weekly post between England and India may be
said to have had the same effect upon Indian correspondence that the penny post has had upon English
letter-writing, viz. that while correspondence has enor-
mously increased, letter-writing as an accomplishment has
ceased to exist. Munro's letters were decidedly long, but
they were extremely interesting, and written, as they
invariably were, in a clear and legible hand, must have
been very charming letters to receive. Those to his
father, from some of which extracts have been given,
relate almost exclusively to his official duties, to the
condition of the country in which he was employed, and
to questions of public policy. They constitute a most
valuable supplement to Munro's official correspondence.
Those to his sister deal with a different description and a
greater variety of topics. They treat of the incidents and
prospects of his private life, of marriage, of the books he
had been reading, and of the popular topics of the day,
and they reveal a fund of humour and imagination for
which probably few persons who had only a superficial
acquaintance with the writer would have given him
credit; for Munro appears throughout his life to have
been somewhat reserved in his manner to strangers and

ordinary acquaintances, although quite the reverse with his intimates. The following are extracts from letters written to his sister in 1795. They express, in a vein of lively and sarcastic humour, the contempt which he felt for unpractical theories and crotchets of every description. It is evident that had he lived in the second half of the nineteenth century, he would have had no sympathy with, or toleration for, the principles of the Peace Society.

All nations are now, it seems, to be of one family, and we are to have no more quarrelling, no more fighting, except intellectual combats; and every man of us is to cultivate philosophy and the arts, and to talk of nothing but urbanity, and humanity, and gentleness, and delicacy, and sympathy, and love—every desert spot is to be converted into a garden, and the whole face of the earth is to swarm with the sons and daughters of reason and liberty. What then? Suppose all these fine things realized, shall we have changed for the better? Let agriculture and manufactures be carried to their utmost possible extent, where does it all end, but in our being more effeminate in our dress, and more epicurean in our food than we are now? We must also admit that the increase of the population has kept pace with the improvement of the arts; and that the whole face of the country will be covered with habitations, except what is required for the purposes of agriculture; but this cannot be a very extensive space, for as the earth will then be forced to yield at least an hundredfold more than at present, I reckon an area of twenty feet square a very ample allowance for each person. This is making a very great concession; for you know that every inch of dry land might be covered with houses, and the inhabitants, by having terraced roofs, might on the top of them raise food enough for their sustenance, as was formerly done by the Babylonians in their hanging gardens; but as I wish, contrary to the practice of the learned, to be moderate in argument, I give you twenty feet square for your maintenance and recreation. What will be the consequence of this advanced state of society? We shall not be able to walk out without being jostled on all sides by crowds of enlightened men and women. All the sports of the field and all rural pleasures will be at an end. There will be no rambling across the meadows, for every man will fence his territorial possessions of twenty feet against all intruders. There will be no hunting or shooting, for all wild animals will have been destroyed; and there will be no fishing, because every living thing in the rivers will have been poisoned by manufactures. There will be no poetry, no silence, no solitude; and if, by chance, some genius should arise and invoke the muse, he will sing more of being lulled to sleep by the clattering of fulling-mills and other machinery, than by the whispering of the zephyrs, or the sweet south, upon a bank of violets. The hard-handed peasant will then wear dogskin gloves, silk stockings, and a solitaire, and be wrapped in silk from top to toe like a cocoon; and as the plough will then, by the power of machinery, go by itself, he will look at its motions, mounted on the horse which in these barbarous times would be employed in drawing it. And the rich man, dressed in the finest stuffs that art can produce, will sit in his marble palace gasping for fresh air; for amidst the steam of human bodies, and the smoke of engines and workshops, it will be impossible to get a mouthful, unless by going to the sea. When the world, by the progress of knowledge, shall come to this pass, if the art of war, after being lost for many ages, is again discovered, it will be hailed as a noble invention, and the author of it will perhaps receive the honours of the Pantheon, for giving elbow-room to the half-stifled inhabitants of the globe, by such ingenious machinery as fire-arms, instead of its being effected by pestilence and famine; it will no doubt be considered as a learned profession, and probably be classed as one of the branches of the medical art. Now, supposing that the economists have accomplished their great plan of filling the world with farmers and manu-facturers, and made the whole face of the earth one great city, it does not appear that the more important end of in-creasing the happiness of mankind would be attained. . . .

I am still of opinion that war produces many good consequences: those philosophers who prophesy that the

millennium is to follow universal civilization, must have
shut their eyes to what is passing in the world, and trusted
entirely to intellectual light; otherwise they would have
seen that in proportion to the progress of science and the
arts, war becomes more frequent and more general, and
this I consider to be the true end of civilization. In
former ages of barbarity and ignorance, two petty States
might have fought till they were tired, without one of
their neighbours minding them, and perhaps without those
who were at a little distance ever hearing anything of the
matter; but in these enlightened times of mail-coaches
and packet-boats, no hostility can be committed in one
corner of Europe but it is immediately known in the
other, and we all think it necessary to fall to immediately.
I should be glad to know in what uncivilized age a fray
in Nootka Sound would have produced a bustle at
Portsmouth. Barbarous nations, when at war, generally
returned to their homes at the harvest season and took
the field again in the holidays, to fight by way of pastime,
and they were not afraid to leave their towns with no
other guard than their women, because no other nation
was supposed to be concerned in their quarrel; but now,
by the happy modern discovery of the balance of power,
all Europe is fraternized—every nation takes as least as
much interest in the affairs of other nations as in its own,
and no two can go to war without all the rest following
their example.

We are not, like barbarians, contented·with one or two
campaigns; the riches of commerce and the improvement
of science enable us to amuse ourselves much longer,
and we are now seldom contented with less than seven.
Why do our men of genius speculate, and our manu-
facturers toil unceasingly, but that we may collect money
enough to treat ourselves now and then to a seven years'
jubilee of warfare? The only instance in which civilized
is less destructive than barbarous war, is in not eating our
prisoners; but this I do not yet despair of seeing accomplished, for whenever any philosopher or politician shall
demonstrate that eating prisoners will improve the cotton
manufacture, or augment the revenue, an Act of Parliament
will soon be passed for despatching them as soon as

possible. War is to nations what municipal government is to particular cities: it is a grand police which teaches nations to respect each other, and humbles such as have become insolent by prosperity.

If you are not satisfied with political arguments, I shall give you some of a higher nature. Do not all religious and orthodox books insist strongly on the manifold benefits resulting from the chastisement and visitations of stiff-necked and stubborn generations? Now, what better visitation can you wish for than forty or fifty thousand men going into a strange land and living there at free quarters for two or three years? Don't you think that the calamities of the American War have made us more virtuous than we were, and that more Britons have gone to heaven since their chastisements, than they did in all the preceding part of the century? And I therefore, for my own sake, thank Providence that such a visitation happened in my life. It is in vain to look for the termination of war from the diffusion of light, as it is called. The Greeks and Romans in ancient times were, and the Germans, French, and English in modern times are, the most enlightened and warlike of nations; and the case will be the same till the end of the world, or till human nature ceases to be what it is. As long as nations have different governments and manners and languages, there will be war; and if commerce should ever so far extend its influence as that trading nations shall no longer fight for territory, they will never refuse to take up arms for cloth, and then the age of chivalry will have given place to that of economists: prisoners will no more be released on parole; the privates and subs. will be employed in coal-heaving and other works serviceable to the State, and those of superior rank ransomed; and if they are dilatory in settling accounts, they will, perhaps, be tossed in blankets of a particular manufacture to promote the circulation of cash. Those who rail against war have not taken a comprehensive view of the subject, nor considered that it mingles, in a greater or lesser degree, with the most refined of our pleasures. How inspired would poetry be without romances and heroic poems, and history without convulsions and revolutions? What would a library be with nothing but Shenstone and a few volumes of sermons? What would become of all those patriotic citizens who spend half their lives in coffee-houses talking of the British Lion, if he were to be laid to sleep by an unfortunate millennium?

Munro remained at his post in the Baramahal until February, 1799, when war with Tippoo having again broken out, and Read, who had attained the rank of lieutenant-colonel, having been appointed to command a force which was formed to reduce the adjoining district of Mysore, and to collect supplies for the army moving under General Harris against Seringapatam, Munro accompanied him as his secretary.

CHAPTER III.

THE war with Tippoo, which took Read and Munro from the Baramahal, had for some time been inevitable. Tippoo had always regarded the English with mixed feelings of hatred and dread, and since the Treaty of Seringapatam, when he was compelled to sign away a considerable portion of his territory, his hatred of the detested nation which had brought this humiliation upon him had become intensified from year to year. To the Muhammadans in the East he had given himself out as the champion of the Muhammadan faith, who was to expel the English Kafirs from India. He had sent a mission to Constantinople, and had opened communications with Zemán Shah, the ruler of Afghanistan, whom he invited to invade India, offering to co-operate with him in a grand effort for the establishment of Muhammadan supremacy throughout the country. At the same time he was engaged in intrigues with the Mahrattas, and was in active communication with the French, on whose help he mainly relied for the accomplishment of his designs against the English. The war would very probably have been postponed for some years, had there not been a change in the office of Governor-General, Sir John Shore, afterwards Lord Teignmouth, who had followed the Marquis of Cornwallis in the Governor-Generalship, having been succeeded by the Earl of Mornington in 1798. It was the opinion of some thoughtful men, and among others of Munro, that advantage should be taken of the defeat of Tippoo, in 1792, to cripple his power more completely than Lord Cornwallis had deemed advisable, when he made the Treaty of Seringapatam. Writing in 1796, Munro says:

We are now obliged to arm to prevent Tippoo from attacking some of our Mahratta friends. This was to be expected from our absurdity in leaving him so strong at the end of the last war. . . . To save the Ráo and Scindia from being crushed by this formidable conspiracy, we are now arming and endeavouring to form a camp by drawing together the fragments of battalions scattered between Ceylon and Amboyna. What is now going forward was to be expected. It was foreseen by every man who has reflected much on Indian politics, and is the only consequence of leaving Tippoo so strong at the end of the last war.

Lord Cornwallis had acted on the policy—and this policy had not been departed from by his successor—that it was expedient to maintain a balance of power in India by supporting Tippoo and the Nizam against the Mahrattas. Munro, as we have seen, at an early period had formed the opinion that Tippoo, and in a lesser degree the Nizam, was a power far more formidable to the English than all the Mahratta chiefs combined; and further reflection and observation, as years went by, only served to confirm him in this opinion. He wrote:

By applying European maxims to India, we have formed the chimerical project of maintaining the balance of power, by joining sometimes one party of Mahrattas and sometimes another, but chiefly by supporting Tippoo and the Nizam as a barrier between ourselves and the whole nation. We take it for granted that, if this fence were ever removed, they would instantly break in upon us, overrun the whole country, and drive us into the sea. I am so far of a different opinion, that I am convinced that the annihilation of both these powers would rather strengthen than weaken the security of our possessions. Experience has shown that augmentation of territory does not augment the force of the Mahrattas : it only serves to render the different chiefs more independent of the Poona Government, and to lessen the union of the confederacy. With more territory, they are not half so formidable as they were fifty years ago; but Tippoo is, what none of them are, complete master of his army and his country. Every additional acre of land and rupee of revenue increases his force in the same manner as among European nations. He introduces modern tactics and all the improvements of musketry and artillery into his army. . . . The Nizam has not followed the same plan, but an abler successor may. The present minister has evidently begun them by attempting in several instances to reduce the great jágírdárs or feudal vassals. Mussulmans, from the spirit of conquest mixed with their religion, are much more disposed than Hindus to spread among their armies all the advantages of foreign discoveries. Whenever the Nizam adopts them, he will become the most powerful prince in India, for he has now in his dominions great numbers of excellent horses and brave men, who want nothing but discipline. He and Tippoo, with regular armies, would be far more dangerous neighbours than the Mahrattas. Their system will be conquest, that of the Mahrattas only plunder. Ours ought, therefore, be, to let the Mahrattas strip the Nizam of as much of his dominions as they please, and to join them on the first favourable occasion to reduce Tippoo entirely. When this is effected, it may be said they would turn their whole force against us; but the interests of their leaders are so various, that we should never find much difficulty in creating a division among them; and admitting the worst, that we did not succeed, their united force would be able to make no impression on us. I have seen enough of their warfare to know that they could do little in action, and that their mode of laying waste the country would be more destructive to themselves than to us, and would never effectually stop our operations. It would not hinder us from making ourselves masters of the Malabar coast, nor from re-establishing the Rájás of Udaipúr and Jaipúr, and many other princes who are impatient to recover their independence. They would soon get tired of the war, make peace with us, and resume their old disputes about the Peshwa and his minister. Their government, which was long conducted by a Peshwa, or minister, in the name of the Rájá, has for more than twenty years been held by the ministers of his minister; and they are now going to decide by the sword whether minister the first or minister the second shall usurp the sovereign power. From a government whose members are scarcely ever united—where there is a perpetual struggle for the supreme authority—which forms no French alliances—and whose armies are constituted in the same way that they were last century, we have surely much less to apprehend than from such an enemy as Tippoo. By our scheme of politics, he is to save us from Mahratta invasions, but is not to extend his dominions; but as he is always contriving means to do it, we are, at every alarm, to be at the expense of taking the field, or going to war to keep him within the bounds which we have prescribed to him; but we are never to go so far as to overturn him entirely. The consequence of all these whimsical projects will be that we shall at last make the native powers so warlike, that in order to enable us to oppose them, we shall be obliged to sink the whole of our revenue in augmenting our armies. Any one who compares our present military establishment, King's and Company's, with what it was twenty years ago, will see how fast we are advancing to this point. The Company may flatter themselves that by their late arrangements they have set limits to their expenses on this head; but they must go on increasing, while the cause which produces them exists—a prince to meet us with regular armies in the field.

These views were very much in accordance with the views which were formed by the new Governor-General at an early period after his nomination to the office. Lord Mornington had previously paid some attention to Indian affairs, having held a seat at the Board of Control. Touching at the Cape of Good Hope on his voyage to India, he there met Lord Macartney, who had been Governor of Madras during a great part of the second war with Mysore, Lord Hobart, who was then on his way home from the same government, and Major Kirkpatrick, at that time Resident at the court of the Nizam. He also found despatches from the Governments in India to the Court of Directors, containing the latest information regarding the position of affairs. The information which he thus received, followed as it was, shortly after his arrival at Calcutta, by the receipt of authentic intelligence from Mauritius that a proclamation had been issued in that island, then a French dependency, inviting volunteers to take service under the Sultan of Mysore in a war which he was about to wage against the English, and that a body of men, recruited for that purpose, had been despatched to the western coast of India, convinced the Governor-General that no time was to be lost in anticipating Tippoo's designs, and crippling his power far more effectually than had yet been done.*

* Lord Mornington attached considerable importance to the correspondence which had been going on between Tippoo and the Afghan chief Zemán Shah. Writing to Mr. Dundas from the Cape of Good Hope on the 28th of February, 1798, he said : 'No mode of carrying 'on war against us could be more vexatious, or more distressing to 'our resources, than a combined attack upon Oudh and the Carnatic. 'It is not impossible that the late intercourse between Tippoo and 'the Zemán Shah had for its object, on the part of the former at 'least, some such plan of joint operation.' In the same letter he wrote : 'The balance of power in India no longer exists upon the 'same footing on which it was placed by the peace of Seringapatam. 'The question therefore must arise how it may be brought back again 'to that state in which you have directed me to maintain it. My 'present view of the subject is that the wisest course would be to 'strengthen the Mahrattas and the Nizam, by entering into a defensive 'alliance with the former against Zemán Shah, and by affording to 'the latter an addition of military strength and the means of extri- 'cating himself from the control of the French party at Hyderabad.' After Lord Mornington's arrival at Calcutta both these measures were proceeded with. The proposed defensive alliance with the Mahrattas failed, but Zemán Shah's projected invasion of Hindostan was prevented by an invasion of his own territories by the Persians. The subversion of French influence at Hyderabad was effectually

He at once ordered preparations to be made for war.* Owing to the scattered position and insufficient strength

carried out, within a few months after Lord Mornington's arrival in India, by the despatch of a British force to Hyderabad, in the presence of which the French officers were dismissed, and the native troops under their command, numbering some 14,000 men, disarmed. Munro refers to this force and its projected dispersion in one of his letters in the following terms :—

'The Nizam has for several years had a few corps of sepoys, 'officered by Europeans of different nations, but the whole commanded 'by Monsieur Raymond. They were for a long time neither well paid 'nor well armed, nor were they dangerous either from their numbers 'or discipline; but after the late war Raymond was permitted to 'make new levies. He obtained a large tract of country in jágír for 'their maintenance, and was enabled to pay them regularly, to clothe 'and arm them completely, and to bring them into a high state of 'order. He was soon at the head of 15,000 men, with a train of 'artillery; he hoisted the tricoloured flag on all occasions, and at last 'became formidable to his master. Could any strong body of French 'troops have been landed in India, it is most likely he would have 'joined them and Tippoo against the English and the Nizam; but 'whatever his projects might have been, he, fortunately for us, died 'in the midst of them, about two months ago. He has left no 'successor of equal ability or influence; and as the different com- 'mandants have various interests, and show but little deference to 'their present chief, the Nizam has, either of himself, or by the 'interference of the Supreme Government, conceived the design of 'breaking them altogether, or, at least, of disbanding all the corps 'that are suspected of being under French influence. A strong 'detachment has been formed in Guntúr, to march in case of necessity 'to Hyderabad. The sooner they move the better, for no time ought 'to be lost in destroying this party so hostile to our interests in the 'Deccan. Raymond owed the rapid increase of his power to the weak, 'timid policy of ——, who might have suppressed it in the beginning, 'if not by remonstrance, at least by menace; but he chose rather to 'sit and view its progress quietly than to do anything to risk, or what 'he thought was risking, hostilities.'

The disbandment of the troops under French command was accom- panied by the establishment at Hyderabad of a British subsidiary force, which, under the command of Colonel Wellesley, took part in the final campaign against Tippoo. This force, composed partly of British and partly of native regiments of the Madras army, has been ever since maintained at Hyderabad, under the designation of the Hyderabad Subsidiary Force. To meet the cost of its main- tenance, the districts of Ballári, Cuddapah, etc., now known as the Ceded Districts, were ceded to the East India Company in 1800.

* The Governor-General was debarred by an Act of Parliament

of the Madras troops available for an expedition against
Mysore, and the utter want of transport and commissariat,
some delay unavoidably occurred; but under the energetic
supervision of the Governor-General, who repaired to
Madras at the end of the year for the purpose of assuming
the immediate direction of the political and military
arrangements, an army of 20,000 men was collected at
Vellore early in February, 1799, and was supplemented
by a force of 13,000 men furnished by the Nizam, under
the command of Colonel Arthur Wellesley; while another
force of 6400 men was ordered to co-operate from the
Bombay side, besides smaller bodies under Colonels Read
and Brown. The command of the whole was entrusted to
General Harris, the Commander-in-chief at Madras. On
the 4th of May the war was practically brought to an end
by the capture of Seringapatam and the death of Tippoo,
who was killed in the assault. Read's force was not
present at the taking of the fortress, having been left
behind the main body of the army for the purpose of
reducing various small forts in their rear and collecting
supplies. It was subsequently employed in taking possession of Bangalore and other forts; but early in June
Munro left it and returned to Seringapatam, having been
nominated one of the secretaries to the Commission
appointed by the Governor-General to consider and
arrange measures for the future disposal of the Mysore

passed in 1793 from either declaring war, or commencing hostilities,
or entering into any treaty for making war, against any of the
country princes or states in India, except in the case of hostilities
having been commenced or hostile preparations having been made by a
native prince. Lord Mornington regarded the Mauritius proclamation—the genuineness of which he considered to have been established
—as affording sufficient evidence that Tippoo was engaged in making
hostile preparations against the English, and this was the view taken
by the President of the Board of Control. The opinion of the Court
of Directors was more guardedly expressed; but their orders conveyed the requisite authority to the Governor-General to declare
war, if he was satisfied of Tippoo's hostile intentions.

territory, and to settle other questions arising out of the
recent conquest. The Commission consisted of General
Harris, Colonel Barry Close, Colonel Arthur Wellesley,
Mr. Henry Wellesley, and Colonel Kirkpatrick—Captain
(afterwards Sir) John Malcolm was Munro's colleague as
secretary. The labours of the Commission, conducted in
close correspondence with the Governor-General, who had
remained at Madras for the purpose of superintending
their work, resulted in the treaty of partition which
divided the Mysore territory between the East India
Company and the Nizam, and the subsidiary treaty which
made over a considerable portion of the Company's share
to a member of the old Hindu dynasty subverted by Hyder
Ali, but now revived in the person of the late Mahárájá of
Mysore.

It was while employed on this Commission that Munro
was first brought into close intercourse with the future
Duke of Wellington, then Colonel Arthur Wellesley, with
whom he contracted a lasting friendship. There were
many points of resemblance in the characters of the two
men. Simple in their habits, practical and clear-sighted
in their views, earnest in the discharge of duty, cordially
detesting everything that savoured of sham or pretension
of whatever description, it was hardly possible that they
should be brought much together without being speedily
inspired by sentiments of mutual regard and esteem. And
similar as they were in character, there was enough difference in the views which they held on some subjects, to
give zest to their intercourse. Munro, at this period of
his life, was an ardent supporter of the policy of extending British rule in India. His observation of the effects
of native misgovernment in the Baramahal, his patriotic
desire for the aggrandizement of his country, and the poor
opinion which he entertained of the power of most of the
native states—all impelled him to advocate the extension

of British rule whenever and wherever opportunity offered. The resolution of the Governor-General to set up another native dynasty in Mysore, notwithstanding the conditions annexed to the measure, whereby, in the words of Lord Mornington, 'the most unqualified community of interests ' was established between the Government of Mysore and 'the Company,' and the Rájá was placed in a position of strict dependence upon the Government of British India, was viewed by Munro with but little satisfaction. If he had had any voice in the decision of the question, he 'certainly would have had no Rájá of Mysore, in the ' person of a child dragged forth from oblivion, to be placed ' on a throne on which his ancestors, for three generations, ' had not sat during more than half a century.' Colonel Wellesley, on the other hand, appears to have been favourable to the arrangement, and though by no means opposed to the general policy of his brother, which was essentially the reverse of a policy of inactivity, he regarded, perhaps, with greater apprehension than Munro the consequences of moving too rapidly.

In one of his letters addressed to Munro in the following year, he writes: 'I fancy that you will have the pleasure ' of seeing some of your grand plans carried into execution.' In another the following sentence occurs: 'This is ex- 'pensive, but if you are determined to conquer all India ' at the same moment, you must pay for it.' * We may be

---

* The following is the text of the two letters in question. The original manuscripts are in the British Museum. The first does not appear to have been published before it appeared in the first edition of this work.

'MY DEAR MUNRO,   'Camp at Hoobly, October 6th, 1800.

          'I have received your letter of the 27th September.   I ' have been ordered by Government to remain for some time in this ' country, and I have come in order to eat rice, which I propose to ' draw from the borders of Soonda without using that brought from ' Nagpore by my brinjarries. You will therefore perceive the necessity ' that my brinjarries should return to me to the northward, but I am ' not in a hurry about them, and it does not much signify if they do

certain that in those few weeks in the summer of 1799
which Munro spent at Seringapatam, there was many an
'not go to Cundapore and Mangalore to receive their loads. I fancy
'that you will have the pleasure of seeing some of your grand plans
'carried into execution: all I can say is that I am ready primed,
'and that if all matters suit I shall go off with a dreadful explosion,
'and shall probably destroy some *campoos* and *pultons* which have
'been indiscreetly pushed across the Kistna—that is to say, if the
'river remains full.

'I have written to tell Colonel Close about your money which I
'shall want. The only reason why I cannot get it is that you are
'obliged to keep enough in your hands to pay the troops in Kanara,
'etc., till January. I have written to desire that a sum of money for
'that purpose may be sent round from Madras in one of the ships of
'the squadron, and whatever sum I hear that they will send I will
'draw an equal one from you. That is the only mode that occurs of
'procuring the supply of money which I shall want in December.

'Believe me, yours most sincerely,
'ARTHUR WELLESLEY.'

'Camp at Hoobly, October 10th, 1800.
'DEAR MUNRO,
'Webbe informs me, in a letter of the 4th instant, that
'you are appointed to be Collector of the countries ceded to the
'Company by the Nizam, and has desired me to write to you to state
'at what place it will be most convenient that you should join me.
'You had better come here and through Soonda. I am sadly pressed
'for troops for all our extensive objects, and I must draw copiously
'upon Kanara in order to be able to make up a detachment at all
'equal to taking possession of the ceded countries. I shall in the
'first place want three companies for Nuggur from Cundapore, and
'eight companies of the 75th for Malabar, in lieu of five companies of
'the 12th which must go into the ceded countries. I recommend it
'to you, therefore, to keep in employment in Kanara all your peons.
'You will thus have plenty of troops and no enemy.

'After all my efforts to provide a proper detachment for the ceded
'districts, I shall be able to collect only one regiment of Europeans,
'one battalion and eight companies of sepoys, with as many guns as
'they please. I should recommend that this detachment should be
'kept together in one body, to be thrown on any point where their
'assistance may be wanted; that the common business should be
'done by peons till more troops can be spared from other services.
'You will thus have no enemy.

'This is expensive, I acknowledge, but if you are determined to
'conquer all India at the same moment you must pay for it.

'Don't forget to recommend my brinjarries to the gentleman whom
'you leave in charge of Kanara.

'Believe me, ever yours most sincerely,
'Major Munro.'   'ARTHUR WELLESLEY.

argument in the Darya Daulat Palace, between the future conqueror of Napoleon and the future Governor of Madras,

The subjoined extracts are interesting as setting forth the views of the two men.

Extract from letter from Major Munro to Colonel Wellesley, dated August 14th, 1800.

' I confess for my own part that, as we have thought it necessary ' to appear in India as sovereigns, I think we ought to avail ourselves, ' not of the distresses of our neighbours, but of their aggressions, to ' strengthen ourselves, and to place ourselves in such a situation as ' may be likely to prevent such attacks hereafter. Sindia has been ' allowed to increase his power by the subjugation of the Jaipúr and ' Udaipúr Rájás, and also in a great measure of the Peshwa. We ' want money to oppose him, and money, too, more particularly since ' the increase to the pay of the native troops ; and if, in order to ' attain those objects, we retain in our possession certain territories ' which pour forth invaders upon us, we can hardly be charged with ' having violated the laws of nations. I am for making ourselves as ' strong as possible before the French return to India, and set Sindia ' at war with us after completing his demi-brigades with pretended ' deserters.'

Extract from letter from Colonel Wellesley to Major Munro, dated August 20th, 1800.

' My ideas of the nature of Indian governments, of their decline ' and fall, agree fully with yours, and I acknowledge that I think it ' probable that we shall not be able to establish a strong government ' on this frontier. Scindiah's influence at Poona is too great for us, ' and I see plainly, if Colonel Palmer remains there, we shall not be ' able to curb him without going to war. There was never such an ' opportunity for it as the present moment, and probably by bringing ' forward and by establishing in their ancient possessions Pursuram ' Rhow's family, under our protection, we should counterbalance ' Scindiah and secure our own tranquillity for a great length of time. ' But I despair of it, and I am afraid that we shall be reduced to the ' alternative of allowing Scindiah to be our neighbour upon our old ' frontier, or of taking this country ourselves. If we allow Scindiah ' to be our neighbour, or if the country goes to any other through his ' influence, we must expect worse than what has passed—thieves of ' all kinds, new Dhondees, and probably Dhondee himself again. If ' we take the country ourselves I don't expect much tranquillity.

' In my opinion the extension of our territory and influence has ' been greater than our means. Besides, we have added to the number ' and description of our enemies by depriving of employment those ' who heretofore found it in the service of Tippoo and the Nizam. ' Wherever we spread ourselves, particularly if we aggrandize our- ' selves at the expense of the Mahrattas, we increase this evil. We regarding the sanguine projects of the latter for the extension of British rule—projects which Munro lived to see

'throw out of employment, and of means of subsistence, all who have
'hitherto managed the revenue, commanded or served in the armies,
'or have plundered the country.

'Upon all questions of increase of territory, these considerations
'have much weight with me, and I am in general inclined to decide
'that we have enough; as much at least, if not more than we can
'defend.

'I agree with you that we ought to settle this Mahratta business
'and the Malabar Rajahs before the French return to India; but I
'am afraid that to extend ourselves will rather tend to delay than
'accelerate the settlement, and that we shall thereby increase, rather
'than diminish, the number of our enemies.

'As for the wishes of the people, particularly in this country, I
'put them out of the question. They are the only philosophers about
'their governors that ever I met with—if indifference constitutes that
'character.'

From Major Munro to Colonel Wellesley, dated August 29th, 1800.

'Your arguments against extension of territory are certainly very
'strong, but still I cannot help thinking that you allow too much
'for its increasing the number of our enemies and weakening our
'means of defence. There are three things that greatly facilitate our
'conquests in this country. The first is, the whole of India being not
'one nation, always parcelled out among a number of chiefs, and
'these parcels continually changing masters, makes a transfer to us
'to be regarded, not as a conquest, but merely as one administration
'turning out another. The second is the total want of hereditary
'nobility and country gentlemen, or that there is no respectable class
'of men who might be compelled, by a sense either of honour or of
'interest, to oppose a revolution. And the third is our having a
'greater command than any of the native powers of money—a strong
'engine of revolution in all countries, but more especially in India.

'As to the enemies we create by driving men out of employment,
'I do not apprehend it ever can do us any serious mischief. We have
'already, in overthrowing Tippoo, seen more of it than we can ever
'see again, because his service contained so great a number of
'Mussulmans. Let us suppose Savanúr to fall into our hands: the
'only person almost in the revenue line who would suffer is Bál Kishan
'Ráo: all the headmen of villages would remain exactly as they are;
'ten or a dozen of Bál Kishan's gomashtas might be changed, but as
'we must have men of the same description, their places would be
'supplied by a dozen other gomashtas, and as the whole of both sets
'would probably be natives of Savanúr, the result would be that
'among the revenue people of the country there would be twelve outs
'in favour of the Mahrattas, and twelve ins in favour of the Company.

'But it may be said we should have the military against us. The carried out far in excess of his early expectations, and which Wellesley only a few years later did much to further

'chiefs would certainly be against us; but their resentment would be 'very harmless, because the payment of their men is the only hold 'they have upon them; and as the means of doing this would be lost 'along with the revenue, they would be left without troops. These 'troops, if natives of the country, either have land themselves, or a 'share of what is held by their fathers and brothers; and as the 'labouring part of the family would prefer the Company's govern- 'ment on account of; being more moderately taxed, they would in 'most cases be able to keep the military part quiet. Many of the 'young men among the disbanded troops would find employment in 'the Company's army; and even the older, though they would be 'rejected themselves, would by degrees become attached to it by their 'younger brothers or sons entering into it. There is no army in 'India which supports decently, or even liberally, so great a number 'of what may be called the middling class of natives as our own. It 'is true it offers no field to your Nawábs and Fonjdárs, but what of 'that? These men have no influence but while in office. They are 'frequently raised from nothing, and often dismissed without any 'reason; and the people, by being accustomed to see so many 'successions of them, care about none of them; so that although these 'officers, by losing their places, become our enemies, yet, as they have 'no adherents, they can do us no harm.

'Sindia is at this moment as much our enemy as we can make 'him. If he does not break with us, it is because he fears us, and an 'extension of territory, by giving us greater resources, would make 'him still more cautious. The acquisition of Savanúr would give us 'a frontier that would not require more troops to defend than our 'present one. But I have not the least doubt myself that from the 'nature of Indian governments, every inch of territory gained adds to 'our ability both of invading and defending. Every province that 'falls into our hands diminishes the force of the enemy by the loss of 'the revenue destined to support a certain number of troops, and it 'increases our force in a greater ratio, because the same province 'under us will pay as many troops, and of a much better quality. A 'Mahratta or Nizamite army invading our territory can make no 'lasting impression upon it : they cannot take forts, and we have no 'great feudal vassals to revolt to their standard. They might for a 'time ravage the country, but they would soon be obliged to fall back 'by their brinjarries, etc., being intercepted, and probably by dis- 'turbances at home. But we, in entering their territory, would find 'little difficulty in reducing every place that came in our way, and we 'should everywhere find Ráos and Bhows and Nawábs ready, if not to 'join us, at least to throw off their dependence upon the enemy.

'All that India can bring against us is not so formidable as the 'confederacy of Hyder and his Mahrattas was in 1780, when we had by his decisive victory over the Mahrattas at Assye. It may be a question whether, if Munro had lived in the days of Lord Dalhousie, he would have approved the annexation policy of that ruler in all its details. It may be that he would have doubted the justice of suppressing native rule in Nagpore, and the policy of annexing Oudh ; but there can be no manner of doubt that the proposal to restore Mysore to native rule, after it had enjoyed for nearly fifty years the benefit of British administration—a proposal which, having been repeatedly negatived by the highest authorities, was eventually sanctioned in 1867— would have encountered from him an opposition not less strenuous than that which was offered to it by Lord Canning and his successor in the Governor-Generalship.

Among the territories which under the partition treaty became British, was the district of Canara, a tract lying along the western coast between Mysore and the sea, which, having been governed by successive Hindu dynasties up to 1773, was in that year subjugated by Hyder and annexed to Mysore. It was necessary at once to appoint an officer of revenue experience to administer this district, and the choice fell upon Munro. The arrangement was one which by no means accorded with Munro's personal wishes; for his desire was to return to the Baramahal,

'but a small force, with a frontier as difficult to defend as our present
'one. The increase of our resources have enabled us to double our
'army, and has given us an excellent body of cavalry, and a few more
'lakhs of pagodas of country will give us the means of making this
'cavalry so strong that nothing in India will look at them. I am
'therefore for going to the Malpurba in the mean time, unless you are
'determined on going to the Krishna at once, which unluckily must
'be our fate sooner or later. The business must be settled at Poona, and
'the territory may be said to be made over to us, either for a subsidy,
'or for the expenses of the war and future aid against new Dhondees.
'Sindia cannot well act against us in the peninsula, unless by usurping
'the Poona Government, and then we should be able to bring a strong
'confederacy against him—all the friends of the Peshwa, the Nizam
'in order to recover the valuable territory he lost before the last war,
'and the Rájás of Udaipúr and Jaipúr, supported by the royal army.'

where, as his late chief, Read, was about to leave India, he naturally hoped to succeed him. Munro was, as we have seen, much attached to that country and to its people. He had laboured hard in bringing it into order, and he longed to return and complete his work. Moreover, he shrank from the separation from old friends which his removal to Canara would necessarily entail. But Munro's personal desires and the public interests were on this occasion deemed by the authorities to be incompatible. Malabar, the district adjoining Canara on the south, which had been brought under British rule in 1792 by the Treaty of Seringapatam, partly owing to the inefficiency of the arrangements made for its management by the Government of Bombay, and partly owing to the refractory and turbulent character of the petty chiefs, who were numerous in the district, had given, and still was giving, a good deal of trouble. It was feared that the example of the unruly chiefs of Malabar would not be without its influence upon the petty chiefs and ryots of Canara, and it was felt that if order was to be introduced into the latter province, its management must be entrusted to an officer of proved firmness and capacity. Munro was not the man to decline a disagreeable duty when he was told that the public interests required him to undertake it, and as soon as his business at Seringapatam was done, he started for Canara.

The gloomy anticipations with which Munro entered upon his new charge, were not destined to be agreeably disappointed. Canara had been at one time a very thriving country, filled with industrious inhabitants, more lightly taxed than those of any other Indian province; but it had been grievously oppressed by the exactions of Hyder and Tippoo. It had been the scene of four wars, and during the latter years of Tippoo's reign misgovernment had produced insurrections, and with them a spirit of anarchy

which indisposed the people to submit to settled rule.
Just before Munro entered the district, one portion of it
had been ravaged by the Coorgs, and another had been
invaded by the followers of Dhundaji—a Mahratta adven-
turer who had escaped from Seringapatam, and had set the
British authorities in Mysore at defiance. Jamalábád, a
strong hill-fort, was in the hands of rebels, and in several
parts of the district bodies of marauders of various classes
were at large. Munro's earlier experiences of the ryots of
Canara were by no means favourable. He met with the
greatest difficulty in even commencing a settlement of the
revenue, the ryots refusing to attend for the purpose, save
under certain conditions, and sending him a paper wherever he went, 'a kind of bill of rights,' the terms of which
they required to be conceded before they would discuss the
subject of the assessment. He wrote:

The ryots themselves are a most unruly and turbulent
race. This, however, without ascribing to them any
naturally bad disposition, may be easily accounted for,
when we know that they have twice lost the advantageous
tenures by which they held their lands—once by Hyder's
conquest, and now by that of the Company, Before they
fell under the Mysore Government their land-tax was
probably as light as that of most countries in Europe.
When Tippoo's finances became totally deranged about
four years ago, when he did not receive fifty per cent. of
his revenue, they joined the Sirkár servants in plundering,
and recovered in some measure their lost rights by being
permitted to withhold twenty or twenty-five per cent. of
their rents. On my arrival they wanted not only to keep
what they had got, but also to get more; while I was
resolved, after making allowance for the desolation of two
wars, to bring the revenue back to what it had been in
1789, the last year of any regular government in Tippoo's
reign, and then to leave it to Government to relinquish as
much of it as they might think fit. As soon as they
discovered my intention, they entered into combinations

to bring me to terms. These sort of combinations had been very general under the weak and profligate set of rulers they had had since 1792. They were even encouraged; because men in office always contrived to receive something for settling them; and the inhabitants too gained their ends, in some measure, by obtaining a remission of rent on account of the loss they were supposed to have sustained from the neglect of cultivation during their temporary insurrection. They sent me proposals from all quarters, demanding, in general, a remission of all assessments since the conquest of Hyder, as the only condition on which they would agree to enter into any discussion about a settlement. I, of course, rejected all preliminaries but such as I might think it necessary, upon examination, to prescribe to myself. This was considered by them as a declaration of war, and they lost no time in taking the field; that is to say, they refused to come to the cutcherry. They absconded when peons were sent for them. They almost starved some of the amildárs I had detached, by preventing them from getting fire and water; and whenever I approached a village, the inhabitants went off to another, so that I was sometimes several weeks in a district without seeing one of them. Reports had been circulated among them that the country was soon to be placed under the Bombay Government; and they therefore hoped that by keeping aloof for a time, they would either see me removed, or constrain me to submit, lest the season should pass away before I could make a settlement. Perseverance on my part, however, at last brought over some deserters; and by talking to them, as your friend Cleveland would have done, they brought over more, and I am now getting on as well as I can expect; but they are such a different kind of people to any ryots to the eastward of the Gháts, that I have still but very little confidence in their engagements, and am very far from being satisfied that they will perform them—and I can hardly venture to say that I shall come within ten per cent. of the settlement : six months, however, will decide the question.

After a time, however, patience and firmness, which were marked features in Munro's character, prevailed, and by a careful examination into the circumstances of the district, and a scrutiny into its ancient records, he was able to make a settlement, which has formed the basis of all subsequent arrangements with reference to the land revenue of Canara, now and for many years past one of the most flourishing provinces in India. The labour which Munro underwent in his investigation into the Canara land tenures and in settling the assessment, was very great. He says in one of his letters : 'In this one year 'I have gone through more work than in almost all the 'seven I was in the Baramahal.' He examined a number of ancient registers,* in which he traced the tenures and the assessments which had prevailed as far back as the middle of the fourteenth century, when Canara was subject to the Rájá of Vijayanagar, and when the assessment which formed the basis of that which he found in operation, was introduced. This ancient assessment, which was called the rekhá or shist, Munro found still written, ' not only in all general accounts of districts, but 'in those of every individual landholder.' Additions had been made to it by the Bednore Government, but not such as materially to affect the prosperity of the people. The amount even then would seem not to have exceeded one-

* Writing on the 7th of June, 1800, to his friend Mr. Cockburn, a Member of the Board of Revenue, he says : ' I wished to have traced 'the nature of landed property in Súnda, if such property actually 'existed there, by a chain of sanads up to the eighth century, but the 'sanads take too much time; many of them are intricate and 'obscure, and after translating a dozen sometimes, I meet with 'nothing to illustrate the object of my search. Time slips away; 'business accumulates, and I am in danger of neglecting the present 'generation, while I am attempting to ascertain whether their fore- 'fathers were permitted to eat a greater proportion of the land than 'they do. With the view of clearing away difficulties for new men I 'shall exact the payment of balances more rigorously than I would 'have done had I wished to take a lease of the country. This will bear 'hard upon some individuals; *but where there has been nothing but* '*anarchy for the last seven years, order can only be established by being* '*inflexible—indulgence can be thought of afterwards.*'

fourth of the gross produce. The revenue was easily
realized and outstanding balances were almost unknown.
It was not until after the conquest of Hyder that any
serious pressure was put upon the landholders. From
that time one addition after another was made to the
assessment, and the country ' was regarded as a fund from
' which he (Hyder) might draw without limit for the
' expenses of his military operations in other quarters.'
The whole course of the administration of Hyder's
deputies is described by Munro as ' a series of experi-
' ments made for the purpose of determining the extent '
to which the assessment could be raised, and ' how much
' it was possible to extort from the farmer without dimin-
' ishing cultivation.' Under Tippoo the state of things
was even worse. He destroyed many of the principal
towns near the coast, and forced their inhabitants to
remove to Jamalábád and other unhealthy situations near
the hills : in one night he seized all the Christian men,
women, and children, numbering above sixty thousand,
and sent them into captivity to Mysore. He prohibited
all foreign trade, and permitted a system of corruption
and disorder in all departments of his administration; and
when many of the ryots had been compelled by his
exorbitant exactions to abandon their holdings, he forced
those who remained to cultivate, in addition to their own
land, the land of those who had gone, for which they did
not possess the necessary stock, thereby intensifying their
difficulties and ultimately diminishing the revenue.

Land in Canara had always been regarded as private
property. Its transfer,

by sale or otherwise, was unrestrained. Nothing but
gift, or sale, or non-payment of rent, could take it from
the owner. If he absconded with balances standing
against him, it was transferred to another person; but if
he or his heir returned at ever so distant a period, it was

restored, on either of them paying a reasonable compensation for the balance, and such extra expenses as might have been incurred on account of improvements. No crime in the proprietor could extinguish the right of the heir to the succession.

Most of these proprietors had tenants under them with rights of occupancy more or less permanent.

Though the estates held immediately of Government were so small that the rent of each did not exceed fifty pagodas, yet the proprietors had under them an infinite number of lesser proprietors, holding their lands of them, with all the same proprietary rights as those under which they held their own of Government. It was usual for the original proprietors to rent, either for a term of years or for ever, such a portion of their lands as was sufficient to discharge the whole of their public rent, and to keep the rest in their hands. The tenants for ever became a second class of proprietors, whom nothing could deprive of their rights of possession, unless their own act of gift or sale. On failure of heirs, the lands reverted to the original superior landlord; but a reversion of the estate of the superior landlord to the sirkár did not take place if the inferior could be found.

Much of the land in Canara had a saleable value. Munro had met with some instances in which particular fields had been sold as high as twenty-five or thirty years' purchase of the Government assessment. This state of things had been seriously altered for the worse by the misgovernment of the Mysore rulers. In many cases the ancient proprietors had become extinct. In all, the value of the rights which the landholders possessed had been seriously diminished; but what remained was 'still as 'much cherished, and the title to it as obstinately con-'tested, as it ever was perhaps at any former period.'

Munro's earlier impressions of the actual condition of the landholders were more unfavourable than those which

he was led to form on further acquaintance with the
district. In his first report, dated the 3rd of May, 1800,
he described the landlords, who all lived chiefly on their
rents, as having hardly any rent at all. 'Few of them,'
he wrote, 'have sufficient to constitute of itself the fund
'of their subsistence.' But shortly after this paper was
written, he was led by facts which came under his notice
to judge more favourably of their condition. His attention
was attracted to the extraordinary number of suits about
land; Canara in this, as in other respects, presenting a
remarkable contrast to the Baramahal. In the Baramahal
a dispute about land had scarcely come before him once
in six months; in Canara land produced nineteen in
twenty of all the complaints he had to deal with. 'The
'accumulated suits of half a century appeared to have
'broken loose at once,' and every moment that he could
spare from his ordinary business had been given to the hearing of them without having sensibly reduced their number.
In making his first settlement of the district, Munro had
not deemed himself at liberty, on his own authority, to
reduce the assessment much below the standard which
he found in operation. He had made 'no other reduction
'in the assessment of Tippoo Sultán than such as was
'absolutely necessary in order to ensure the collection of
the rent.' He had regarded himself merely as a Collector
who was to investigate and report upon the state of the
country, but he had urged upon the authorities at Madras
a considerable reduction, which was sanctioned by the
Government as a temporary arrangement. This recommendation he was now led to modify, partly by the con-
clusions which he drew from the extent of litigation about
land, partly by the facts that the assessment which he
had imposed was generally paid with considerable punc-
tuality, and that cultivation was increasing, and partly
by other evidence which satisfied him that the landholders

did not require the amount of relief which he had at first
suggested.

The settlement which Munro recommended for Canara,
was in its leading principles ryotwár; that is to say, it
was a settlement of the revenue with the actual landowners,
the holders for the most part of small estates, without the
intervention of any middle men in the shape of renters or
zemindárs. It differed, however, from the ryotwár settlement which had been made in the Baramahal, and from
that which was subsequently carried out in the Ceded
Districts, in two important particulars. In the first place,
the settlement was made, in many cases, not with the
actual cultivator, but with a landholder, who, owing to
the lightness of the assessment, was able to let a portion
of his land to a tenant or tenants, from whom he received
a rent, and who, as we have said, had rights of occupancy
more or less permanent. In the second place, the assessment was laid, not as in the other two cases referred to,
upon each field, but upon each estate or warg. In this, as
in other cases, the salient feature of Munro's revenue
policy was to accept the existing institutions of the country
as he found them, and not to introduce any alterations
which were not absolutely necessary. He found in
Canara a very widely established system of private property in land, which, although it had suffered damage
from the oppression and exactions of the late rulers of the
country, was still cherished and valued by the people, and
his policy was, not to supersede it by any new system, but
to restore and strengthen it by moderate assessments and
by the impartial administration of justice. But in those
days very different views obtained in the highest quarters
as to the proper mode of administering the land revenues
of India. The zemindári settlement effected by Lord
Cornwallis in Bengal, under which the Government
received the revenue from a limited number of large

landholders, holding under a permanent assessment, was regarded as the model on which all revenue settlements throughout India should, as far as possible, be based, and before Munro left Canara he received orders to submit proposals for dividing the country into large estates, to which the principles of the Bengal permanent assessment was to be applied. Munro was much opposed to the arrangement. He held that although in countries where private property in land was unknown, and where the general poverty of the cultivators disabled them from making any improvement, the division of land into large estates, and giving them away, or disposing of them for a price to men of property, where such could be found, might possibly have some advantages—in Canara, where almost all land was private property, derived from gift or purchase, or descent from an antiquity too remote to be traced; where there were more title-deeds; and where the validity of these deeds had probably stood more trials than all the estates in England, great proprietors could not be established without annihilating all the rights of the present landlords. Nor did he believe that by any arrangement for 'placing a number of small estates under the collection of one landlord,' any facility of collection, or any security for revenue, would be obtained, that might not be secured by letting the estates remain as they then stood. In his opinion, any advantages that might be gained from introducing a system of great estates could only be temporary, owing to the absence of any exclusive rights of primogeniture and the consequent tendency to a subdivision of property.   He wrote:

The expenses of Indian must not be measured by those of European husbandry. Exclusive of tanks, there is hardly any expense which may not be defrayed by the smallest, as easily as by the great proprietors; and even tanks themselves are unnecessary in Canara. The small estates are in general better cultivated than the great ones; and their owners are as regular as the great owners in discharging their kists.* Among the numerous instances which have come before me, of their having been violently dispossessed of their lands, or of their having fled and left them waste on account of balances under the late Government, there is not one in which these balances can fairly be attributed to the rent alone, nor in which they have not arisen from fines, anticipations, and other acts of oppression. In whatever way I view the question of great and small proprietors, I am perfectly satisfied that the preference ought to be given to small ones, and that Government ought to make its settlements immediately with them. Under such a system, the gross produce of the country will be greater, and the collection of the revenue will be as regular as under that of great landholders.

Munro, however, invariably obeyed orders, and accordingly, after stating his objections to the arrangement proposed, he submitted a plan for giving effect to it, which, however, was not carried out, and, owing to a change which took place some years later in the views of the Madras Government and of the Court of Directors, was eventually abandoned.

But the settlement of the land revenue and the investigation of suits about land were not by any means the only matters which engaged Munro's attention in Canara. The disturbed state of the district, when it was first occupied, made it necessary to establish not less than fourteen different military posts in it, and Munro had to correspond with the commandants of each one of these posts. Indeed, it may be said that the general direction of the military arrangements was practically in his hands, although his military rank did not admit of his being formally invested with the command, as Read had been in the Baramahal.

* *Kist*—instalment, the portion of the annual revenue to be paid at specified periods in the course of the year.

With Colonel Wellesley, who had been left at the head of affairs, both military and civil, in Mysore, Munro was engaged in constant correspondence, a great part of which had reference to the arrangements for provisioning the army employed under the former in his pursuit of the rebel Dhundaji. He was also required to write several elaborate memoranda, for the information of the Governor-General, regarding matters on which Lord Mornington consulted him. One of these was on the defences of the Malabar coast, with reference to the contingency of a French invasion, of which at that time there was some apprehension. The following is an extract from Munro's paper * on the subject :—

An enemy landing on this coast with an intention of penetrating into the Mysore country, while we have an army there, or even of establishing themselves below the Ghâts, would find it a very arduous task ; for in either case they must bring with them almost everything but rice. To penetrate into Mysore or Coimbatore, they must not only be masters of the sea for a time, but they must reduce the low country ; and when this is done, they must bring tents, bazars, draught cattle, carriage and slaughter cattle, sheep, etc., from Guzerat or the Concan—countries from which, even supposing the communications to be uninterrupted, they would probably not be able to draw the supplies wanted, and certainly not within the requisite period ; for they must establish themselves upon the Malabar coast, receive their supplies, and ascend the Ghâts between the months of September and May, which it is utterly impossible that they could do. . . . While we are strong in Mysore, there are so many insurmountable obstacles to an invasion of that country from Malabar, that any enemy that hazards it must perish in the attempt. It is not only impossible for an enemy to make any impression upon Mysore from that quarter, but it is almost

* The original manuscript of this paper, in Munro's handwriting, is in the Manuscript Library of the British Museum. It was published for the first time in the first edition of this memoir.

equally so for him to take possession of the coast for any
length of time, because, in order to do this, he must land
as great a force as we could bring against him; but it is
not at all likely that France will ever be able to do this,
and if she could, she would land it on the Coromandel, and
not on the Malabar coast. Supposing, however, that any
body of Europeans, from 5000 to 10,000, were landed in
Malabar, the only chance they would have of maintaining
possession of their ground would be by getting possession of some posts which might be capable of sus-
taining a long siege, and by being joined by the Nair
Rájás and the other petty chiefs between Cochin and
Sadásivaghar. We ought therefore to have no forts of
great strength on the coast of Malabar. Those which we
already have, are sufficiently strong to guard against a
surprise, and to resist any enemy who has no cannon,
which is all that is necessary. Were the French to get
possession of them, they could easily be driven out again
by an army from Mysore; and as the Nairs, etc., would see
that their footing was precarious, they would be afraid to
join them. Were we however, to make any place particularly strong, one of those unforeseen events which frequently happen in war, might throw it into the power of the
enemy. After they were in it, it would be difficult to dis-
lodge them, and they might in consequence be able to stir
up the neighbouring petty princes of the country to insurrection. If we wish to be secure against a foreign enemy,
we ought to strengthen none of the forts on the coast. If
we wish to be secure against our own subjects, we ought
to disarm them.

Munro did not remain in Canara much more than sixteen
months. He had never thoroughly liked the district. He
greatly disliked the climate, which is extremely relaxing,
and although he had considered it his duty to undertake
the charge when pressed upon him on public grounds, he
had from the first expressed a wish to be removed to some
other part of the country, as soon as he should have succeeded in introducing a settled system of revenue, and
substituting order for the anarchy which Tippoo's *régime*

had left behind it. To Munro, who had been accustomed to the drier climates of the Carnatic and the Baramahal, Canara, with its damp and steamy atmosphere and long rainy season, was as distasteful as Calcutta is to the Punjáb official of the present day. With all his love for beautiful scenery, which may be said to abound in all parts of Canara, Munro seems to have been to the last unable to acquire any enthusiasm for a country in which there are five months of almost continuous rain, and where the difficulties of locomotion, even now considerable, were at that time unusually great.

No man (he wrote) who has not seen Canara and Súnda, can have the least idea of the endless vexatious interruptions the nature of the climate, of the country, and of the people oppose to the progress of revenue settlements. From the beginning of June to the end of October, the proper season for settlements, there is no certainty of a fair day. No wheel carriage can be used, not even a bullock bandy. In many of the inland cross-roads bullocks cannot travel loaded, and tents must be carried by coolies. My cutcherry tent stands pitched at Bárkúr, where I first got it. I could only bring with me two very small captain's marquees and three private tents. How, you will ask, does your army move? It usually sends its tents by sea, marches along the coast, and occupies the houses of the inhabitants. If it moves inland, as it did to Jamalábád, it marches parallel to the course of the rivers, and probably only crosses one. The large tents are then carried on elephants; but an elephant would not answer my purpose, because I never move without crossing a river, and often two or three. The business of loading and unloading him would take up the whole day. Even with bullocks, the business of swimming them over takes up so much time, that I am always obliged to wait an hour or two for my tent, the same as if I was in camp. It cannot be sent on the night before, because it is both difficult and dangerous in small canoes to pass rivers in the dark, towing cattle alongside. If I send it on the day before, I lose the use

of it for my cutcherry people. . . . Peons, on account of
rivers and also the number of thieves, travel only in the
day, and not more than twelve or thirteen miles on an
average. They seldom come in less than fifteen days from
Mangalore. The tappál* does not go thirty miles a day,
and letters by it, though they are sometimes more expe-
ditious than peons, are sometimes again much longer in
reaching, either from mistakes in the department or from
my being out of the road, and the people missing me. My
correspondence with the more distant districts is much
more tedious than that between Madras and Bengal. It
would be much easier for me to manage all the countries between the Krishna and the Colleroon than this Collectorate.

It is not surprising that, with so great an aversion to
Canara, Munro should have sought for a change as soon
as he had accomplished the principal objects of his mission.
Towards the end of 1800, the change came in the shape of
a transfer to the charge of the districts south of the Tongabadra, which had just been ceded to the Company by
the Nizam. It was not without reluctance that the Madras
Government sanctioned this transfer. Munro's services in
Canara were very highly valued. He had in a wonderfully
short time put down crime and rebellion, and substituted
settled government for anarchy and disorder. It was not
an easy matter to replace him. But the management of
the newly ceded country was a task not less arduous than
that which Munro had accomplished in Canara, and it
would have been difficult to find another man equally
qualified for it. Accordingly, it was resolved to divide
Canara into two charges, each under a separate Collector,
and to appoint Munro Principal Collector of the Ceded
Districts.

* *Tappál*—the post.

CHAPTER IV.

THE CEDED DISTRICTS.

Munro entered upon his new charge when the first year of this century was drawing to a close. The territory which he was deputed to administer was a very extensive one. It comprised an area little short of twenty-seven thousand square miles, including the present districts of Ballári, Cuddapah, and Karnúl, and also the Palnád, now a táluq or subdivision of the Krishna district. Karnúl was at that time a principality under a Muhammadan chief, a tributary of the Nizam, whose rights over Karnúl, as well as over the remainder of the Ceded Districts, were transferred to the Company. With the internal administration of this principality the Company's representative had little or no concern, so long as the tribute was regularly paid, and so long as there was an absence of such disorder as might threaten the peace of the adjoining districts. But in the adjoining districts,* or rather provinces, of Ballári and Cuddapah, which constituted the remainder of the Principal Collector's charge, and which included an area of twenty-one thousand square miles, there were elements of work sufficient to tax the powers and to engage the unremitting attention of the

---

* The term 'district,' which is now the official designation of the collectorates, or zillahs, into which the several Presidencies or provinces are divided, is generally applied by Munro to the smaller divisions, now commonly called táluqs.

ablest administrator. If Canara had suffered from thirty-six years of misgovernment by Hyder Ali and Tippoo, the Ceded Districts had been for upwards of two centuries a scene of successive invasions and a constant prey to internal conflict and misrule. From the middle of the fourteenth to the middle of the sixteenth century these provinces had formed a part of the Hindu kingdom of Vijayanagar, which in the early part of the sixteenth century appears to have included the whole of the peninsula south of the river Krishna. That dynasty, as we have seen, had established in Canara a system of landed tenure which had secured the prosperity of the country, and enabled it to pass through the period of Mysore misgovernment without any serious damage. But the rule of the Vijayanagar Government over the Ceded Districts was brought to an end in 1564, when the Hindu king was defeated by a confederacy of the Muhammadan chiefs of Bíjapúr, Golconda, Daulatábád, and Berár, and the greater part of the Ceded Districts fell into the hands of a number of petty chiefs, called poligárs. In 1680, these districts were invaded and a portion of them conquered by Sivají, the founder of Mahratta rule. Subsequently they were invaded by Arangzib, and later they formed part of the viceroyalty of the Nizam of the Deccan, until in 1778 they fell to the arms of Hyder Ali, and were incorporated in the kingdom of Mysore. By the treaty of 1792 the greater part of the Ceded Districts reverted to the Nizam, and the remainder was included in the share of Tippoo's dominions which was allotted to the Nizam in 1799. The Hyderabad administration was extremely weak, and the country was kept in a state of continual disturbance by the rebellious poligárs, who set the Government at defiance. These poligárs were petty chiefs, who from time to time had acquired power and territory owing to the weakness of the ruling prince.

Some of them had begun as leaders of banditti, who, on
the principle of set a thief to catch a thief, had been
invested with police authority. Others were descendants
of the ancient Rájás or their principal officers. Others
had been granted villages as a reward for services. Others
had gained possession of tracts of country by usurpation.
Others had begun as rulers of districts or as revenue
officers, and some as mere headmen of villages. In one
of his first letters after assuming his new charge, Munro
wrote :

We have now a great empire in the southern part of
India ; and if we can only keep the French out at the
general peace, it will, after remaining as long undisturbed
as Bengal has now been, yield a very noble revenue, drawn
with ease from willing subjects. But before such a
desirable change can be effected, we shall have to remove
many powerful and turbulent poligárs, and many petty
ones of modern origin, who have taken advantage of the
troubles of the times, in order to withhold their rents for
a few years and then to declare themselves independent.
The reduction of these vagabonds, who are a kind of
privileged highwaymen, will render us more able to resist
our external enemies ; for in all late wars we have been
obliged to employ a great number of troops to secure
internal tranquillity, instead of sending them to augment
the army in the field.

Again :

The country is overrun with poligárs. I have between
twenty and thirty who send me vakíls. They are not
confined to one corner, but are in every district. I am
trying, with the help of Dugald Campbell, General of
Division here, to get rid of as many as possible ; but it
will take some campaigns to clear them out.

Latterly the evil had been intensified by the weakness
of the Nizam's administration.

In that part of the Ceded Districts which fell to the

Nizam, his officers, from indolence and weakness, were utterly unable to cope with the poligárs. They were constantly in rebellion, and their rebellion and their reduction were alike disastrous to the country, The Mysore system,* which removed all poligárships, expelled their turbulent chiefs, and levied an additional body of troops to prevent their return, was in every respect preferable to that of the Nizam, which at a greater expense suffered them to retain their power, to commit every kind of degradation, and to set the Government itself at defiance.†

Nor were the turbulence and excesses of the poligárs the only source of trouble. The troops of the Nizam, with their pay in arrears, as is so often the case with the armies of Oriental rulers, had resorted to forced levies from the overtaxed inhabitants of the country. Munro wrote :

This last year a mutinous army was turned loose during the sowing season to collect their pay from the villagers. They drove off and sold the cattle, extorted money by torture from every man who fell into their hands, and plundered the houses and shops of those who fled, by which means the usual cultivation has been greatly diminished.

The first thing to be done was to reduce the poligárs, and, owing to the energetic measures taken by Munro

* The following allusion to the Mysore system of dealing with poligárs occurs in a letter from Colonel Wellesley to Munro, dated 26th October, 1800 :—
    'I think Pournaya's mode of dealing with these Rajahs (Harpo-
'nelly and Anagoondy) is excellent. He sets them up in palanquins,
'elephants, etc., and a great sowarry, and makes them attend to his
'person. They are treated with great respect, which they like, but
'they can do no mischief in the country. Old Hyder adopted this
'plan, and his operations were seldom impeded by poligár wars.'
    The poligár of Anagoondy (properly Anagundi) was a descendant of the old Rájás of Vijayanagar.
    † Manual of the Ballári District, compiled under the orders of the Madras Government, p. 117.

and General Campbell, within a year from the transfer of the country considerable progress was made in effecting this object. Many of the most powerful and turbulent among the poligárs were expelled from the Ceded Districts, and those who remained were forced to disband their armed retainers and to abstain from unauthorized exactions from the ryots. The removal of the Nizam's troops had, of course, followed immediately on the cession.

As in Canara, so in the Ceded Districts, the suppression of disorder was accompanied by a settlement of the land revenue. But the state of things to be dealt with in the two provinces was very different. That which was so marked a feature in Canara—private property in land—had no existence in Ballári or Cuddapah. In the latter districts the land had always been regarded as the property of the State. There were no traces of its having ever been the property of the cultivators or of the renters. The Inám* sanads † granted by the Vijayanagar princes, as well as by rulers of more ancient date, invariably granted the soil as well as the assessment, thus proving that the land was considered to belong to the sovereign. Accurate records of ancient assessments, such as Munro had discovered in Canara, had no existence in the Ceded Districts. The little that was known of the revenue of these districts under the Vijayanagar Government, did not amount to more than a tradition that it used to be assessed in kind in the proportion of half the produce—a much higher rate than that demanded in Canara—and that this half was converted into money at a price unfavourable to the cultivator. Of the state of things under the rulers

---

* *Inám*—an Arabic word of which the original meaning is gift, benefaction, a gift from a superior to an inferior. In the south of India the term is especially applied to grants of land held free, either wholly or in part, from the payment of revenue to the State.

† *Sanad*—a grant or document conveying titles, privileges, or emoluments.

who succeeded the Vijayanagar kings, the accounts were
extremely fragmentary, until the occupation of the country
by Hyder Ali, from which time the records appear to have
been tolerably complete.

With the information thus available Munro proceeded
to institute a survey and assessment of the country under
his charge. In the performance of this duty he was
aided by four English assistants, members of the Civil
Service, to each of whom, partially following the example
of Read in the Baramahal, he assigned a separate charge,
retaining under his own immediate management the
southern portion of the Ballári district. The system of
revenue which was introduced was ryotwár, differing from
the system followed in Canara in that the assessment was
fixed upon each separate field instead of including the
entire holding, and that it was based upon a detailed
measurement of the land and classification of the productive capacities of the various soils. The two processes
of survey and assessment, which were conducted separately,
were carried out very much upon the same principles as
those which have regulated the surveys and assessments
made in India in more modern times, although they were
probably less accurate, owing to the inferior character of
the native agency which in those days was available. The
survey was commenced in 1802 and finished in 1805. The
classification of the land began in 1804, and was completed in 1806. Pending the completion of these operations, a rough settlement of the revenue was made through
the potails, or heads of villages. The survey and assessment, imperfect as they may have been, were the most
complete that had yet been made in any Indian province.
They established once for all Munro's reputation as a
revenue administrator, and served as a model, to be
improved upon in future years, for the subsequent revenue
settlements of Southern India.

This duty, performed as it was in the midst of others of a multifarious character, was extremely harassing. Munro wrote to Read:

It is needless to tell you how I pass my time; for you know well enough what kind of life that of an itinerant Collector is. I have all the drudgery without any of the interesting investigations which employed so much of your time in the Baramahal. The detail of my own division, near ten lakhs of star pagodas, and the superintendence of others, leave me no leisure for speculations. The more common business of amildárs' letters, complaints, etc., often occupy the whole of the day. Besides, I am taken up an hour or two almost every other day in examining spies, and sending out parties of peons in quest of thieves and refugee poligárs. I am also obliged to furnish grain for three regiments of cavalry and the gun bullocks, and to transmit a diary every month to the Board to show that I am not idle. My annual circuit is near a thousand miles, and the hours I spend on horseback are almost the only time I can call my own.

Two years later, he wrote to the same correspondent:

Many causes have concurred to keep me at a distance from society, and to force me to travel about my districts alone, when I have more business of different kinds than I can well manage. The subordinate Collectors having been all removed, and a complete new set given to me last year, has been a great hindrance to my operations; for it has obliged me not only to continue to retain the greatest part of the country in my own hands, but to look after, for a time, the internal management of the other divisions. I am also a kind of commissary or agent for the army, for almost all their supplies are drawn from this province. I should have thought nothing of it, had it been only to equip them at first starting, but the demand is increasing. Ever since November, 1802, when the preparations for war began, I have never had less than ten thousand, and sometimes above thirty thousand bullocks in motion; and though peace has now been concluded, I am at this moment sending off ten thousand Warda bullocks with

rice for General Wellesley's army beyond Árangabad. I
have not only had the purchase of the supplies, but the
payment of most of the bullocks. This bullock business,
together with sheep, boats, pay of boatmen, and I do not
know what, and the endless disputes and correspondence
about accounts, bills, etc., leave me very little time for
revenue. For more than three years I have not had a
single holiday, and have very rarely risen from business
before sunset. I could not have believed, had I not made
the experiment, that it was possible to undergo such a
constant drudgery; but, after all, my time is in some
respects very unprofitably employed. You did infinitely
more in one month, in investigating the condition of the
inhabitants and the principles of revenue, than I do in
twelve. Two very bad seasons in this country, and all
over the Deccan, have greatly augmented the usual
difficulty of finding subsistence for the armies. In some
parts of the Deccan there is a famine, and the scarcity
here very nearly approaches to that calamity. The
revenue of course has suffered greatly, and now stands at
about fourteen lakhs of pagodas, instead of sixteen, to
which it would have risen this year, had the two last been
ordinary seasons.

The seven years which Munro spent in the Ceded
Districts were probably the most important period in his
official life. In the Baramahal his position had been a
subordinate one. In Canara, where for the first time he
was invested with an independent charge, his tenure of
office had been too short to admit of his doing more than
to suppress disorder, and to lay down principles of revenue
administration which his successors could work out. In
the Ceded Districts he remained long enough to guide
and direct the development of the system which he introduced, and by constant intercourse with the people to
habituate them to the spectacle of a ruler, who with
inflexible firmness in securing the just rights of the State,
and maintaining order and obedience to the law, combined
a patient and benevolent attention to the well-being of all

classes. The natives of India are not destitute of gratitude, nor are they deficient in the capacity to discern and appreciate the qualities which characterize a just, firm, and beneficent ruler. Towards Munro the ryots of Ballári and Cuddapah were led to entertain feelings of confidence and attachment which but few officials have been able to inspire, and when he left the province, his departure was lamented by all classes of the population. Nor was the memory of his good work one of those transient recollections which often pass away so speedily. The appellation by which Munro was most commonly known to the people of the Ceded Districts, was that of the 'Colonel Dora,' * with reference to the military rank which he held during the greater part of his service as Principal Collector; and to this day it is considered a sufficient answer to inquiries regarding the reason for any revenue rule, that it was laid down by the Colonel Dora.

But while Munro was thus winning the confidence and confirming the loyalty of the people committed to his charge, and at the same time consolidating the system of revenue with which his name has ever since been identified, the influences which had compelled him, though not without a vigorous protest, to submit a plan for the introduction of middle men between the State and the landlords of Canara, were still actively at work, and naturally were even more antagonistic to the adoption of a system of direct revenue settlements in a country in which there was no private property in land, and where the holdings on the average were even smaller and more numerous in proportion than in Canara. Nor was this antagonism confined to the authorities in Bengal. It was shared by eminent civil servants in the Madras Presidency, some of

* *Dora* means 'gentleman.' It is equivalent to the English 'Mr.' It is synonymous with the Hindustáni word 'Sahib.'

whom either were, or shortly afterwards became, members
of the Board of Revenue, and brought all the weight of
their official authority to bear upon the decision of the
question. Thus, during the latter years of Munro's resi-
dence in the Ceded Districts, much of his time was occupied in discussions of the relative merits of the ryotwár
and zemindári systems. From the Governor of Madras,
Lord William Bentinck, who at an early period became
convinced of the correctness of Munro's views, he received
active and consistent support, and it was not until after
Lord William Bentinck had left India, and Munro had
retired from his post in the Ceded Districts, that the
changes long threatened were carried into effect. But
from Sir George Barlow, a Bengal civilian who succeeded
Lord William Bentinck as Governor, and who, first as
Secretary under Lord Cornwallis, and afterwards as a
member of Lord Wellesley's Council, had been an active
supporter of the zemindári settlement of Bengal, the
ryotwár system encountered a determined opposition—an
opposition which, as we have said, was not destitute of
local support. The result was that shortly after Munro
left India, the ryotwár method of settlement, which in the
Baramahal had been already replaced by the múttadári *
system, was in the Ceded Districts superseded by a system
of triennial leases, under which the revenue of an entire
village was farmed to the potail or principal ryot, or, in
the event of his refusing to accept the lease, to a stranger.
These triennial leases were followed by leases for ten
years, both being regarded as preliminary to the adoption
of a permanent settlement; but under both there were
heavy losses of revenue to the State and much damage to

---

* *Múttadári*—properly *muthádári*, from *muthá*—an estate composed of one or more villages. The word is nearly synonymous with
zemindári, but it is usually applied to smaller estates than those held
by the zemindárs in the Madras Presidency.

the prosperity of the country, and after eight years' trial of the plan of leases to middle men, a recurrence to the ryotwár system was ordered by the Court of Directors.

It would be foreign to the scope of this memoir to enter into an elaborate disquisition on the arguments adduced by the respective advocates of the two principles of revenue administration; but a few words on the salient points of the controversy, which was hotly maintained for many years, and which even now has not entirely died out, will not be out of place. The question at issue was not so much the question of permanent *versus* temporary settlements, as whether the State should receive its revenues direct from a large body of small landholders—for the most part the actual cultivators of the soil—or from a more limited body of middle men, who, either as zemindárs, or as múttadárs, or as renters of villages, should collect the revenues from the ryots, receiving a percentage for their trouble and responsibility. Allusion has already been made to Munro's views on the question of fixity of assessment. It may be said that he was entirely in favour of an assessment so far fixed that its terms were not to be liable to frequent or arbitrary variations, but at the same time were not to preclude the State, in times of exceptional financial pressure, from levying a special assessment to meet a special emergency. This was, of course, an important qualification, and it may fairly be argued that it deprived the settlement of that element of certainty which is essential to encourage agricultural improvement; but it is clear from Munro's writings that though, looking to our position in India at that time and to the additional demands upon the treasury which the military expenditure was certain to involve, he considered it prudent to attach this qualification to the terms of our revenue settlements, he was prepared to abandon it, provided that the State did not sacrifice the prospective increase of revenue that might be derived from the many millions of acres still remaining uncultivated, but which in Bengal, under the settlement made by Lord Cornwallis, had been surrendered in perpetuity to the zemindárs. What Munro mainly objected to was the creation of middle men extemporized for the purpose. His contention was, that where large landholders did not exist, it was not wise, either from an economic or from a political point of view, to create them by an artificial process. As I have already said, one of his guiding principles was to accept existing institutions as he found them, and to reform and strengthen, but not to improve them off the face of the earth. Thus, when some years later he had, as Governor of Madras, to deal with the zemindáries of the Northern Sirkars and of North Arcot, some of which were of very ancient date, he did not scruple to propose a law of entail with the avowed object of giving security and permanency to that description of tenure. But what he contended for in regard to the Ceded Districts, and in regard to the greater part of Southern and Western India, was that the ancient land tenure of the country was not zemindári or múttadári, or any other tenure implying the existence of a middle man between the cultivator and the ruling power, but pure and simple ryotwár. Nor did he admit that a system involving the direct collection of the revenues of the State from a large body of small landowners, was of necessity unworkable or even inconvenient.

His views on this point are well expressed in the following extract from a letter addressed to the Board of Revenue shortly before his departure from the Ceded Districts:—

The chief arguments against the ryotwár system, are the great detail of accounts, and the consequent difficulty of management; the interference of revenue officers in cultivation; the expense of collection; and the fluctuation in the annual amount of the public revenue. But there seems to be nothing very serious in those objections. When a country is surveyed and the rent of every field fixed, the accounts become perfectly simple—they are nothing more than a list of ryots and fields; and if the ryots do not next year take up new or throw up old land, the same register will serve again; and as curnums must always be kept, there is no more difficulty in getting from them the accounts of a hundred ryots, than of one múttadár. The accounts of the customs, which yield so small a portion of revenue, are infinitely more intricate and troublesome than those of the land-rent. If such a remission is granted as will leave the ryots a private rent, after discharging the public one, the interference of revenue servants will be unnecessary. Their own interest will stimulate them to cultivate, as in Canara, where no revenue officer ever thinks of calling upon the owner to plough or sow his fields. The additional expense of collection in the ryotwár settlement would be gradually compensated by the rent of waste lands brought into cultivation, and the fluctuation in the annual amount of the revenue would be gradually lessened, as the ryots became attached to their farms, by the benefits of a low assessment, and retaining them as a lasting possession, instead of changing them, partly or wholly, almost every year.

Munro held strongly the opinion that the ryotwár system was the ancient system of India, and he argued that any system which might be introduced would have a tendency, in the absence of artificial restraints, to resolve itself into ryotwár, 'because the duration of great property 'in any family was opposed by early and universal mar- 'riage, and by equal division among all the sons.' If, in despite of this tendency, some of the larger landholders, created under the new arrangements, should develop into armed chiefs, like some of the large zemindárs, the result in his opinion would be 'detrimental to the country and 'dangerous to the Government.'

G

Writing on this subject some years later, Munro observed :

Most of the well-intentioned, but visionary, plans for the improvement of India by the creation of zemindárs of whole districts, or of simple villages, appear to have originated in extreme ignorance of the state of the landed property of the country and the rights of the persons by whom it was held. It has been supposed by some that the zemindárs were the landlords or proprietors, and the ryots their under-tenants or labourers, and by others that the sovereign was the sole landlord, and the ryots were cultivating tenants. But the ryot is the real proprietor, for whatever land does not belong to the sovereign, belongs to him. The demand for public revenue, according as it be high or low in different places and at different times, affects his share ; but whether it leaves him only the bare profit of his stock, or a small surplus beyond it as landlord's rent, he is still the true proprietor, and possesses all that is not claimed by the sovereign as revenue. . . . The distribution of landed property differs in every country : it is different in Ireland from what it is in England, and in India from what it is in other countries. But we ought to take it as we find it, and not attempt, upon idle notions of improvement, to force a distribution of it into larger properties, when every local circumstance is adverse to its continuance in that state. The experiment has already been tried by the establishing of village zemindárs or múttadárs, and has already very generally failed. The event could not possibly have been otherwise, of a measure whose object was to bring a new class of proprietors into villages where the produce was too little for the old ones. Even in those villages which are still in the hands of múttadárs, the object of having larger landed properties will entirely fail, because the properties, by sale and division among heirs, are fast subdividing, and will soon dwindle into portions smaller than the properties of individual ryots. There are instances in which this has already happened, and they will soon become so numerous, that the system must at no distant period die a natural death.

It must not, however, be supposed that in affirming the ryotwár to have been the ancient system of India, Munro overlooked the fact that it had been preceded by a system of common or joint tenures by village communities. The latter system had to a great extent died out in the Madras Presidency, and had been superseded by a system of separate holdings. When the change took place, was not exactly known. Munro believed that in many places it dated back to a very remote period. He observed :

Such a change is the natural course of things, and must always precede every material improvement, and is only restrained from becoming general by over-assessment or by difficulties regarding water. If one part of the lands of a village has advantages over the other in these respects, the common tenure will be acceptable to the proprietors by giving to all in their turn the benefit of the favoured land; but where the advantages of the several lots of land are nearly equal, the occupants will in general wish to keep their own permanently, because no man ever labours with the same spirit to improve what he is to share with another, as what he is to retain exclusively for himself. The common tenure has existed in many nations, but usually in the rude and early stages of agriculture, and has always, I believe, been considered as hostile to improvement.

But even if the joint tenure system had been more pre-valent in South India than it was, this fact would not have affected Munro's argument against the creation of a quasi-landlord class to act as middle men between the ryots and the State. Though for the reasons above given Munro preferred separate tenures to joint tenures, there can be little doubt that, had the latter system remained in full force, he would have been as much opposed to sup-plementing it by an arbitrary creation of middle men, as he was to supplementing the system of separate tenures by a similar device.

The views of Munro's opponents, like those of Lord Cornwallis and his Council, were entirely derived from English precedents. To them it appeared to be contrary to all sound principles that the State should deal directly with a numerous body of small landholders. They contended that, as a matter of fact, an intermediate agency— including under that term the native collectors of revenue, such as tahsildárs, amildárs, etc.—had always existed between the Government and the ryots; and they argued that the creation of a body of large landowners, where it did not already exist, would be followed by a better system of agriculture, by the protection of the ryots from oppression, and by establishing 'that just gradation of 'rank which is so essential to the existence and prosperity 'of every well-ordered society.'

Upwards of three-quarters of a century have elapsed since the commencement of this controversy. During that period the two rival systems have had an ample trial, and it cannot be said that the result has been adverse to Munro's views. The latest public utterance on the subject is contained in the Report of the Indian Famine Commissioners, who contrast the position of the Madras and Bombay ryots as 'independent landholders,' possessing a 'tenure as secure and simple as can well be con- 'ceived,' with that of the 'tenant of the north, often hold- 'ing his land at a rack rent and with no permanent 'interest in the land,' and who state that they 'have 'received a large amount of evidence, remarkable in its 'weight and unanimity, to the effect that in the Bengal 'province the relations of landlord and tenant are in a 'specially unsatisfactory condition.'

After Munro had been about two years in the Ceded Districts, the second war with the Mahrattas took place. The alliance which had subsisted between the Mahrattas and the Company in 1792, when a Mahratta force cooperated with the British army in the war against Tippoo, had been succeeded by sentiments of distrust and hostility on the part of the Mahrattas. In the last war against Tippoo they had failed to send the contingent which they were bound to furnish by the Treaty of Seringapatam ; and, in fact, the Peshwa and Sindia had planned an attack upon the Nizam, the ally of the British, while his army was engaged at the siege of Seringapatam. At the close of the Mysore War the Peshwa had declined to accept a share of the conquered territory offered to him by the Governor-General subject to the condition that he, like the Nizam, should accept a British subsidiary force. Although the nominal head of the Mahratta confederacy, the Peshwa had been for some time little more than a puppet in the hands of Sindia ; but war having broken out between Jeswant Ráo Holkar and Sindia, which resulted in an attack on Poona and the defeat by Holkar of the combined armies of Sindia and the Peshwa, the latter had escaped to Bassein, near Bombay, and there, on the 2nd of December, 1802, had made with the British a separate treaty ' of defensive alliance and reciprocal ' protection,' under which he agreed to receive a subsidiary force, assigning certain districts for their support.

The Treaty of Bassein gave great offence to the other Mahratta chiefs, who saw plainly enough that the system of subsidiary alliances with the British was fatal to the independence of native States; and a confederation was speedily formed between Sindia and the Rájá of Berár to oppose the English—a confederation to which the Peshwa, notwithstanding the treaty, was secretly a party. The immediate casus belli was the position taken up by the troops of Sindia and the Berár Rájá on the confines of the Nizam's territories. The Governor-General resolved to attack the Mahrattas in Hindustan, Guzerat, and Cuttack, as well as in the Deccan, and for this purpose four *corps d'armée* were formed, numbering altogether about 55,000 men. The two most important of these bodies were placed under the respective commands of General Lake, the Commander-in-Chief in Bengal, and of General Arthur Wellesley, who still held the military, as well as the civil command in Mysore. The latter speedily captured Ahmednagar, a strong and important fortress, and on the 3rd of September, 1803, defeated the united forces of Sindia and Berár at Assye, after one of the severest engagements that had yet been fought in India. The capture of Burhanpur and of Asírghar, another fortress of considerable strength and the last of Sindia's possessions in the Deccan, speedily followed, and the defeat of the Berár troops at Argáon on the 28th of November finished the war in that part of India. On the 1st of the same month the battle of Laswári, in which General Lake completely defeated Sindia's northern army, ended the war in the north. The result of these operations was a considerable addition to the Company's territories, including the greater part of the districts which now form the North-Western Provinces, and the Delhi territory, as well as Cuttack and a part of Guzerat.

Munro, as may be supposed, was a keenly interested observer of the events of the war. Indeed, before it commenced, and before the Treaty of Bassein was executed, on hearing of Holkar's victory at Poona, he addressed a letter to the Governor-General, urging that the opportunity should be taken for imposing a subsidiary alliance upon the Peshwa, and obtaining from him in return a portion of the Southern Mahratta country. The latter object, to which Munro, from the time of the conquest of Mysore, had attached very great importance, regarding the possession of the districts in question as essential to secure our territories against incursions from the Mahrattas, was not accomplished until 1818, when Munro, in command of a division of the Madras army, had the satisfaction of effecting it. ·

During this war, as during the operations against Dhundaji a few years before, Munro maintained a constant correspondence with General Wellesley, whose army depended for its supplies mainly on the districts under Munro's charge. This correspondence includes an interesting letter from General Wellesley to Munro, explaining his tactics at Assye, and commencing with the remark : 'As you are a judge of a military operation, and 'as I am desirous of having your opinion on my side,' etc., etc. Munro's reply is characteristic—modest, cordial, and friendly, but frank in its criticism, and affording evidence of considerable strategic ability on the part of the writer.*

---

* These letters are so interesting that copies of them are subjoined.

From General Wellesley to Major Munro.

'Camp at Cherikain, November 1st, 1803.
'MY DEAR MUNRO,

'As you are a judge of a military operation, and as I am 'desirous of having your opinion on my side, I am about to give you 'an account of the battle of Assye in answer to your letter of the 19th 'October; in which I think I shall solve all the doubts which must 'naturally occur to any man who looks at that transaction without a 'sufficient knowledge of the facts. Before you will receive this, you 'will most probably have seen my public letter to the Governor- 'General regarding the action, a copy of which was sent to General 'Campbell. That letter will give you a general outline of the facts. 'Your principal objection to the action is that I detached Colonel 'Stevenson. The fact is, I did not detach Colonel Stevenson. His 'was a separate corps equally strong, if not stronger than mine. We 'were desirous to engage the enemy at the same time, and settled a 'plan accordingly for an attack on the morning of the 24th. We 'separated on the 22nd: he to march by the western, I by the eastern 'road round the hills between Budnapoor and Jaulna ; and I have to 'observe that this separation was necessary—first, because both corps 'could not pass through the same defiles in one day; secondly, because 'it was to be apprehended that if we left open one of the roads through 'those hills, the enemy might have passed to the southward while we 'were going to the northward, and then the action would have been 'delayed, or probably avoided altogether. Colonel Stevenson and I 'were never more than twelve miles distant from each other, and when

Another event which occurred while Munro was in the
Ceded Districts, was the mutiny of the native troops at

'I moved forward to the action of the 23rd, we were not much more
'than eight miles. As usual, we depended for our intelligence of the
'enemy's position on the common hircarrahs of the country. Their
'horse are so numerous, that without an army their position could not
'be reconnoitred by a European officer ; and even the hircarrahs in
'our own service, who are accustomed to examine and report on
'positions, cannot be employed here, as, being natives of the Carnatic,
'they are as well known as a European.
    'The hircarrahs reported the enemy to be at Bokerdun. Their
'right was at Bokerdun, which was the principal place in their
'position, and gave the name to the district in which they were
'encamped ; but their left, in which was their infantry, which I
'was to attack, was at Assye, which was six or eight miles from
'Bokerdun.
    'I directed my march so as to be within twelve or fourteen miles
'of their army at Bokerdun, as I thought, on the 23rd. But when I
'arrived at the ground of encampment, I found that I was not more
'than five or six miles from it. I was then informed that the cavalry
'had marched, and the infantry were about to follow, but were still on
'the ground. At all events, it was necessary to ascertain these points,
'and I could not venture to reconnoitre without my whole force. But
'I believed the report to be true, and I determined to attack the
'infantry if it remained still upon the ground. I apprised Colonel
'Stevenson of this determination, and desired him to move forward.
'Before marching on, I found, not only their infantry, but their cavalry
'encamped in a most formidable position, which, by-the-by, it would
'have been impossible for me to attack, if, when the infantry changed
'their front, they had taken care to occupy the only passage there
'was across the Kaitna.
    'When I found their whole army and contemplated their position,
'of course I considered whether I should attack immediately, or should
'delay till the following morning. I determined upon the immediate
'attack, because I saw clearly that if I attempted to return to my
'camp at Naulniah, I should have been followed thither by the whole
'of the enemy's cavalry, and I might have suffered some loss : instead
'of attacking, I might have been attacked there in the morning ; and
'at all events I should have found it very difficult to secure my
'baggage as I did, in any place so near the enemy's camp, in which
'they should know it was ; I therefore determined upon the attack
'immediately.
    'It was certainly a most desperate one, but our guns were not
'silenced. Our bullocks, and the people who were employed to draw
'them, were shot, and they could not all be drawn on ; but some
'were, and all continued to fire as long as the fire could be of any use.
    'Desperate as the action was, our loss would not have exceeded

Vellore. Munro had observed, not without anxiety, the large proportion which, owing to successive augmentations

'one-half of its present amount, if it had not been for a mistake in
'the officer who led the picquets, which were on the right of the first
'line.
    'When the enemy changed their position, they threw their left to
'Assye, in which village they had some infantry; and it was sur-
'rounded by cannon. As soon as I saw that, I directed the officer
'commanding the picquets to keep out of shot from that village;
'instead of that, he led directly upon it; the 74th, which were on the
'right of the first line, followed the picquets, and the great loss we
'sustained was in these two bodies. Another evil which resulted
'from this mistake was the necessity of introducing the cavalry into
'the cannonade and the action, long before it was time, by which that
'corps lost many men and its unity and efficiency, which I intended
'to bring forward in a close pursuit at the heel of the day. But it
'was necessary to bring forward the cavalry to save the remains of
'the 74th and the picquets, which would otherwise have been entirely
'destroyed. Another evil resulting from it was, that we had then
'no reserve left, and a parcel of straggling horse cut up our wounded;
'and straggling infantry, who had pretended to be dead, turned their
'guns upon our backs.
    'After all, notwithstanding the attack upon Assye by our right
'and the cavalry, no impression was made upon the corps collected
'there, till I made a movement upon it with some troops taken from
'our left after the enemy's right had been defeated; and it would
'have been as well to have left it alone entirely till that movement
'was made. However, I do not wish to cast any reflection upon the
'officer who led the picquets. I lament the consequences of his mis-
'take; but I must acknowledge that it was not possible for a man to
'lead a body into a hotter fire than he did the picquets on that day
'against Assye.
    'After the action there was no pursuit, because our cavalry was
'not then in a state to pursue. It was near dark when the action
'was over; and we passed the night on the field of battle.
    'Colonel Stevenson marched with part of his corps as soon as he
'heard that I was about to move forward, and he also moved upon
'Bokerdun. He did not receive my letter till evening. He got
'entangled in a nullah in the night, and arrived at Bokerdun, about
'eight miles from me to the westward, at eight in the morning of
'the 24th.
    'The enemy passed the night of the 23rd at about twelve miles
'from the field of battle, twelve from the Adjuntee Ghaut, and eight
'from Bokerdun. As soon as they heard that Colonel Stevenson was
'advancing to the latter place, they set off, and never stopped till
'they had got down the Ghaut, where they arrived in the course of
'the night of the 24th. After his difficulties of the night of the 23rd,

of the native army, the native troops bore to the European
force. In a letter to General Wellesley written two years

'Colonel Stevenson was in no state to follow them, and did not do so
'till the 26th. The reason for which he was detained till that day
'was that I might have the benefit of the assistance of his surgeons
'to dress my wounded soldiers, many of whom, after all, were not
'dressed for nearly a week for want of the necessary number of
'medical men. I had also a long and difficult negotiation with the
'Nizam's sirdars to induce them to admit my wounded into any of the
'Nizam's forts; and I could not allow them to depart until I had
'settled that point. Besides, I knew that the enemy had passed the
'Ghaut, and that to pursue them a day sooner or a day later would
'make no difference. Since the battle Stevenson has taken Burhan-
'poor and Asseerghur. I have defended the Nizam's territories. They
'first threatened them through the Casserbarry Ghaut, and I moved
'to the southward to the neighbourhood of Arungabad. I then saw
'clearly that they intended to attempt the siege of Asseerghur, and I
'moved up to the northward and descended the Adjuntee Ghaut and
'stopped Scindiah. Stevenson took Asseerghur on the 21st. I heard
'the intelligence on the 24th, and that the Rajah of Berar had come
'to the south with an army. I ascended the Ghaut on the 25th, and
'have marched a hundred and twenty miles since in eight days, by
'which I have saved all our convoys and the Nizam's territories. I
'have been near the Rajah of Berar two days, in the course of which
'he has marched five times; and I suspect that he is now off to his
'own country, finding that he can do nothing in this. If that is the
'case, I shall soon begin an offensive operation there.
  'But these exertions, I fear, cannot last, and yet, if they are
'relaxed, such is the total absence of all government and means of
'defence in this country, that it must fall. It makes me sick to have
'anything to do with them; and it is impossible to describe their
'state. Pray exert yourself for Bistnapah Pundit, and believe me,
                                  'Ever yours most sincerely,
                                          'ARTHUR WELLESLEY.'

From Major Munro to General Wellesley.
                          'Khádirabad, 28th November, 1800.
'DEAR GENERAL,
    'I have received your letter of the 1st instant, and have read
'with great pleasure and interest your clear and satisfactory account
'of the battle of Assye. You say you wish to have my opinion on
'your side; if it can be of any use to you, you have it on your side,
'not only in that battle, but in the conduct of the campaign. The
'merit of this last is exclusively your own; the success of every
'battle must always be shared, in some degree, by the most skilful
'general with his troops. I must own I have always been averse to
'the practice of carrying on war with too many scattered armies, and

before the Vellore mutiny took place, he gave expression to
his apprehensions on this subject in the following terms :—

'also of fighting battles by the combined attacks of separate divisions.
' When several armies invade a country on separate sides, unless each
' of them is separately a match for the enemy's whole army, there is
'always a danger of their being defeated one after another, because,
'having a shorter distance to march, he may draw his force together
'and march upon a particular army before it can be supported. When
'a great army is encamped in separate divisions, it must of course be
'attacked in separate columns. But Indian armies are usually
'crowded together on a spot, and will, I imagine, be more easily
'routed by a single attack than by two or three separate attacks by
'the same force. I see perfectly the necessity of your advancing by
'one route, and Colonel Stevenson by another, in order to get clear of
'the defiles in one day. I know also that you could not have recon-
'noitred the enemy's position without carrying on your whole army;
'but I have still some doubts whether the immediate attack was,
'under all circumstances, the best measure you could have adopted.
' Your objections to delay are, that the enemy might have gone off
' and frustrated your design of bringing them to battle, or that you
' might have lost the advantage of attack by their attacking you
'in the morning. The considerations which would have made me
'hesitate, are that you could hardly expect to defeat the enemy with
'less than half the loss you actually suffered; that after breaking
'their infantry, your cavalry, even when entire, was not sufficiently
'strong to pursue any distance, without which you could not have
'done so much execution among them as to counterbalance your own
'loss; and, lastly, that there was a possibility of your being repulsed,
'in which case the great superiority of the enemy's cavalry, with
'some degree of spirit which they would have derived from success,
'might have rendered a retreat impracticable. Suppose that you had
'not advanced to the attack, but remained under arms, after recon-
'noitring at long-shot distance, I am convinced that the enemy would
' have decamped in the night, and as you could have instantly followed
' them, they would have been obliged to leave all or most of their guns
'behind. If they ventured to keep their position, which seems to me
' incredible, the result would still have been equally favourable ; you
' might have attacked them in the course of the night ; their artillery
' would have been of little use in the dark ; it would have fallen into
'your hands, and their loss of men would very likely have been
'greater than yours. If they determined to attack you in the morning,
'as far as I can judge from the different reports that I have heard
'of the ground, I think it would have been the most desirable event
' that could have happened, for you would have had it in your power
' to attack them either in the operation of passing the river, or after
'the whole had passed, but before they were completely formed.
' They must, however, have known that Stevenson was approaching,

The Indian armies in the different augmentations that have been made since the fall of Seringapatam, have received no proportionable increase of Europeans, and the European force is in consequence much below the proportion which it ought always to hold to the native battalions. Though we have but little reason to apprehend any danger from our native troops, yet it is not impossible that circumstances may induce them to listen to the instigations of enterprising leaders, and support them in mutiny and revolt. After seeing what has happened among our own soldiers and sailors in England, we cannot suppose that it is impossible to shake the fidelity of our sepoys. The best security against such an event would be an increase to our European force, which ought to be, I think, to our native in proportion of one to four, or at least one to five.

The facts of the Vellore mutiny are well known, at all

'and that he might possibly join you in the morning, and this assist-
'ance alone would, I have no doubt, have induced them to retreat in
'the night. Your mode of attack, though it might not have been the
'safest, was undoubtedly the most decided and heroic. It will have
'the effect of striking greater terror into the hostile armies than
'could have been done by any victory gained with the assistance of
'Colonel Stevenson's division, and of raising the national character,
'already high in India, still higher.

'I hear that negotiations are going on at a great rate. Sindia
'may possibly be secure, but it is more likely that one view at least
'in opening them is to encourage his army, and to deter his tributaries
'from insurrection. After fighting so hard, you are entitled to dictate
'your own terms of peace.

'You seem to be out of humour with the country in which you
'are, from its not being defensible. The difficulty of defence must,
'I imagine, proceed either from want of posts, or from the scarcity of
'all kind of supplies. The latter is most likely the case, and it can
'only be remedied by your changing the scene of action. The Nizam
'ought to be able to defend his own country, and if you could contrive
'to make him exert himself a little, you would be at liberty to carry
'the war into the Berár Rájá's country, which, from the long enjoy-
'ment of peace, ought to be able to furnish provisions. He would
'probably make a separate peace, and you might thus draw from his
'country supplies for carrying on the war with Siudia.

     'Believe me, dear General,
       'Yours truly,
        'THOMAS MUNRO.'

events to most Anglo-Indian readers. Vellore was the fortress in which the members of Tippoo's family were placed after his death and the capture of Seringapatam. The garrison at that time consisted of four companies of His Majesty's 69th Regiment, one complete regiment of Native Infantry, and six companies of a second. Early in the morning of the 10th of July, 1806, the sepoys rose upon their European officers and upon the British part of the garrison, and killed thirteen officers and a considerable number of men. Intelligence of the outbreak having been conveyed to Arcot, nine miles distant, Lieutenant-Colonel Gillespie, then in command of the 19th Dragoons, galloping over to Vellore with a squadron of his regiment, a troop of Native Cavalry, and two galloper guns, rescued the survivors, who had established themselves in the ramparts partially under cover, where they were able to keep their assailants at bay. The fort was speedily in the possession of the British troops, and three or four hundred sepoys were cut down or bayoneted, and a still larger number made prisoners.

There was considerable difference of opinion as to the cause of the outbreak. Many persons, and among them the Governor of Madras, attributed it to a wide-spread plot to massacre the English and to restore Mussulman rule in Mysore, if not also in the Carnatic and other parts of the Presidency—a plot to which it was supposed that some of the poligárs in the Ceded Districts were privy. Others ascribed it to certain regulations recently issued, prohibiting the sepoys from wearing caste marks when in uniform and from wearing beards, and prescribing a head-dress, which, somewhat resembling an English hat, was supposed to have been ordered with the intention of compelling the sepoys to become Christians. Munro held the latter opinion. Replying to a letter on the subject from Lord William Bentinck, he stated that 'the restoration of

'the Sultan never could alone have been the motive for
'such a conspiracy. Such an event could have been
'desirable to none of the Hindus who form the bulk of
'the native troops, and only to a part of the Mussulmans.
'The general opinion of the most intelligent natives' in
the Ceded Districts 'was that it was intended to make the
'sepoys Christians.' This was also the view taken by the
Home authorities, who recalled the Governor, Lord
William Bentinck, and also the Commander-in-Chief, Sir
John Cradock.

CHAPTER V.

LIEUTENANT-COLONEL MUNRO (he had attained that rank in 1804) resigned his appointment in the Ceded Districts in October, 1807, preparatory to returning to England on furlough. He had held his office for seven years—a long time for the tenure of an office in India, where, owing to the climate and the consequent failure of health, changes in the *personnel* of the English officials are so frequent. He had gained the approbation of his official superiors, the esteem and regard of his subordinates, and the confidence and veneration of the people. In announcing to the Court of Directors Munro's relinquishment of the office of Principal Collector, the Madras Government expressed their hope that the exertions which had been 'made by Lieutenant-Colonel Munro in the advancement 'of the public service under circumstances of extreme 'difficulty, and with a degree of success unequalled in the 'records of this, or probably of any other Government,' would 'receive a corresponding recompense in the appro- 'bation' of the Honourable Court. They observed that while gradually augmenting the annual revenues from twelve and a half lakhs to eighteen lakhs of star pagodas, Lieutenant-Colonel Munro had 'produced a general 'amelioration and improvement in the manners and 'habits' of the inhabitants of the Ceded Districts, under the influence of which, 'from disunited hordes of lawless 'plunderers and freebooters,' they had become 'as far 'advanced in civilization, submission to the laws, and 'obedience to the magistrates as any of the subjects' under the Madras Government. 'The revenues,' they wrote, 'are collected with facility, every one seems satisfied with 'his situation, and the regret of the people is universal on 'the departure of the Principal Collector.'

The foregoing encomium was contained in an official despatch, based upon a Minute recorded by Mr. Petrie, who acted as Governor of Madras during the interregnum between the departure of Lord William Bentinck and the arrival of Sir George Barlow. Lord William Bentinck had left India a few weeks before Munro. He was, as I have said, a consistent supporter of Munro's ryotwár policy, and entertained a very high opinion of his services. In a letter which he addressed to Munro, not long before they both left India, he expressed himself in the following terms :—

I trust I need not take any pains to convince you of the sincere concern which I have felt at your intended departure. I say to you now, what I shall recommend to be stated in the most public manner, that the thanks of this Government are, in an especial manner, due to you for the distinguished and important services which you have been performing for the East India Company for so many years. These have been no ordinary revenue duties: on the contrary, the most difficult work that can be assigned to man has been most successfully accomplished by you. You have restored the extensive provinces committed to your charge, long infested by every species of disorder and calamity, private and public, to a state of prosperity, and have made them a most valuable acquisition to your country. It is satisfactory to know that the most important part of the revenue arrangement, the survey, which could scarcely have been executed under any other superintendence, has been completed before your departure. This will make the road, in respect to the revenues, easy for your successors. But I fear that in

provinces not long since so very much disturbed, a continuance of the same good policy will be indispensable.
It is to your advice that I must refer for determining by
what arrangement these districts shall be hereafter
managed — whether by a Principal and Subordinate
Collectors, or by two or three separate zillah Collectors.
The zillahs are the cheapest and most convenient mode.
Are the servants at present there equal to the charge?
The present arrangement was always, according to my
judgment, the most eligible. A Principal Collector par-
taking of the confidence of Government is more particularly
necessary as your successor. It may be expected that the
absence of your authority and arrangements must be
attended with some injurious effects. These effects may
grow into serious consequences if there is not immediately
established an able and efficient superintendence. It had
occurred to me that Mr. Thackeray might be inclined, and
would be the most proper person, from various considerations, to succeed you, in case the same arrangement as
now obtains should be continued. I am desirous in the
first instance to receive your sentiments upon this subject.
My great and anxious object is to preserve to the Ceded
Districts, as far as possible, a continuance of the same
system, in all its parts and branches, by which such vast
public benefits have been obtained.

But it was not only by his official superiors that testi-
mony was borne to Munro's merits as a public servant.
Shortly after his return to England he received the
following letter, signed by eight civil servants who had
served under him in the Ceded Districts or in Canara:—

16th February, 1808.

Dear Sir,
        We have all had the happiness of serving under
you, either in the Ceded Districts or in Canara. We ad-
mire the generosity, the kindness, and the magnanimous
equality of temper which for eight years we constantly
experienced from you, amidst sickness, difficulties, and
fatigue. As public servants we can bear witness to the

H

justice, moderation, and wisdom with which you have managed the important provinces under your authority. We know that the Ceded Districts hold your name in veneration and feel the keenest regret at your departure. As for ourselves, we attribute our success in life, in a great measure, to you, and think if we are good public servants, we have chiefly learnt to be so from your instruction and example. We are at a loss how to express our feelings; but we request your acceptance of a cup which Mr. Cochrane, your former deputy in the Ceded Districts, will have the honour to present to you.

And of the confidence with which Munro had inspired the natives of the districts committed to his charge, very remarkable evidence is furnished by the following anecdote, mentioned in Colonel Wilks' 'Sketches of the South of India':—

I will not deny myself the pleasure (says Colonel Wilks) of stating an incident related to me by a respectable public servant of the Government of Mysore, who was sent in 1807 to assist in the adjustment of a disputed boundary between that territory and the district in charge of the Collector. A violent dispute occurred in his presence between some villagers, and the party aggrieved threatened to go to Anantipur and complain to their *father*. He perceived that Colonel Munro was meant, and found upon inquiry that he was generally distinguished throughout the district by that appellation.

Munro left India in October, 1807, and reached England in the April of the following year, after an absence of more than twenty-eight years. He had left England a lad of eighteen; he returned a middle-aged man of forty-six. He did not quit India without those misgivings which every man must feel after so prolonged an absence from his native country and from his family. Writing to his sister two years before his departure from the Ceded Districts, he remarked that correspondence between India and Scotland, between persons who had not seen each other for nearly thirty years, and who might never meet again, was like letters from the dead to the living.

We are both so changed from what we were, that when I think of home and take up one of your letters, I almost fancy myself listening to a being of another world. No moral or religious book, not even the Gospel itself, ever calls my attention so powerfully to the shortness of life, as does in some solitary hour the recollection of my friends and of the long course of days and years that have passed away since I saw them.

As the time drew near for his departure, these sentiments became mingled with anxiety as to how he should employ his time in England. He wrote:

What I am chiefly anxious about is what I am to do when I get home. I have no rank in the army there, and could not be employed upon an expedition to the Continent or any other quarter; and as I am a stranger to the generous natives of your isle, I should be excluded from every other line as well as military, and should have nothing to do but to lie down in a field like the farmer's boy and look at the lark sailing through the clouds. I wish to see our father and mother, and shall therefore make the voyage, but I much fear that I shall soon get tired of an idle life and be obliged to return to this country for employment.

The wish expressed in the latter part of the foregoing extract was not destined to be gratified as regards one of his parents; for his mother had already died before his letter was written, and by the time he reached Scotland, his father, who had watched his career with pride, and up to a short time previously with unflagging interest, had begun to fail in mind, as well as in body, and was but little capable of enjoying the pleasure which, under other circumstances, he would have derived from renewed intercourse with his son.

Munro remained in England upwards of six years. During the earlier part of this period he spent a good deal of his time in Scotland, principally in Edinburgh; but he subsequently removed to London, where he was much consulted on questions at that time engaging the attention of the Court of Directors and of the Government. When Munro returned from India in 1808, the charter, under which the East India Company were invested with the government of India and carried on their trade, had only five years to run, and preparations were already being made, on the one side by the Directors of the Company to defend, and on the other by their enemies, to attack the further continuance of the privileges, especially in respect of the trade, which had been continued to the Company by the Charter Act of 1793.

No serious opposition was offered to the continuance to the Company of their territorial powers, if we except a remarkable speech by Lord Grenville, who denounced the union of the functions of a sovereign with those of a trader, and declared that 'twenty years was too long a 'period for farming out the commerce of half the globe 'and the government of sixty millions of people,' and that the government of India ought to be vested in the Crown; the patronage difficulty being got rid of by the adoption of a system of open competition for the Civil Service, and by conferring the military cadetships, by some fixed plan, upon the sons of officers who had died in the discharge of their duties. But these sentiments were nearly half a century in advance of the time at which they were uttered, and did not find supporters. As regards the continuance of the trade monopoly, the case was different. Here the claims advanced by the Company, who sought to maintain their privileges intact, encountered a strenuous opposition, and the result was, that while the monopoly of the trade with China was continued to the Company for a further period of twenty years, as well as liberty to pursue its trade with India, the latter trade was thrown open to the nation, though with the restriction that no private vessel employed in it should be of larger dimensions than four hundred tons.

The question upon which the most animated discussion took place, was that of extending the export and import trade with India to the provincial ports, as they were then called, of Great Britain. When the provisions of the new charter were first brought under consideration, the Government proposed to limit the extension of the trade to vessels sailing from and to the port of London ; but as the discussion advanced, the merchants of Liverpool, Glasgow, and the other leading provincial ports brought so much pressure to bear upon the Government, that, not-withstanding the most urgent protests of the Court of Directors and of the Court of Proprietors of the East India Company, the proposed limitation was abandoned.

This question of throwing open the trade with India was one which could not have been postponed for many years ; for the trade had grown beyond the capacity of a single company, whose servants were engaged in the arduous task of forming and consolidating an extensive empire, to make adequate provision for it. Fifteen years before, Lord Wellesley had found it necessary to give additional facilities to the merchants of Calcutta, by chartering a number of vessels built at that port, where shipbuilding was being extensively carried out, and reletting them to private merchants, with liberty to make their own arrangements with the proprietors. This measure, though highly disapproved of by the Court of Directors at the time, was necessary in order to secure to Great Britain the trade of India, then being rapidly diverted to foreign countries, to whose vessels the Indian ports were free. In 1797, the imports and exports of.

American, Portuguese, and Danish vessels had exceeded a million and a half sterling, and in September, 1800, there were 8500 tons of foreign shipping, under foreign colours, lying in the Hooghly, while the India-built shipping anchored at the port amounted to 10,000 tons. Moreover, during the interval which elapsed before the renewal of the charter, two circumstances occurred which tended to hasten the removal of the restrictions on the Indian trade. One was the rapid advance of English manufactures; the other, the war in Europe, which closed the ports of the Continent to British trade. Another question which was much discussed at this time was the expediency of permitting a free resort to India of Englishmen not in the service of the East India Company.

Besides such questions as these, which, affecting as they did the personal interests of Englishmen, excited considerable interest in Parliament and throughout the country, there were others, connected with the internal administration of India—such as the system of land tenure, the judicial system, and the police—which underwent careful investigation, and in reference to which consultation was held with some of the most eminent Indian officials in England at the time. A searching inquiry was instituted by a Select Committee of the House of Commons, whose celebrated Fifth Report constitutes a most valuable repertory of information regarding the progress of Indian administration up to 1812.

On all the questions which were thus brought under investigation, Munro was consulted, and in most cases the information which he contributed, and the opinions which he expressed, largely influenced their settlement. The evidence given by him before the House of Commons, and the promptitude and clearness of his replies, produced a most favourable impression. It was mainly, if not entirely, owing to his influence that the plan of applying the Bengal system of land revenue to the rest of India was finally abandoned, and the ryotwár system authorized for the districts in the Madras and Bombay Presidencies which had not been already brought under permanent settlement. And his views on the judicial system and the police so highly commended themselves to the most influential persons at the Board of Control and in the Court of Directors, that it was resolved to send him back to Madras on a special commission, for the purpose of preparing on the spot a scheme for giving effect to them.

On the question of throwing open the trade Munro was in favour of tentative measures. He had little sympathy with the outcry raised against the Company's monopoly, which, in his opinion, had been the source of many great national advantages, enabling it to acquire the extensive dominions then under British rule in India. He observed :

These territories never could have been acquired, had there not existed a Company possessing the exclusive trade, directing their undivided attention constantly to India, and employing their funds in extending their dominions. The whole of the merchants of Britain, trading separately, could neither have undertaken nor accomplished so magnificent an enterprise.

The Company are willing that the trade should be thrown open to the port of London ; but this, it is asserted, will not afford a wide enough range for the skill and enterprise of British merchants. But are these qualities monopolized by the outports ? Have not the London merchants their full share, and have they not capital sufficient to carry on all the Indian trade which the most visionary theorist can look for ? If freedom of trade is claimed on the ground of right, and not of expediency, every port in the kingdom ought to enjoy it; for they have all the same right abstractedly. But unfortunately it is necessary to withhold the benefit from them, because the warehouse system and custom houses are not yet sufficiently spread along our coasts; or, in other words, because a great increase of smuggling would undoubtedly ensue. The East India Company are attacked from all quarters, as if they, alone in this kingdom, possessed exclusive privileges. But monopoly pervades all our institutions. All corporations are inimical to the natural rights of British subjects. The corn laws favour the landed interest at the expense of the public. The laws against the export of wool, and many others, are of the same nature; and likewise those by which West India commodities are protected, and enhanced in price. It would be better for the community that the West India planter should be permitted to export his produce direct to all countries, and that the duties on East India sugar, etc., should be lowered. When the petitioners against the Company complain that half the globe is shut against their skill and enterprise, and that they are debarred from passing the Cape of Good Hope and Cape Horn, and rushing into the seas beyond them, with their vessels deeply laden with British merchandise, they seem not to know that they may do so now; that all private traders may sail to the western coast of America, to the eastern coast of Africa, and to the Red Sea; and that India, China, and the intervening tract only are shut. Some advantage would undoubtedly accrue to the outports by the opening of the trade. But the question is, would this advantage compensate to the nation for the injury which the numerous establishments in the metropolis connected with India would sustain, and the risk of loss on the Company's sales, and of their trade by smuggling? . . .

It yet remains doubtful whether or not the trade can be greatly increased; and as it will not be denied that London has both capital and mercantile knowledge in abundance to make the trial on the greatest scale, the danger to be apprehended from all sudden innovations ought to induce us to proceed with caution, and rest satisfied for the present with opening the trade to the port of London. Let the experiment be made; and if it should hereafter appear that London is unable to embrace the increasing trade, the privilege may then, on better grounds, and with less danger, be extended to other places. If Government cannot clearly establish that no material increase of smuggling, and no loss in the Company's sales, and consequent derangement of their affairs, would ensue from allowing the outports to import direct from India, they should consider that they are risking great certain benefits for a small contingent advantage.

Munro did not anticipate any considerable increase in the demand for British manufactures by the natives of India, unless by very slow steps, and at a very distant period. He wrote:

No nation will take from another what it can furnish cheaper and better itself. In India, almost every article which the inhabitants require is made cheaper and better than in Europe. Among these are all cotton and silk manufactures, leather, paper, domestic utensils of brass and iron, and implements of agriculture. Their coarse woollens, though bad, will always keep their ground from their superior cheapness: their finer camblets are warmer and more lasting than ours.

Glass-ware is in little request, except with a very few principal natives, and among them is confined to mirrors and lamps; and it is only such natives as are much connected with Europeans who purchase these articles. They keep them, not to gratify their own taste, but to display to their European friends, when they receive their occasional visits: at all other times they are put out of the way as useless incumbrances. Their simple mode of living, dictated both by caste and climate, renders all our furniture and ornaments for the decoration of the house and the table utterly unserviceable to the Hindus: living in low mud houses, eating on the bare earth, they cannot require the various articles used among us. They have no tables; their houses are not furnished, except those of the rich, which have a small carpet, or a few mats and pillows. The Hindus eat alone, many from caste in the open air, others under sheds, and out of leaves of trees in preference to plates. But this is the picture, perhaps, of the unfortunate native reduced to poverty by European oppression under the Company's monopoly? No, it is equally that of the highest and richest Hindu in every part of India. It is that of the Minister of State. His dwelling is little better than a shed : the walls are naked, and the mud floor, for the sake of coolness, is every morning sprinkled with a mixture of water and cow-dung. He has no furniture in it. He distributes food to whoever wants it, but he gives no grand dinners to his friends. He throws aside his upper garment, and, with nothing but a cloth round his loins, he sits down half-naked, and eats his meal alone, upon the bare earth, and under the open sky.

In regard to imports from India, Munro remarked that India was capable of supplying to any extent most of the articles at that time imported, and that every measure by which the demand could be enlarged, and the supply facilitated, of those commodities which do not interfere with our own manufacture, would promote the national prosperity. The demand for Indian cotton goods in the English market had already begun to fall off, owing to the improvement of the manufacture in England, and Munro foresaw that it would fall still lower, though apparently he did not anticipate the great extent to which the native manufacture would be superseded, at no very distant date, by the produce of the Lancashire mills. His views on the trade question, and his opposition to the complete abolition of the monopoly, if judged by the light which subsequent experience has thrown upon the subject, may perhaps appear to have been deficient in that sagacious foresight which usually characterized his opinions ; but there is enough in the foregoing extracts to show that he was by no means ignorant of the true principles of economic science, and that he was only deterred from assenting to their immediate application to the case under discussion by a consideration of the peculiar and anomalous circumstances under which the British Empire in India, at that time still in a condition of growth, had been formed, and by the conservative tendency which disinclined him to alter any existing institutions that notwith-

standing occasional defects, were on the whole working
well, for the sake of theoretical advantages, the certainty
of which had not been established.

Munro was also opposed to the unrestricted admission
of Europeans into India, but his objections on this point
do not seem to have been very strong. Owing to the
commercial habits of the natives, and the superior economy
of their mode of life, he saw no prospect of any considerable number of Europeans being able to make a livelihood
in the country. He said in his evidence before the House
of Commons :

The people of India are as much a nation of shopkeepers
as we are ourselves. They never lose sight of the shop :
they carry it into all their concerns, religious and civil.
All their holy places and resorts for pilgrims are so many
fairs for the sale of goods of all kinds. Religion and trade
are in India sister arts : the one is seldom found in any
large assembly without the society of the other. It is this
trading disposition of the natives which induces me to
think it impossible that any European traders can long
remain in the interior of India, and that they must all
sooner or later be driven to the coast. What the European
trader eats and drinks in one month, would make a very
decent mercantile profit for the Hindu for twelve. They
do not, therefore, meet upon equal terms : it is like two
persons purchasing in the same market, the one paying
a high duty, the other none. The extra duty paid by the
European is all the difference between his own mode of
living and that of the Hindu.

But the subjects upon which Munro's opinions deservedly
carried most weight, were those connected with the
organization of the army and the great departments of the
civil administration, viz. the revenue, the judicial system,
and the police. On the first of these questions Munro
was a high authority. He had served in all the campaigns
against Hyder Ali and Tippoo after 1780, and had been
a close observer of the recent campaign against the

Mahrattas. Although so much employed on civil duties, he was a soldier at heart, and the satisfaction which he could not help feeling at his success as a civil administrator, was often mingled with regrets at being debarred from opportunities of advancement in his own profession. While deeply impressed with the necessity of maintaining an adequate British force in India, and conscious of the risk to which that empire must always be exposed from defection on the part of the native troops, he had a good opinion of those troops, and believed that their fidelity might be insured by considerate and judicious treatment. The best way, he considered, of insuring the fidelity of our native troops was to show no distrust, but confidence at all times, to treat them well and keep them occupied, to bring all the corps at certain fixed periods back to their respective native districts, and to take care that none of them were permitted to remain too long in any place where they were likely to be tampered with by any native chief. His views as to the number of European officers required for a native regiment were very similar to those which have been acted on since the mutiny of 1857. He regarded the establishment of European officers provided by the organization of 1796 to be excessive, and he disapproved of the plan of appointing young officers on first obtaining their commissions to native regiments. His opinion was that every officer on first going out to India should be employed one or two years with a European regiment, until he had learnt his duty, and that ' he ' ought not to be transferred to a sepoy corps until, by ' previously serving with a European one, he had made ' himself master of all his duties, and likewise, by being ' in some degree acquainted with the character of the ' natives, qualified to command and to act with sepoys.' He greatly deprecated a proposal which about that time had been made to abolish the Company's European regiments, and, on the contrary, was in favour of adding to their number both in infantry and in cavalry.

Enough has been already said of Munro's views on revenue matters. The judicial and police arrangements which had been carried out in Bengal under regulations passed by Lord Cornwallis in 1793, and had been introduced in the Madras Presidency in the earlier years of the present century, were regarded by Munro as involving too great a departure from native institutions to work with success. In both Presidencies there were great complaints of inordinate delay in the disposal of civil suits, and of inefficiency in the repression of crime. The Judge of a district was also Magistrate, and although a stationary officer, was invested with the superintendence of the police. In both Presidencies there were native Judges who disposed of suits of small value, but their salaries were too small to command either efficiency or integrity, and their numbers too limited to enable them to render material aid in disposing of the vast amount of litigation, which was one of the earliest results of settled government. Munro strongly advocated the revival of the native institution called 'panchayat'—a court of arbitration composed of five or more persons—and the transfer of the duty of superintending the police from the Judge to the Collector, who, moving frequently about his district, and mixing with the people, had better means of effectively supervising the police than were available to a stationary judicial officer. The union, for similar reasons, of the offices of Collector and Magistrate, and the utilization of the village officials to deal with petty offences and with petty suits, were also included in his proposals. Instructions in the sense of Munro's recommendations were sent to the two Presidencies, and in the summer of 1814 he sailed for Madras to carry out the special Commission to which he had been appointed.

CHAPTER VI.

SPECIAL COMMISSION AND MILITARY COMMAND.

PUBLIC affairs, much as they occupied Munro's time, were not the only matters which engaged his attention during his stay in England. A few weeks before he sailed for India, he married Miss Jane Campbell, one of the daughters of Mr. Richard Campbell, of Craigie House, Ayrshire— a beautiful and accomplished woman, whose picture by Sir Thomas Lawrence hangs opposite that of the late Marchioness of Tweeddale in the drawing-room of the Government House at Madras. The marriage appears to have been a very happy one. In Mrs. Munro, or to use the name by which she is best remembered, Lady Munro, he found a wife eminently qualified not only to insure his domestic happiness, but to adorn the high position which a few years later he was destined to fill.

Munro's feelings on proceeding a second time to India were very much those which so many Anglo-Indians have experienced under similar circumstances. Writing to his sister from Portsmouth on the eve of embarkation, he says, 'I was in this place thirty-five years ago, and much 'more impatient than now to reach my destination; for 'my head was full of bright visions, which have now 'passed away. I now, I am sorry to say, go out, not to 'hopes, but to certainties, knowing exactly the situation 'in which I am to be employed, what I am to have, and 'when I am to return. This, to many people, would be very

'comfortable ; to me it is dull and uninteresting.' They
reached Madras on the 16th of September, and became at
once involved in a vortex of visits, which in India are paid
in the hottest hours of the day. In a letter written about
a fortnight after their arrival, he says, 'I have been
'attending to nothing but visits. The first operation on
'landing is for the stranger to visit all married people,
'whether he knows them or not. Bachelors usually first
'call on him. Then his visits are returned. Then his wife
'visits the ladies, and altogether there is such calling and
'gossiping and driving all over the face of the country
'in an old hack chaise in the heat of the day, that I can
'hardly believe myself in the same place, where I used, in
'former times, to come quietly, without a single formal
'visit.'

Notwithstanding, however, these social labours, Munro
speedily set to work on the business of his commission.
The duty which had been assigned to him was by no
means free from difficulties. There were not only the
inherent difficulties of the task of remodelling a system
of police and judicature, civil as well as criminal, adapted
to the habits and character of the natives of India, and at
the same time suited to the advancing civilization which
peace and settled government were certain to bring in their
train, but there was the exterior difficulty of the antagonism
of the local authorities to any change in the system then
in force. Allusion has been made to the opposition which
the ryotwár settlement encountered from the Madras civil
servants. There can be no doubt that from the first, on
the part of the members of that service, with a few
honourable exceptions, there was a perhaps not unnatural
jealousy of the military Collectors, of whom Munro was
the foremost ; and when to this feeling was superadded,
in the minds of some, a sincere conviction, however
erroneous, that the measures introduced by Lord Corn-

wallis, and supported by all the weight of the authority of
his gifted successor, Lord Wellesley, were founded upon
sound principles of fiscal and juridical science, it can
scarcely be a matter of surprise that the commission entrusted to Munro, which was supposed to include within
its scope far more sweeping changes than were really
contemplated, should have been viewed with disfavour.
The Governor of the Presidency, Mr. Elliot, whose previous
career had been in the diplomatic service, had taken charge
of his office on the same day on which Munro landed at
Madras, and was therefore of necessity very dependent
upon his constituted advisers in the Council and the Sec-
retariat; and though he appears to have had every disposition to treat Munro with consideration, it was perhaps
hardly in his power to prevent a certain amount of
obstruction being offered to the business of the Commission. And new as he was to the country, and unac-
quainted with native institutions and requirements, it was
not difficult for those by whom he was surrounded, and
upon whose experience he naturally placed a considerable
amount of reliance, to convince him that some of the
changes proposed were inexpedient. Mr. Elliot, Munro
wrote—

received an impression very soon after his arrival that
everything was in the best possible state; that an approxi-
mation had been gradually making of late years to the
system proposed in the judicial despatch of the 29th April,
1814; that much of it, in fact, had been anticipated; that
more could hardly be done without danger; that great
improvements had taken place since I left India; and that
were I now to visit the districts, I would abandon all my
former opinions and acknowledge that the Collector could
not be entrusted with the magisterial and police duties
without injury to the country. Though I knew that there
was no foundation for these assertions, it appeared to me
necessary to wade through all the police reports and the

proceedings of the Committee, in order that I might be enabled to assure Mr. Elliot, not as an opinion of my own, but as a fact drawn from these documents, that things remained just as they were seven years ago.

The opposition continuing, Munro, in a later letter, addressed to an official at the Board of Control, deemed it necessary to point out that if it was expected that the instructions of the Home Government were to be obeyed, the strongest and plainest words must be used. 'For instance,' he wrote, 'the expressions, "It is our wish," '"It is our intention," "We propose," do not, it is main-'tained here, convey orders, but merely recommendations. 'Unless the words, "We direct," "We order," are em-'ployed, the measures to which they relate will be regarded 'as optional.'
Again:

No orders have been issued for carrying into effect the instructions contained in the judicial despatch of the 29th April, 1814, and the Commission consequently still remains at Madras.

Mr. Elliot tells me that the resolutions of Government are printing for circulation, and that they correspond nearly with my view of it, except in not transferring the office of Magistrate to the Collector; but this is the most essential part of the whole, for without it the Collector will be merely the head darogah of·police under the Zillah Judge, and the new system will be completely insufficient. No time should therefore be lost in sending out by the first conveyance a short letter stating the heads of altera-tions in the present system which are imperative, and not optional with the Government here, and ordering them, not recommending, to be carried into immediate execution.

Six months later, after he had been nearly a year in Madras awaiting orders, Munro wrote:

The resolutions of Government of the 1st March and

my letters will have informed you how little has been done,
that no one thing has been finally done, that different
points of the judicial despatch have been referred to the
Sadr Adálat, the Board of Revenue, and the Commission,
that they are respectively to call upon the local officers
for their opinions on certain points, and that they are then
to frame the Regulations.

These Regulations, when framed, will be some months
with the Sadr Adálat, who will report upon them to
Government, and Government will then send them to
Bengal for the sanction of the Supreme Government.
Some months will elapse before this sanction is granted :
they must then be translated, which will consume some
months more, and by the time they can be circulated to all
the districts, the Commission will have expired.   The six
Regulations drawn up by the Commission have been with
the Sadr Adálat about two months, and it is quite uncertain
how much longer they may remain with them.   Only one
will be circulated without reference to Bengal.   It is that
which transfers the police, but not the office of Magistrate,
to the Collector, and will not do any good.   The Council
will oppose the promulgation of the rest without the
authority of the Supreme Government.   They will therefore be sent to Bengal, and as Lord Moira proposes that
the two Governments should deliberate maturely on the
' whole subject of the judicial despatch, and avail them-
' selves of the advantages of a mutual interchange of
' sentiments and suggestions, in the course of the delibera-
' tions respecting so serious an object,' it may be some years
before they are issued.   Why should we amuse ourselves
with interchanges of sentiments on things which have
undergone a ten years' discussion, and which the Government at home has directed to be adopted ?   Or of what
use can it be to import sentiments from Bengal on pan-
cháyats and potails * which most of the public servants in
that Presidency profess never to have heard of.   I see no
way of enabling the Commission to answer any of the

---

* *Potail*—properly pátíl—the headman of the village, who, besides
exercising a petty jurisdiction as a Magistrate, is the local collector
of the revenue.

objects of its institution, but by sending out orders without delay to the Government here to carry into immediate execution, without reference to, or waiting for an answer from, Bengal to any reference that may have been made, all those modifications on which the Government at home have already made up their mind.

At last, however, the operations of the Commission were allowed to proceed, and in 1816 a serious of enactments framed by it, and embodying all the leading features of the scheme of police and judicial reform advocated by Munro, and sanctioned by the Court of Directors and Board of Control, was passed by the Madras Government. In framing these measures, which, in the legislative phraseology of that time, were styled Regulations, Munro was assisted by Mr. Stratton, one of the Judges of the Court of Sadr Adálat, then the chief Court of Appeal and Revision, who at his request had been associated with him on the Commission. The new Regulations effected important changes in the administration of the police and judicature. They transferred the superintendence of the police, and also the functions of Magistrate of the district, from the Judge to the Collector. They expressly recognized the employment of the hereditary village officials in the performance of police duties, and empowered the headmen of villages to hear and determine petty suits. They extended the powers of native judges, they simplified the rules of practice in the courts, and legalized a system of village and district pancháyats, or courts of arbitration—a system to which, as being adapted to native habits and usages, Munro attached special importance. Of the changes thus introduced, it may be said that they were all decided improvements upon the state of things which they superseded, in that they tended to simplify judicial procedure, to utilize native agency to a far greater extent than had yet been tried, to obviate delays in the administration of justice which had become a scandal, and to substitute a system of police superintendence which might possibly work, for one which, from the nature of the case, was necessarily useless. Some of these measures have stood the test of the experience of nearly three-quarters of a century, and have been extended in principle, if not in form, throughout India. The policy of entrusting the superintendence of the police and the duties of chief Magistrate to the administrative head of the district is now universally recognized, and within the last two years the various administrations have been invited to consider the expediency of extending the Madras system of village tribunals to their respective provinces. On two points, however, the reforms of 1816 have not answered the expectations of their authors. The pancháyat system has been so little resorted to, that it may be said to have been practically inoperative, owing probably to the fact that while it was a system adapted to a rude and primitive state of society, and of which the people were ready to avail themselves so long as there was nothing better available, it was less suited to a more advanced civilization, and could hardly be expected to maintain its place by the side of regular courts of justice, which, with all their faults, speedily won the confidence of the natives of India.* Of the police system which was

* In one of his Minutes on the judicial administration, written when Governor of Madras, Munro says of the pancháyat: 'There 'was nothing in which our judicial code on its first establishment 'departed more widely from the usage of the country than in the 'disuse of the pancháyat. When this ancient institution was intro-'duced into our code in 1816, there was so much objection to it, both 'at home and in this country, lest it should become an instrument of 'abuse, that it was placed under so many restrictions as to deprive it 'of much of its utility. It was unknown to some of the Company's 'servants as anything more than a mode of arbitration; it was known 'by others to have been employed by the natives in the decision of 'civil suits, and even of criminal cases, but it was imagined to have 'been so employed, not because they liked it, but because they had 'nothing better; and it was opposed by some very intelligent men on

introduced by Munro, it may be said that it was better than that which it superseded, and that the attempt to impart life and energy to the ancient institution of village police was sound in principle, and has in some parts of the country been fairly successful in practice; but the union of police and revenue functions in the native stipendiary officials of the revenue department, such as tahsildárs, amildárs, etc., has proved to have been a mistake. This part of the machinery not only in many instances failed in the detection and repression of crime, but was too often a prolific source of oppression. It has for many years

'the ground of its form and proceedings being altogether so irregular 'as to be quite incompatible with the system of our courts. All 'doubts as to the popularity of pancháyats among the natives must 'now have been removed by the reports of some of the ablest servants 'of the Company, which explain their nature and show that they were 'in general use over extensive provinces. The defects of the pan-'cháyat are better known to natives than to us; yet, with all its 'defects, they hold it in so much reverence that they say, "Where the 'jury sits, God is present." In many ordinary cases the pancháyat is 'clear and prompt in its decisions; but when complicated accounts 'are to be examined, it is often extremely dilatory. It adjourns 'frequently: when it meets again some of the members are often 'absent, and it sometimes happens that a substitute takes the part of 'an absent member. All this is no doubt extremely irregular. But 'the native government itself is despotic and irregular, and every-'thing under it must partake of its nature. These irregularities are, 'however, all susceptible of gradual correction; and indeed even now 'they are not found in practice to produce half the inconvenience that 'might be expected from them by men who have been accustomed to 'the exact forms of English courts of judicature.' Munro was in favour of withdrawing all suits below a certain amount from the jurisdiction of the regular courts, and transferring them to pan-cháyats. He was also in favour of extending the principle of the system to criminal trials by the employment of a jury, a measure which is now sanctioned by the Indian Code of Criminal Procedure, and is in force in some parts of the country; but however well founded Munro's impressions may have been regarding the popularity of the pancháyat system, as a mode of deciding civil disputes, before the establishment of the regular courts, and notwithstanding that Munro's views have been shared by other eminent men in more recent times, it has not, as a matter of fact, been found possible to give any vitality to the system.

been superseded by a separate body of stipendiary police working under the general supervision of the district Magistrate.

The period for which the Judicial Commission was appointed was three years, but before that term had expired, circumstances occurred which led to Munro's re-employment for a time in a military capacity.

During the twelve years which had elapsed since the retirement of Lord Wellesley, the policy of non-interference with the native princes, or what in these days would be called the policy of másterly inactivity, which had long been prescribed in vain by the Home authorities, had exercised full sway over the counsels of the Indian authorities at Calcutta, as well as in London. Lord Cornwallis, who was appointed Governor-General for the second time on Lord Wellesley's retirement, had gone out to India armed with the most emphatic instructions, both from the India House and from the Board of Control, with the wisdom of which he was himself deeply impressed, to reverse the foreign policy of his predecessor. During the few weeks that he survived his resumption of office, he had done his best to undo the results of the victories achieved by Lord Wellesley over the Mahrattas, and to give the Mahratta chiefs full power to re-establish their authority in Hindustan. He had resolved to abandon to the tender mercies of Sindia and Holkar the less powerful chiefs of Rájputána and Central India, to whom Lord Wellesley had guaranteed the protection of the British Government; and he had gone so far as to order that peace should be made with Sindia, who was at that time forcibly detaining the British Resident at his court. Owing to the manly opposition offered by the Commander-in-Chief, Lord Lake, the latter measure was delayed until the British Resident had been released; but the general policy, so far as the north of India was concerned, had

been carried out by Sir George Barlow, who, on Lord
Cornwallis's death, succeeded for a time to the Governor-
Generalship, and who, it may be remarked, as long as
Lord Wellesley remained in India, had been a cordial
supporter of his measures. Lord Minto, who held the
Government from 1807 until the autumn of 1813, was a
statesman of a different type. He checked Runjeet Sing's
designs upon the protected Sikh states in Sirhind. He
sent an army to defend the Nagpúr state, at that time in
alliance with the British, against the incursions of Amír
Khán, a Pathán chief who for years ravaged Rájputána
and Central India ; and he urgently pressed upon the
Home authorities the necessity of interfering for the
protection of other weak and defenceless states which
were at that time exposed to the ravages of the Pindáris ;
but the policy of strict neutrality was still in the ascendant
in Leadenhall Street and at the Board of Control, and the
inhabitants of Central India and the Deccan were left
for some years longer a prey to outrage and disorder.
Lord Minto's successor, the Earl of Moira, shortly afterwards created Marquis of Hastings, who held the
Governor-Generalship at the time of which I write, had
gone out deeply impressed with the unwisdom of Lord
Wellesley's policy, and resolved to maintain the system of
non-interference prescribed by the Home Government;
but he had not been long in India before he came to the
conclusion that, if the British position in that country
was to be upheld, the only safety lay in establishing
British supremacy throughout India, by holding the other
states 'as vassals, though not in name,' and obliging
them, 'in return for our guarantee and protection, to
'perform the two great feudatory functions of supporting
'our rule with all their forces, and submitting their
'mutual differences to our arbitration.' It was not without difficulty that Lord Moira overcame the reluctance of

his official superiors to sanction any measures that might
possibly result in further extensions of territory. This
was a question upon which successive Presidents of the
Board of Control held views quite in harmony with those
which from the first had been held by the Court of
Directors. Lord Castlereagh, Lord Buckinghamshire, and
Mr. Canning were as much opposed to any increase of
British territory or of British responsibilities in India as
the most commercial members of the Court of Directors.
Mr. Canning was, if anything, the most decided of the
ministers in his opposition to any renewal of the policy
of advance. He was 'unwilling to incur the risk of a
'general war for the uncertain purpose of extirpating the
'Pindaris.' He was prepared even to invoke the aid of
Sindia for the protection of the British territories from
Pindári incursions. Referring to information sent home
as to the suspicious behaviour of certain Mahratta chief-
tains and daring movements on the part of the Pindáris,
he caused a despatch to be addressed to the Governor-
General in Council by the Secret Committee of the Court
of Directors, in which they were made to express ' a strong
' hope that the dangers which arise from both these causes,
' and which *must perhaps always* exist in a greater or less
' degree, may, by a judicious management of our existing
' relations, be prevented from bearing upon us in any very
' formidable force ; while, on the other hand, any attempt
' at this moment to establish a new system of policy tend-
' ing to a wider diffusion of our power, must necessarily
' interfere with those economical regulations which it is
' more than ever incumbent upon us to recommend as in-
' dispensable to the maintenance of our present ascendency,
' and by exciting the jealousy and suspicion of other states,
' may too probably produce or mature those very projects
' of hostile confederacy which constitute the chief object
' of your apprehension.

It must be admitted that some of the views expressed in the foregoing passages were not without a semblance of justification in the circumstances of the Government of India at that time. The financial position was extremely alarming. The charges incurred by Lord Wellesley's wars had imposed a heavy burthen upon the exchequer. A war with the Gúrkhas of Nepál, which had been forced upon Lord Moira shortly after his arrival at Calcutta by their invasion of our territory, had found the treasury nearly empty, and the credit of the Government so low in the money market that the Governor-General was compelled to borrow two crores of rupees (two millions sterling) from the Nawáb of Oudh. And it must be remembered that though the trade with India had been thrown open, the East India Company was still a trading body, established for the purposes of commerce, rather than for the purposes of conquest, and therefore not unnaturally averse to increase responsibilities, already sufficiently onerous, the financial result of which it was impossible to foresee. Nor can it be a matter for surprise that the brilliant statesman who at that time presided at the Board of Control, himself the representative of a great commercial constituency, and in constant communication with the leading members of the Court of Directors, should have been induced for a time to regard the financial aspect of the situation as one of greater gravity than the political.

But on this, as on former occasions, the force of events outweighed the apprehensions of economists, and upset the theories of those who opposed the further extension of the British power in India. A bold raid made by the Pindáris into British territory on the Coromandel coast, accompanied by circumstances of the greatest atrocity, intelligence of which reached England very shortly after the despatch above quoted had been sent out, convinced the Home Government that the policy inculcated in it

must be abandoned, and that effective steps must be taken
to vindicate the British name, and to defend the people
who looked to us for protection. In the revised instructions
which were thereupon sent out, it was significantly added
that 'any connection of Sindia and Holkar with the
'Pindáris against us or our allies would place them in a
'state of direct hostilities to us.'

Before these orders reached India the aggressions of the
Pindáris had forced the British authorities to act against
them. Two expeditions had already taken place, and at
the end of 1816, while the permissive despatch of the
Court of Directors was still on its way, the Governor-
General in Council had resolved on assembling a considerable force for the complete extirpation of these
audacious freebooters. The war which followed was conducted upon a more extensive scale than any which had
yet been undertaken. The armies of the three Presidencies were called out, and including irregulars and the
contingents of the Nizam, Mysore, and other native chiefs,
the force amounted to 116,000 infantry and cavalry, with
300 guns. The result was not only the extirpation of the
Pindáris, but the dethronement of the Peshwa, the annexation of the greater part of his dominions as British
territory, the reduction of Sindia and Holkar to the
position of feudatories, the release of the native states in
Málwa and Rájputána from Mahratta domination, and the
establishment of British supremacy throughout the whole
of India to the banks of the Sutlej. Before the British
forces were put in motion, the Governor-General had
become aware that a confederacy had been formed between the Mahratta powers, of which the Peshwa was the
centre, to oppose the British. The Peshwa had been
secretly hostile ever since the Treaty of Bassein, under
which his independence had been impaired by the subsidiary alliance imposed upon him by Lord Wellesley; and

that hostility had been intensified, a few months before the war began, by an enforced cession of territory which Lord Moira compelled him to make in consequence of the discovery of intrigues in which he was implicated.

By the prompt and decided action of the Governor-General, who also combined with that office the functions of Commander-in-Chief, Sindia was detached from the confederacy; but before the end of the year the Peshwa, the Rájá of Berár, and the troops of Holkar had broken into hostilities, the two former making unsuccessful attacks upon the British Residents stationed at their respective capitals, while Holkar's troops, advancing towards the Deccan to the support of the Peshwa, encountered and were defeated by Sir Thomas Hislop's division at the battle of Mahidpúr.

As soon as it became plain that an important war was impending, Munro applied to the Governor-General for a military command. His application was not in the first instance successful; and after all that has been said and written of late years regarding the impolicy of entrusting military commands to officers who have long been employed upon civil duties, it may appear on a superficial view of the matter that the hesitation to comply with Munro's wishes was not unreasonable. But Munro's case was a very exceptional one. He had served in every campaign in which the Madras army had been engaged since 1780, with the exception of General Wellesley's brief campaign against the Mahrattas in 1803; and although he had been employed for some years in a civil capacity, the nature of that employment, owing to the disturbed condition of the districts administered by him, had been such as to call into frequent exercise those qualities of self-reliance, decision, and readiness of resources which go so far to insure efficiency in military command. Moreover, his military ability was well known and fully recognized

by the highest military authorities, and it was not, therefore, without mortification that when the distribution of
commands was settled, he found himself passed over in
favour of officers junior to him in military rank. But
although Munro was denied a command with the forces
sent in advance, he speedily obtained employment in
which he was able to render valuable services, first in a
civil or semi-military capacity, and very shortly afterwards
in the direction of important military operations, the
brilliancy of which, considering the slender means at his
disposal, has seldom been surpassed. Mention has been
made of the cession of certain districts which had been
exacted from the Peshwa a few months before the war
began. For the charge of these districts, bordering upon
Mysore and upon the Company's territory in Canara and
Ballári, an able and resolute officer was required, and the
choice naturally fell upon Munro. Anxious as he was for
strictly military employment, it was not without reluctance
that he accepted another civil charge; but upon its being
explained to him that his employment upon this particular
duty was considered to be highly desirable on public
grounds, he acquiesced in the decision, and proceeded to
Dhárwár to take charge of the newly acquired territory,
the military as well as civil command of which was placed
under him.

Shortly after his arrival, and before hostilities with the
Peshwa had commenced, Munro was ordered, with the
small force under his command at Dhárwár, to effect
the reduction of Sundúr, a small principality at the
extreme south of the Southern Mahratta country, the
chief of which had managed for twenty-one years to
maintain a position of complete independence. The expedition was sent at the request of the Peshwa, with
whom there was an engagement of some standing on the
part of the Company to effect the reduction of the Sundúr

chief. The latter, conscious of the superiority of the
British power, immediately on the arrival of the force
surrendered his fortress and territory, which, after the
conclusion of the war and the deposition of the Peshwa,
were restored to him on Munro's recommendation. While
Munro was engaged upon this expedition, the war broke
out, and he was at once invested with the rank of brigadier-
general and the command of the reserve division, formed
to reduce the Southern Mahratta country and to oppose
the forces of the Peshwa, who, after his unsuccessful attack
upon the Poona Residency, had moved southwards.

Some time elapsed before Munro was in a position to
enter upon his new command, a considerable body of the
enemy having occupied the country which lay between
him and the division assigned to him; but he did not
allow this difficulty to reduce him to inaction. With the
small force at his disposal, consisting at first of only five
companies of infantry, one gun, and a mortar, and subsequently increased by a small battering train, seven
additional companies of Native Infantry, four companies
of pioneers, and three troops of Native Cavalry, Munro
entered the enemy's country and captured fort after fort
in succession, placing in each, as he took it, a garrison of
peons—a sort of irregular militia—and then moving on
with his small force to another. Of these Badámi and
Belgaum were both fortresses of considerable strength.
These operations occupied Munro from the beginning of
December to the 18th of April, when he was joined by the
main body of his division, and, marching without loss of
time to Sholapúr, captured the fortified pettah, or city,
of that place by assault on the 10th of May, the citadel
capitulating two days later. With the reduction of Sholapúr, the subjugation of the Southern Mahratta country
was complete; and the troops having moved into canton-
ments, Munro, whose health was very indifferent, relin-

quished his command and prepared to return to England.
The vigour and skill with which this campaign was
conducted, the smallness of the force employed during
the greater part of it, and the importance of the results
achieved, at once proved Munro's capacity as a military
commander; but no amount of generalship would have
enabled him to accomplish so much in the time, with the
extremely inadequate force at his disposal during the
greater part of the operations, had it not been for his
thorough insight into the political situation and the influence which he was able to exert over the people of the
country. In the latter respect the reputation which a few
years before he had established in the adjoining district
of Ballári, stood him in good stead. To the Canarese
agriculturists of the Southern Mahratta Provinces he was
known by repute as a just and considerate ruler; and
accordingly, in his military operations, he met with
support instead of opposition from the people of the
country. Munro's services on this occasion elicited high
praise from the Governor-General; and when, after the
termination of the war, Mr. Canning moved in the House
of Commons a vote of thanks to the army and its com-
manders, he referred to Munro in terms of panegyric such
as seldom have been applied to a public servant.

At the southern extremity (Mr. Canning said) of this
long line of operations, and in a part of the campaign
carried on in a district far from public gaze, and without
the opportunities of early special notice, was employed a
man whose name I should indeed have been sorry to have
passed over in silence. I allude to Colonel Thomas Munro,
a gentleman of whose rare qualifications the late House of
Commons had opportunities of judging at their bar, on the
renewal of the East India Company's charter, and than
whom Europe never produced a more accomplished statesman, nor India, so fertile in heroes, a more skilful soldier.
This gentleman, whose occupations for some years must

have been rather of a civil and administrative than a military nature, was called early in the war to exercise abilities which, though dormant, had not rusted from disuse. He went into the field with not more than five or six hundred men, of whom a very small proportion were Europeans, and marched into the Mahratta territories to take possession of the country which had been ceded to us by the Treaty of Poona. The population which he subjugated by arms, he managed with such address, equity, and wisdom, that he established an empire over their hearts and feelings. Nine forts were surrendered to him or taken by assault on his way, and at the end of a silent and scarcely observed progress, he emerged from a territory heretofore hostile to the British interest, with an accession instead of a diminution of force, leaving everything secure and tranquil behind him. This result speaks more than could be told by any minute and extended commentary.

During the whole of these operations much of Munro's time was occupied with the discharge of civil functions; for, in addition to the arduous duties of his military command, he retained the office of Commissioner for the districts ceded by the Treaty of Poona. He was his own civil and political officer, and until the head-quarters of the reserve division joined him, he had no military staff. Writing on the 24th of March to his friend and colleague in the Judicial Commission at Madras, Mr. Stratton, who had applied to him for assistance in some matter connected with the business of that Commission, which he was engaged in winding up, Munro says :—

I can be of no use to you while the war lasts. I shall never be able to command six hours' leisure, which you think enough; and even if I had this leisure, I should be thinking of more immediate concerns than laws and regulations. I have five and twenty amildárs on my hands, with a list of about seven thousand peons, or what is called in the newspapers, irregular infantry. I have

also the command of regular troops, the political management of the southern jágírdárs, and much more than I can
well attend to. I should be delighted to have a few weeks'
leisure with you at Madras to finish whatever is wanting;
but you must expect nothing from me while I am on this
side of the Tongabadra. You can do what is wanting
yourself better than any one else.

Munro's duties at this time brought him into constant
correspondence, both official and private, with Mr. Mount-
stuart Elphinstone, then Resident at the Court of the
Peshwa, and shortly afterwards Governor of Bombay, of
whose ability Munro entertained a high opinion, and with
whom his relations were most cordial. Another frequent
correspondent was Sir John Malcolm, Munro's colleague
at Seringapatam in 1799, between whom and Munro there
had ever since existed a fast friendship. When one thinks
of the personal jealousies which in India, as in other parts .
of the world, so often disturb the relations of public officers
to the great detriment of the public service, it is refreshing to observe the utter absence of all such feelings in the
intercourse of these three eminent men. Thus, when the
question of the arrangements to be made for the management of the newly conquered provinces was under consideration, we find Munro writing to Malcolm that nobody
was so well qualified for the duty as Elphinstone; and
when the military operations in that part of the country
had been completed by the capture of Sholapúr, we see
Elphinstone foremost in bringing to notice the brilliancy
of the services rendered by Munro; while at an early
stage of the operations Malcolm describes them in the
following glowing terms :—

I send you a copy of a public letter from *Tom Munro
Sahib*, written for the information of Sir Thomas Hislop.
If this letter makes the same impression upon you that it
did upon me, we shall all recede as this extraordinary man

comes forward. We use common vulgar means, and go on zealously and actively and courageously enough; but how different is his part in the drama! Insulated in an enemy's country, with no military means whatever (five disposable companies of sepoys were nothing), he forms the plan of subduing the country, expelling the army by which it is occupied, and collecting the revenues that are due to the enemy, through the means of the inhabitants themselves, aided and supported by a few irregular infantry whom he invites from the neighbouring provinces for that purpose. His plan, which is at once simple and great, is successful in a degree which a mind like his could alone have anticipated. The country comes into his hands by the most legitimate of all modes, the zealous and spirited efforts of the natives to place themselves under his rule and to enjoy the benefits of a government which, when administered by a man like him, is one of the best in the world. Munro, they say, has been aided in this great work by his local reputation, but *that* adds to his title to praise. His popularity in the quarter where he is placed is the result of long experience of his talents and virtues, and rests exactly upon that basis of which an able and good man may be proud.

The letters written by Munro about this time contain interesting remarks on various matters connected with the political situation. Nearer acquaintance with the Mahrattas and their system had led him to form a more unfavourable opinion of their power for mischief than at one time he had entertained. He wrote:

The Mahratta Government has been one of the most destructive that ever existed in India. It never relinquished the predatory spirit of its founder, Sivají. That spirit grew with its power, and when its empire extended from the Ganges to the Cávery, this nation was little better than a horde of imperial thieves. All other Hindu states took a pride in the improvement of the country, and in the construction of pagodas, tanks, canals, and other public works. The Mahrattas have done nothing of this

K

kind: their work has been chiefly desolation. They did not seek their revenue in the improvement of the country, but in the exaction of the established chout from their neighbours and in predatory incursions to levy more.

Again:

It is fortunate for India that the Peshwa commenced hostilities and forced us to overthrow his power, for the Mahratta Government from its foundation has been one of devastation. It was continually destroying all within its reach and never repairing. The effect of such a system has been the diminution of the wealth and population of a great portion of the peninsula of India.

On the other hand, Munro considered the power and the numerical strength of the Pindáris to have been from the first greatly exaggerated. He did not estimate the aggregate number of their troops at more than seven or eight thousand men.

All the possessions of the Pindáris were confined to a few small districts in Málwa, which would not have maintained half that number. If we suppose that as many more were maintained by plunder, it is making a great allowance; for plundering, though destructive to the inhabitants, is not always profitable to the plunderers, who often lose more than they gain, by various accidents, before they reach their homes through a hostile country. The Pindári chiefs cannot bring large bodies into the field; but it is a part of their system to magnify their force, in order to strike terror and to prevent resistance. Secrecy and expedition are essential to their success, and it is only in small parties that they can move rapidly and elude pursuit.

They never would have ventured to enter our territory, had they not discovered that we were restrained from following them into their own. This conduct of the Indian Government, which I suppose was owing to orders from home, produced the consequence which everybody here foresaw. The Pindáris, when they saw that they had nothing to fear if they could only get safe back with their plunder to their own country, were encouraged to repeat their depredations in ours.

It will be remembered that at one time Munro was an ardent supporter of the system of subsidiary alliances with native states. He had now come to the conclusion that any further development of the system was inexpedient. The increased power of the British Government in India, and the comparative weakness of the native states, combined with other considerations, led him to think that this part of Lord Wellesley's policy should not be carried further. The following cogent remarks on the subject are contained in a letter addressed to the Governor-General before the commencement of the war :—

There are many objections to the employment of a subsidiary force. It has a natural tendency to render the government of every country in which it exists, weak and oppressive, to extinguish all honourable spirit among the higher classes of society, and to degrade and impoverish the whole people. The usual remedy of a bad government in India is a quiet revolution in the palace, or a violent one by rebellion or foreign conquests. But the presence of a British force cuts off every chance of remedy, by supporting the prince on the throne against every foreign and domestic enemy. It renders him indolent by teaching him to trust to strangers for his security, and cruel and avaricious by showing him that he has nothing to fear from the hatred of his subjects. Wherever the subsidiary system is introduced, unless the reigning prince be a man of great abilities, the country will soon bear the marks of it in decaying villages and decreasing populations. This has long been observed in the dominions of the Peshwa and the Nizam, and is now beginning to be seen in Mysore. The talents of Purnayya, while he acted as Diwán, saved that country from the usual effects of the system, but the Rájá is likely to let them have their full operation. He is indolent and prodigal, and has, besides the current revenue, dissipated about sixty lakhs of pagodas of the treasure laid up by the late Diwán. He is mean, artful, revengeful, and cruel. He does not take away life, but he inflicts the most disgraceful and inhuman punishments on men of every rank, at a distance from his capital, where he thinks it will remain unknown to Europeans, and, though young, he is already detested by his subjects.

A subsidiary force would be a most useful establishment, if it could be directed solely to the support of our ascendency, without nourishing all the vices of a bad government; but this seems to be almost impossible. The only way in which this object has ever in any degree been attained, is by the appointment of a Diwán. This measure is no doubt liable to numerous objections; but it is still the only one by which any amends can be made to the people of the country for the miseries brought upon them by the subsidiary force in giving stability to a vicious government. The great difficulty is to prevent the prince from counteracting the Diwán, and the Resident from meddling too much; but where this is avoided, the Diwán may be made a most useful instrument of government.

There is, however, another view under which the subsidiary system should be considered—I mean that of its inevitable tendency to bring every native state into which it is introduced, sooner or later, under the exclusive dominion of the British Government. It has already done this completely in the case of the Nawáb of the Carnatic. It has made some progress in that of the Peshwa and the Nizam, and the whole of the territory of these princes will unquestionably suffer the same fate as the Carnatic. The observation of Moro Dekshat, in speaking of the late treaty to Major Ford, that 'no native Power 'could, from its habits, conduct itself with such strict 'fidelity as we seemed to demand,' is perfectly just. This very Peshwa will probably again commit a breach of the alliance. The Nizam will do the same, and the same consequences, a further restriction of their power for our own safety, must again follow. Even if the prince were himself disposed to adhere rigidly to the alliance, there will always be some amongst his principal officers who will urge him to break it. As long as there remains in

the country any high-minded independence which seeks
to throw off the control of strangers, such counsellors will
be found. I have a better opinion of the natives of India
than to think that this spirit will soon be completely
extinguished, and I can therefore have no doubt that the
subsidiary system must everywhere run its full course and
destroy every government which it undertakes to protect.

In this progress of things, the evil of a weak and
oppressive government, supported by a subsidiary alliance,
will at least be removed; but even if all India could be
brought under the British dominion, it is very question-
able whether such a change, either as regards the natives
or ourselves, ought to be desired. One effect of such a
conquest would be that the Indian army, having no longer
any warlike neighbours to combat, would gradually lose
its military habits and discipline, and that the native
troops would have leisure to feel their own strength, and,
for want of other employment, to turn it against their
European masters. But even if we could be secured
against every internal convulsion, and could retain the
country quietly in subjection, I doubt much if the condition of the people would be better than under their
native princes. The strength of the British Government
enables it to put down every rebellion, to repel every
foreign invasion, and to give to its subjects a degree of
protection which those of no native Power enjoy. Its laws
and institutions also afford them a security from domestic
oppression unknown in those States; but these advantages
are dearly bought. They are purchased by the sacrifice
of independence, of national character, and of whatever
renders a people respectable. The natives of the British
provinces may without fear pursue their different occupations as traders, mirásidárs, or husbandmen, and enjoy
the fruits of their labours in tranquillity; but none of
them can look forward to any share in the legislation or
civil or military government of their country. It is from
men who either hold or are eligible to public office that
natives take their character: where no such men exist,
there can be no energy in any other class of the community. The effect of this state of things is observable in
all the British provinces, whose inhabitants are certainly

the most abject race in India. No elevation of character
can be expected among men who in the military line
cannot attain to any rank above that of subahdár, where
they are as much below an ensign as an ensign is below
the Commander-in-Chief, and who in the civil line can
hope for nothing beyond some petty judicial or revenue
office, in which they may by corrupt means make up for
their slender salary.

If the British Government is not favourable to the improvement of the Indian character, its control through a
subsidiary force is still less so. Its power is now so great
that it has nothing to fear from any combination, and it
is perfectly able to take satisfaction for any insult, without any extension of the subsidiary system being necessary.
It will generally be found much more convenient to carry
on war where it has not been introduced. This was the
case in both the wars with Tippoo Sultan. The conquest
was complete, because our operations were not perplexed
by any subsidiary alliance with him. The simple and
direct mode of conquest from without is more creditable,
both to our armies and to our national character, than that
of dismemberment from within by the aid of a subsidiary
force. However just the motives may be from which such
a force acts, yet the situation in which it is placed, renders
its acting at all too like the movement of the Prætorian
bands. It acts, it is true, only by the orders of its own
Government, and only for public objects; but still it is
always ready in the neighbourhood of the capital to dictate
terms to, or to depose, the prince whom it was stationed
there to defend.

I have said that Munro was compelled, by the state of
his health, to relinquish his appointments, both civil and
military, in the Southern Mahratta country. Although
his general health was good, the heavy work he had gone
through, coupled with exposure to the sun, had so much
impaired his eyesight that rest from all work for a time
was considered essential. He returned to Madras in the
autumn of 1818 for the purpose of at once returning to

England, but, owing to the difficulty of obtaining a
passage in a suitable vessel, was detained until the 24th of
January, 1819, when he and Mrs. Munro embarked, and
touching at Ceylon and at St. Helena, reached England
towards the end of June. Their eldest son, the present
Sir Thomas Munro, was born on the voyage.

CHAPTER VII.

GOVERNMENT OF MADRAS—DEATH.

MUNRO's stay in England on this occasion was very short. A few weeks after his arrival, he received intimation that he had been nominated Governor of Madras in succession to Mr. Elliot. For many years the custom had been to appoint to the Governor-Generalship and to the Governorship of Madras persons not connected with the Indian services. Since the retirement of Warren Hastings in 1785, Sir John Shore (afterwards Lord Teignmouth) and Sir George Barlow had been the only Governors-General appointed from home who had risen in the Indian service, and in the case of Sir George Barlow the appointment had only been made as a temporary measure, and notwithstanding the strenuous efforts of the Court of Directors to obtain its confirmation for the usual period, had been cancelled by the ministry after the lapse of a few months. Similarly in Madras, from the date of Lord Macartney's accession to the Government in 1781, with the exception of occasional intervals, when, in pursuance of the Act of 1784, the Senior Member of Council acted as Governor between the departure of one Governor and the arrival of his successor, the only Indian official who had held the office was Sir George Barlow, to whom it was given as some compensation for the loss of the Governor-Generalship. In Bombay more delay had occurred in giving effect to the new policy, Mr. Jonathan Duncan, an eminent Bengal civilian, having held the Governorship from December, 1795, until his death in August, 1811 ; but his successor, Sir Evan Nepean, was a stranger to India, and the intention was to adopt in future, in regard to Bombay, the policy which had of late years been followed in respect of Bengal and Madras.* There was much to be said in favour of that policy. The low standard of official morality which prevailed in India a hundred years ago, and the necessary unfitness for offices demand-ing high administrative capacity, of men whose duties, for the most part, had been of a commercial character, went far to justify the policy of looking beyond the civil servants of the Company for persons qualified to fill the chief places in the several Presidencies. But during the thirty-four years which had elapsed since the passing of Mr. Pitt's India Bill, great changes had taken place. The

* In the Diary of Lord 'Ellenborough, published some years ago, there is the following curious account of a conversation with the Duke of Wellington, at the time Prime Minister, regarding the appointment of a Governor of Bombay :—
'After seeing the Chairs spoke to the Duke about the Bombay
'succession. He asked what I meant to do with Elphinstone. I con-
'sidered he had left India altogether. The Duke thought he must
'return—that he would go to Bombay again, with the expectation of
'afterwards going to Madras. I think the Duke has an idea of
'making him Governor-General. I mentioned Mr. Chaplin. The Duke
'mentioned Mr. Jenkins, of whom he thought highly. He had done
'well at Nagpore, and he had had some correspondence with him
'when in India, which gave him a good opinion of him. The Duke
'spoke of Mr. Russell, but thought he had been mixed up with the
'Hyderabad transaction. I then mentioned Clare. The Duke thought
'him better than any of the others mentioned—that it was a great
'thing to have a man of rank; he must be well supported ; *he had not*
'*a very strong mind.* However, on the whole he seemed better than
'the others, and I am to propose him. I am very glad to have Clare.
'I have a great respect and regard for him—*but I have a little hesita-*
'*tion as to his fitness.* He will, however, be a most zealous and honour-
'able servant of the public, *and his good manners will keep people in*
'*good humour and in order.*'
Lord Clare is not the only Indian Governor in regard to whose fit-ness for the office doubts must have been entertained by those who sent him out.

Government of the Company, engaged at the beginning of
that period in a struggle for existence, the issue of which
was then uncertain, had succeeded in 1818 in establishing
its supremacy throughout the whole of the peninsula. In
the course of the war just brought to a close, and during
many years preceding it, services of the most conspicuous
merit, administrative, political, and military, had been
rendered by servants of the Company—services which it
was not only just, but eminently politic, to recognize in a
special manner. Mr. Canning, who still presided at the
Board of Control, discerning the requirements of the
situation with that enlightened and liberal statesmanship
which marked the whole of his political career, and recog-
nizing the expediency of a temporary departure from the
policy of his predecessors, resolved on appointing some of
the most distinguished servants of the Company to Indian
Governorships as vacancies occurred. Such a vacancy
was at the moment impending at Bombay, and Mr.
Canning accordingly sent an intimation of his views to the
Court of Directors, coupling with it the names of Sir
John Malcolm, Mr. Elphinstone, and Colonel Munro. Mr.
Elphinstone was appointed to Bombay, and when, in the
following year, the appointment of a successor to Mr.
Elliot at Madras was brought under consideration, Munro
was selected.

Honourable as the appointment was, and much as it
would have gratified Munro some years previously, it was
not without reluctance that he decided on accepting it.
He was already fifty-eight years of age. He had served
in India upwards of thirty-two years, much of that service
having been passed in very trying climates, and latterly
under circumstances involving great exposure. His duties
during the greater part of the time had been most arduous.
More than most men he had been used ' to scorn delights
' and live laborious days,' and it was not unnatural that he

should long for a life of greater leisure, in which he could visit new and interesting scenes, and pass the residue of his days in the society of his family and friends. From an expression in a letter written to his sister in 1815, it would seem that he had contemplated the possibility, though not the probability, of his being promoted to high office. 'There is no situation,' he wrote, 'likely to fall 'to me in this country that I care about. There is but 'one that I think of any consequence, and even that in a 'few years will be indifferent to me.' And when the appointment to which the foregoing remark not improbably referred, had been offered to and accepted by him, he could not help feeling that at his time of life the expatriation which it involved, was not without its drawbacks.

This country (he wrote, as he was waiting at Deal to embark) is the country of all our relations and of early life, and of all the associations connected with it. It is also the country of all the arts of peace and war, and of all the interesting struggles among statesmen for political power, and among radicals for the same object. It is near France and Italy and all the countries of the Continent, which I have earnestly wished to visit ever since I first read about them. The only objection I feel to going again to India is my age. I might now perhaps find employment in this country, and I have health enough to travel over Europe and visit whatever is remarkable for having been the scene of great actions in ancient times; but when I return from India, it will be too late to attempt to enter upon a new career in this country, and my eyes will probably be too old, if I am not so in other respects, to permit me to derive any pleasure from visiting the countries of the Continent.

It was with these feelings that Munro embarked for India in the last days of 1819. He had been appointed a Companion of the Bath for his military services in the Mahratta War, and before his departure he was promoted

to the rank of Knight Commander. In conformity with
the custom obtaining in those days, shortly before he sailed
he was entertained by the Court of Directors at a banquet,
at which Mr. Canning gave expression in eloquent terms
to the sentiments of general satisfaction with which
Munro's appointment was regarded.

We bewilder ourselves (Mr. Canning said) in this part
of the world with opinions respecting the sources from
which power is derived. Some suppose it to arise with the
people themselves, while others entertain a different view.
All, however, are agreed that it should be exercised *for*
the people. If ever an appointment took place to which
this might be ascribed as the distinguishing motive, it was
that which we have now come together to celebrate, and
I have no doubt that the meritorious officer who has been
appointed to the Government of Madras, will in the
execution of his duty ever keep in view those measures
which will best conduce to the happiness of twelve millions
of people.

Sir Thomas and Lady Munro reached Madras on the
8th of June, 1820, having spent a fortnight on the way
at Bombay as the guests of Mr. Elphinstone, with whom
Munro wished to discuss various public matters. He took
his seat as Governor immediately on landing, and at once
entered upon the business of the office. At that time, as
now, the Government of Madras consisted of a Governor
and three Members of Council, of whom the Commander-
in-Chief was one, and the other two were members of the
civil service. To a Governor possessing no previous
acquaintance with Indian administration, the Council is
a valuable and necessary aid; but in the case of a man
of Munro's antecedents, such assistance was certainly not
necessary, and it would not have been surprising if in the
earlier period of his government he had found himself
somewhat embarrassed by the opposition of his colleagues;
for on some of the most burning questions of the day his

policy was but little in accord with the views hitherto maintained in the Council, and only a few years had elapsed since his functions on the judicial Commission had been for a time paralysed by the opposition which they encountered. But it does not appear that from the time of his assumption of the Governorship Munro experienced any difficulty in his relations with his Council. It is not improbable that his path was smoothed to some extent by the support which his views had already received from the Home Government; but, making every allowance for this consideration, much must be attributed to the fact that Munro possessed in an eminent degree those qualities of earnestness, patience, and toleration for the opinions of others, which go so far to disarm opposition. There never was a more constitutional Governor than Munro. The law having provided that he should discharge the duties of his high office in conjunction with a Council, he acted up to its provisions in the spirit as well as in the letter, treating his colleagues with invariable confidence and unreserve; and thus it came to pass that while there never was an Indian Government in which there was less friction between the Governor and the Council, there never was a Government which was more essentially the Government of the Governor, than the Madras Government was while Munro presided over it.

The unceasing work which had been Munro's lot in the more subordinate employments hitherto filled by him, was not destined to be materially diminished in his new office. The Governor had less of the drudgery of detail than the district officer. Questions came before him more fully prepared. As a general rule his duty was rather to decide on facts ascertained by the investigations of others than to go through the laborious task of investigating. But if the quality of the work was different, the quantity was much the same. The ordinary business was heavy.

Before Munro had been many weeks in office, he found that not only was his time occupied by the necessary business of administration, but that much of it was taken up ' in ' reading masses of papers and useless altercations between ' different departments.' He wrote:

These require all my patience and a great deal more, for I have very little left. Nothing is so tiresome as to waste time in discussions of matters of no importance in themselves, but which derive some from the absurd heat of the combatants.

The remark made by an English statesman, which is quoted in Sir John Kaye's ' Life of Lord Metcalfe,' that ' eloquence in India evaporates in scores of paragraphs,' was only an epigrammatic description of the fact with which the new Governor found himself confronted. He wrote to Mr. Canning:

By not coming to India you have escaped the irksome task of toiling daily through heaps of heavy long-drawn papers. I never had a very high opinion of our records; but it was not until my last return that I knew that they contained such a mass of useless trash. Every man writes as much as he can, and quotes Montesquieu and Hume and Adam Smith, and speaks as if we were living in a country where people were free and governed themselves.

But besides the current work there were questions of special importance which pressed for settlement when Munro arrived at Madras, and chief among these was the condition of some of the districts, and especially of his old charge, the Ceded Districts, which had suffered grievously from the revenue experiments to which they had been subjected. The abolition of the ryotwár system, and the substitution for it of village leases to renters without any reduction in the assessment, had been very disastrous. Most of the renters had failed; the ryots were impoverished and the villages thrown back on the Government. In the Raidrúg táluk of the Ballári district most of the ryots had emigrated. The state of many of the other districts was no better. Most of the headmen were reduced to poverty. Many of them had been sent to jail. The substantial ryots, whose stock supported the agriculture of the villages, were gone. An immediate reduction of the assessment, which, indeed, had been recommended by Munro before he left the Ceded Districts in 1807, was necessary, with full liberty to the ryots to increase or diminish their cultivation, and these measures Munro and his Council ordered in anticipation of the sanction of the Court of Directors. But the issue of orders is one thing : their execution is another ; and before the reforms directed by Munro could be brought into operation in such a manner as to effect their object, he had to remove two Collectors, of whom one by his obstinacy, and the other by his indolence, had practically defeated the intentions of the Government. In dealing with this matter, as with many others, Munro acted on the principle of seeing for himself, by visiting the districts concerned and ascertaining their condition on the spot. His thorough knowledge of Indian district administration and his command of the native languages were, of course, enormous advantages, and added greatly to the value of the tours through the country which he made frequently. On these occasions he invariably travelled by short stages, just as he had done as a Collector, though necessarily with a larger camp, making himself thoroughly accessible to the people. He usually took with him one of the Secretaries to Government and a Member of the Board of Revenue acquainted with the districts through which he was to pass, and at the end of his tour he embodied the results of his observations in a Minute, which was laid before the Council and formed the basis of the orders subsequently issued.

Two other matters, closely connected with each other,

which engaged Munro's early attention, were the disparity
of the emoluments in the two great departments of the
internal administration, the revenue and judicial departments, and the training of the junior civil servants.
Under the arrangements made some years previously, the
salaries of the revenue officials had been fixed on a scale
far below that assigned to the judicial officers, and not
only were the judicial salaries higher than the revenue
salaries, but the number of well-paid appointments in the
former department considerably exceeded the number of
those in the latter. The necessary result was that the
ablest men in the service were attracted to the judicial
branch and every Collector aspired to promotion as a
Judge. This state of things Munro regarded as extremely
mischievous, attaching, as he did, great importance to the
office of Collector.

Nothing is so expensive as inexperienced Collectors.
Much more than the amount of their allowances is lost
every year in revenue from their mismanagement, and
when the affairs of their districts have in consequence
fallen into disorder, we are obliged to submit to the
additional expense of a commission to inquire into the
causes of it. We must, under every system, expect to
have some bad servants, but when the system itself is bad,
we can expect to have but few that are good.

We should form a very erroneous judgment of the important influence of the office of Collector, if we supposed
that it was limited merely to revenue matters, instead of
extending to everything affecting the welfare of the people.
In India, whoever regulates the assessment of the land-
rent, holds in his hand the mainspring of the peace of the
country. An equal and moderate assessment has more effect
in preventing litigation and crimes, than all our civil and
criminal regulations. When the lands are accurately surveyed and registered, the numerous suits which occur
where this is not the case, regarding their boundaries and
possession, are prevented, and when the assessment is

moderate, every man finds employment, and the thefts and robberies which are committed, in consequence of the want of it and of other means of subsistence, almost entirely cease. When the people are contented, those incorrigible offenders who live as banditti and make robbery a trade, find no protection or encouragement, and are all gradually taken or expelled from the country.

On the question of the proper training of the junior civil servants Munro held very decided opinions. He deemed it essential that every civil servant should pass the earlier years of his service in the revenue line. His reasons cannot be better expressed than in his own words :

We have now in our widely extended territory an ample field for the training of the junior servants in revenue affairs, and we ought to avail ourselves of it for that purpose. A knowledge of revenue will be useful in whatever department they may be afterwards employed; but a knowledge of the natives is still more essential, and this knowledge is only to be acquired by an early and free intercourse with them, for which the revenue presents infinitely more facilities than any other line.

It ought to be our aim to give to the younger servants the best opinion of the natives, in order that they may be better qualified to govern them hereafter. We can never be qualified to govern men against whom we are prejudiced. If we entertain a prejudice at all, it ought rather to be in their favour than against them. We ought to know their character, but especially the favourable side of it; for if we know only the unfavourable, it will beget contempt and harshness on the one part and discontent on the other. The custom of appointing young men, as soon as they leave college, to be Registrars to Zillah Courts is calculated rather to produce than to obviate this evil. . . . There are some men who overcome all difficulties, and become valuable public officers, in whatever line they are placed, and whatever may have been that in which they are first employed; but in making rules we must look to men such as they generally are. When a young man is

L

transferred from college to the office of Zillah Registrar,
he finds himself all at once invested with judicial functions.
He learns forms before he learns things. He becomes full
of the respect due to the court, but knows nothing of the
people. He is placed too high above them to have any
general intercourse with them. He has little opportunity
of seeing them except in court. He sees only the worst
part of them, and under the worst shapes. He sees them
as plaintiff and defendant, exasperated against each other,
or as criminals; and the unfavourable opinion with which
he too often at first enters among them, in place of being
removed by experience, is every day strengthened and
increased. He acquires, it is true, habits of cautious examination, and of precision and regularity; but they are
limited to a particular object, and are frequently attended
with dilatoriness, too little regard for the value of time,
and an inaptitude for general affairs which require a man
to pass readily from one subject to another.

In the revenue line he has an almost boundless field,
whence he may draw at pleasure his knowledge of the
people. As he has it in his power at some time or other
to show kindness to them all in settling their differences,
in occasional indulgence in their rents, in facilitating the
performance of their ceremonies, and many other ways;
and as he sees them without official forms or restraint,
they come to him freely, not only on the public, but often
on their private concerns. His communications with
them are not limited to one object, but extend to everything connected with the welfare of the country. He
sees them engaged in the pursuits of trade and agriculture, and promoting by their labours the increase of its
resources,—the object to which his own are directed. He
sees that among them there is, as in other nations, a mixture of good and bad; and that, though many are selfish,
many likewise, especially among the agricultural class,
are liberal and friendly to their poorer neighbours; and
he gradually learns to take an interest in their welfare,
which adheres to him in every future situation.

If a young man be sent at once from college to the
revenue line, the usual effect will be to render him attached
to the natives; if to the judicial, to increase the dislike

towards them with which he too often sets out. The main object, therefore, in beginning with the revenue, is not to teach him to collect the kists, which is a very secondary consideration, but to afford him an opportunity of gaining a knowledge of the inhabitants and their usages, which is indispensable to the due discharge of his duty in the judicial, as well as in the revenue line.   An acquaintance with the customs of the inhabitants, but particularly of the ryots, the various tenures under which they hold their lands, the agreements usual among them regarding culti-vation, and between them and soukárs respecting loans or advances for their rents, and the different modes of assess-ment, is essential to a Judge; for questions concerning these points form the chief part of his business.   A Judge who is ignorant of them, must often be at a loss on the most simple points; but as a knowledge of them can hardly be attained excepting in the revenue, it may be said that no man can be a good Judge who has not served in it.   If this kind of knowledge be indispensable in a Zillah Judge, it is equally so in the Judges of the higher courts and the Secretaries of Government.   It is on the right administration of the revenue that the prosperity of the country chiefly depends.   If it be too heavy, or very unequally distributed, the effects are felt in every de-partment.   Trade is depressed as well as agriculture. Numbers of the lower orders of people are driven by necessity to seek a subsistence in theft and robbery.   The better sort become dissatisfied, and give no help in check-ing the disorder.   The roads become unsafe and the prisons crowded; and we impute to the depravity of the people the mischief which has probably been occasioned by in-judicious taxation, or the hasty abolition or resumption of long-established rights and privileges.   It is of importance that the higher officers of Government should always be able to trace the good or bad state of the country to its true cause, and that, with this view, they should in the early part of their service be employed in the revenue line in the provinces, because it is only there that they can completely see and understand its internal structure and administration.

The observations embodied in the foregoing extracts
may now appear to be trite expressions of long-established truths; but those truths, which in these days are
regarded as axioms of Indian administration, were by no
means so considered sixty years ago, and to Munro the
credit is due of having first put them forward in such a
form as to command the assent of wise and thoughtful men.

Munro had long been impressed with the necessity of
more largely utilizing native agency, and of abandoning
the policy then in vogue of excluding the natives of India
from all situations of trust or emolument.

Writing to Mr. Canning about a year after his arrival
at Madras, he said :

Our present system of government by excluding all
natives from power and trust and emolument is much
more efficacious in depressing, than all our laws and
school-books can do in elevating, their character. We are
working against our own designs, and we can expect to
make no progress while we work with a feeble instrument
to improve, and a powerful one to deteriorate. The improvement of the character of a people, and the keeping
them at the same time in the lowest state of dependence
on foreign rulers to which they can be reduced by conquest, are matters quite incompatible with each other.
There can be no hope of any great zeal for improvement,
when the highest acquirements can lead to nothing beyond
some petty office, and can confer neither wealth nor honour.
While the prospects of the natives are so bounded, every
project for bettering their characters must fail, and no
such projects can have the smallest chance of success
unless some of those objects are placed within their reach,
for the sake of which men are urged to exertion in other
countries. This work of improvement, in whatever way
it may be attempted, must be very slow, but it will be in
proportion to the degree of confidence which we repose in
them, and to the share which we give them in the administration of public affairs. All that we can give them
without endangering our own ascendency, should be given.

All real military power must be kept in our own hands; but they might with advantage hereafter be made eligible to every civil office under that of a member of the Government. The change should be gradual, because they are not yet fit to discharge properly the duties of high civil employment according to our rules and ideas, but the sphere of their employment should be extended in proportion as we find that they become capable of filling properly higher situations.

We shall never have much accurate knowledge of the resources of the country or of the causes by which they are raised or depressed; we shall always assess it very unequally, and often too high, until we learn to treat the higher classes of natives as gentlemen, and to make them assist us accordingly in doing what is done by the House of Commons in England in estimating and apportioning the amount of taxation.

Three years later, in an important Minute on the state of the country and condition of the people, Munro wrote on this subject more at length :

With what grace can we talk of our paternal government, if we exclude the natives from every important office, and say, as we did till very lately, that in a country containing fifteen millions of inhabitants, no man but a European shall be entrusted with so much authority as to order the punishment of a single stroke of a rattan. Such an interference is to pass a sentence of degradation on a whole people, for which no benefit can ever compensate. There is no instance in the world of so humiliating a sentence having ever been passed upon any nation. The weak and mistaken humanity which is the motive of it, can never be viewed by the natives as any just excuse for the disgrace inflicted on them by being pronounced to be unworthy of trust in deciding on the petty offences of their own countrymen. We profess to seek their improvement, but propose means the most adverse to success. The advocates of improvement do not seem to have perceived the great springs on which it depends : they propose to place no confidence in the natives, to give them no authority, and to exclude them from office as much as possible; but they are ardent in their zeal for enlightening them by the general diffusion of knowledge.

No conceit more wild and absurd than this was ever engendered in the darkest ages; for what is, in every age and every country, the great stimulus to the pursuit of knowledge, but the prospect of fame, or wealth, or power? or what is even the use of great attainments, if they are not to be devoted to their noblest purpose, the service of the community, by employing those who possess them, according to their respective qualifications, in the various duties of the public administration of the country. How can we expect that the Hindus will be eager in the pursuit of science, unless they have the same inducement as in other countries? If superior acquirements do not open the road to distinction, it is idle to suppose that the Hindu would lose his time in seeking them; and even if he did so, his proficiency, under the doctrine of exclusion from office, would serve no other purpose than to show him more clearly the fallen state of himself and his countrymen. He would not study what he knew would be of no ultimate benefit to himself: he would learn only those things which were in demand and which were likely to be useful to him, namely, writing and accounts. There might be some exceptions, but they would be few. Some few natives living at the principal settlements and passing much of their time among Europeans, might, either from a real love of literature, from vanity, or some other cause, study their books; and if they made some progress, it would be greatly exaggerated, and would be hailed as the dawn of the great day of light and science about to be spread all over India. But there always has been, and always will be, a few such men among the natives, without making any change in the body of the people. Our books alone will do little or nothing: dry simple literature will never improve the character of a nation. To produce this effect, it must open the road to wealth, and honour, and public employment. Without the prospect of such reward, no attainments in science will ever raise the character of the people.

This is true of every nation, as well as of India. It is true of our own. Let Britain be subjugated by a foreign power to-morrow; let the people be excluded from all share in the government, from public honours, from every office of high trust and emolument, and let them in every situation be considered as unworthy of trust, and all their knowledge and all their literature, sacred and profane, would not save them from becoming, in another generation or two, a low-minded, deceitful, and dishonest race.

Munro's views on this subject were much in advance of those generally entertained by his contemporaries. The Minute from which the foregoing extracts are taken, may be regarded as embodying the first practical suggestion for the employment of natives of India in offices of trust and emolument. It was not without effect in influencing the policy which was subsequently pursued. In less than three years after Munro's death, the Court of Directors sent to India an important despatch on the subject of native education, in which it was laid down that to qualify the natives of India for a larger share in the public administration, was to be regarded as the main object of the educational measures then prescribed. And in the East India Company's Charter Act of 1833 * there was inserted the memorable provision that 'no 'native of the said territory (India), nor any natural-'born subject of His Majesty, shall, by reason of his 'religion, place of birth, descent, colour, or any of them, 'be disqualified from holding any place, office, or employ-'ment under the said Company.' The progress made in giving effect to this policy was, as Munro foresaw, un-avoidably slow; but, as years passed on, there was a gradual and steady improvement, not only in the nature of the duties, but also in the salaries assigned to native officials. For many years past the greater part of the civil business of the country, both administrative and judicial, has been conducted by natives; the work of the

* 3 and 4 William IV., cap. 85, sect. 87.

English officials being mainly that of supervision. The scale of remuneration, though necessarily and justly lower in the case of natives working in their own country, than that which has to be given to Englishmen, has also been considerably raised. The Acts of 1853 * and 1858 †, which threw open all first appointments to the Covenanted Civil Service to open competition, have enabled a few natives to obtain admission to that service; while the Act of 1870‡ has provided additional facilities for the employment of natives ' of proved merit and ability ' in posts previously reserved by law to the Covenanted Service. It may be doubted whether Munro would have approved of the legislation, either of 1833 or of 1853 and 1858, in the shape which it actually assumed. His practical and truthful mind would unquestionably have been opposed to embodying in an Act of Parliament, as was done by the Act of 1833, expectations which could not possibly be realized to the full extent of the language used; for then, as now, it was perfectly clear that there are many posts in India, which, as long as British rule continues, must be filled by Englishmen. It is hardly less certain that Munro would have regarded the admission of natives of India into the Covenanted Service by means of competitive examinations as a measure of very doubtful expediency. The Act of 1870, on the other hand, providing, as it does, for the due recognition of the claims of approved service, while reserving to the Governments in India full discretion as to the extent to which, and the manner in which, effect should be given to that policy, would, we may be sure, have commanded Munro's cordial support. No man would have sympathized more than Munro would have done with the wise and statesmanlike language in which the respon-

---

* 16 and 17 Vict., cap. 95, sects. 36, 37.
† 21 and 22 Vict., cap. 106, sect. 32.
‡ 33 Vict., cap. 3, sect. 6.

sible minister * of the Crown announced the introduction of this Act to the Government of India. That 'our duty 'towards the natives of India, in respect of giving them a 'larger share of employment in the administration of their 'own country, is a duty which must mainly be discharged in ' India on the principle of careful and cautious selection ; ' that 'a more free employment of them in the Uncovenanted ' Service, and promotion *according to tried ability* from that ' service to the Covenanted Service, would seem to be the 'method least beset with difficulties and least open to 'objection ; ' that '*this would indeed be a competitive ex-*'*amination of the best kind ;* ' and, lastly, that 'it should 'never be forgotten, and there should never be any 'hesitation in laying down the principle, that *it is one of* ' *our first duties towards the people of India to guard the safety* '*of our own dominion ;* ' and that 'for this purpose we 'must proceed gradually, employing only such natives as ' we can trust, and these only *in such offices* and *in such* '*places* as, in the actual condition of things, the Govern-' ment of India may determine to be really suited to them ' —these are words which might have been written by Munro, so entirely do they accord with the principles laid down in the remarkable Minutes recorded by him nearly half a century before.

But to Munro it would have been a great disappoint-ment, as it doubtless has been to the framers of the Act, that nearly ten years should have been allowed to elapse before it was brought into practical operation, and that, up to the present time, it has been so worked as rather to afford encouragement to young and comparatively untried officials, than to fulfil the just expectations of men who in a long course of service have proved their fitness for offices higher than those hitherto open to them. It is to be hoped that for this state of things a remedy will be pro-

* The Duke of Argyll.

vided by the orders recently passed in connection with the Report of the late Public Service Commission.

Munro attached little value to schemes for improving the education of natives unless *pari passu* steps were taken for extending to them a greater share in the honours and emoluments of office. His view was that the two things, improved education and higher employment, should go together. Subject to this proviso, he fully recognized the obligation which lay upon the British Government in India to educate the people under its rule. In his opinion, whatever expense the Government might incur in the education of the people would be amply repaid by the improvement of the country; for the 'diffusion of know- 'ledge is inseparably followed by more orderly habits, by 'increasing industry, by a taste for the comforts of life, ' by exertion to acquire them, and by the growing prosperity 'of the people.' It must at the same time be admitted that while entertaining these sentiments, Munro failed to appreciate with his usual discernment the nature of the task which any such measure involved. The funds available were extremely limited, not exceeding Rs. 50,000 (£5000) a year—a mere drop in the ocean in comparison with what was required to meet the cost even of com- mencing anything approaching a complete scheme of public instruction ; and this small sum, which might have done something if it had been applied to the establish- ment of a few schools of a comparatively high order under well-educated English teachers, was frittered away in establishing one central school for training teachers, which was organized upon too cheap a plan to command the sort of agency that was required, and in attempting to establish some four hundred schools of a very elementary character, most of which were little, if at all, superior to the ordinary village schools of the country. The measure was essentially faulty in its design, and its failure was

inevitable. It is one of the few failures which have to
be recorded against Munro. It was reserved for one of
his successors, Lord Elphinstone, some fifteen years later,
to give a fresh start to education in Madras, by establishing a school which, imparting a superior education, not
only served as a nucleus of a comprehensive system of
national education, but gave to that Presidency, in the
course of a few years, a small but influential body of
highly educated native officials, who have done much to
justify Munro's views as to the policy of giving to the
natives of India a more important share in the government
of their country.

Another question which about this time excited a good
deal of discussion in India, was the question of the public
press. In those days there was no native press in India.
In Bengal the English press was subject to restrictions
which varied in their stringency according to the disposition of the head of the Government for the time being.
Under Lord Wellesley and his immediate successors, the
restrictions were extremely severe, and any editor who
made attacks in his paper upon the Government or its
officers, or upon the religion of the natives, was liable to
be deported from India. Lord Hastings allowed the press
very considerable latitude; but Mr. Adam, who succeeded
him in the Governor-Generalship pending the arrival of
Lord Amherst, regarded the press as a dangerous instrument, and deported Mr. James Silk Buckingham, one of
the Calcutta editors, for an infringement of the press
regulations. At Madras there had always been a rigid
censorship of the press, and no paper could be issued until
it had been submitted for the inspection of the Government censor. Munro held very strongly the opinion that
the restrictions upon the press ought not to be removed,
and as the subject was exciting a good deal of attention,
both in England and in India, shortly after he assumed

the Government of Madras, he recorded his views upon it in a comprehensive Minute for the consideration of the Governor-General, and of the Court of Directors. The key-note of Munro's policy on this subject is contained in one of the first sentences of the Minute, in which he states that he ' cannot view the question of a free press ' in India ' without feeling that the tenure with which we hold our ' power, never has been and never can be the liberties of ' the people.' He wrote :

Those who speak of the press being free in this country, have looked only at one part of the subject. They have looked no farther than to Englishmen, and to the press as a monopoly in their hands for the amusement or benefit of their countrymen. They have not looked to its freedom among the natives, to be by them employed for whatever they may also consider to be for their own benefit and for that of their countrymen. A free press and the dominion of strangers are things which are quite incompatible, and which cannot long exist together. For what is the first duty of a free press ? It is to deliver the country from a foreign yoke, and to sacrifice to this one great object every meaner consideration ; and if we make the press really free to the natives as well as to Europeans, it must inevitably lead to this result.

Again :

The advocates of a free press seek, they say, the improvement of our system of Indian government, and of the minds and the condition of the natives; but these desirable ends are, I am convinced, quite unattainable by the means they propose. There are two important points which should always be kept in view in our administration of affairs here. The first is, that our sovereignty should be prolonged to the remotest possible period ; the second is, that whenever we are obliged to resign it, we should leave the natives so far improved from their connection with us as to be capable of maintaining a free, or at least a regular government, among themselves. If these objects can ever be accomplished, it can only be under a restricted press. A free one, so far from facilitating, would render this attainment utterly impracticable; for by attempting to precipitate improvement it would frustrate all the benefits which might have been derived from a more cautious and temperate proceeding.

His chief ground of apprehension was the possible effect of a free press upon the native army. He wrote :

If we, for the sole benefit of a few European editors of newspapers, permit a licentious press to undermine among the natives all respect for the European character and authority, we shall scatter the seeds of discontent among our native troops, and never be secure from insurrection. It is not necessary for this purpose that they should be more intelligent than they are at present, or should have acquired any knowledge of the rights of men or nations. All that is necessary is that they should have lost their present high respect for their officers and the European character; and, whenever this happens, they will rise against us, not for the sake of obtaining the liberty of their country, but of obtaining power and plunder. We are trying an experiment never yet tried in the world,— maintaining a foreign dominion by means of a native army, and teaching that army, through a free press, that they ought to expel us and deliver their country. As far as Europeans only, whether in or out of the service, are concerned, the freedom or restriction of the press could do little good or harm, and would hardly deserve any serious attention. It is only as regards the natives that the press can be viewed with apprehension, and it is only when it comes to agitate our native army that its terrible effects will be felt. Many people, both in this country and in England, will probably go on admiring the efforts of the Indian press, and fondly anticipating the rapid extension of knowledge among the natives, while a tremendous revolution, originating in this very press, is preparing, which will, by the premature and violent overthrow of our power, disappoint all these hopes, and throw India back into a state more hopeless of improvement than when we first found her.

The whole of the Minute from which the foregoing
passages have been extracted, is well worth perusal, as
containing the ablest statement that has been put forward
of the views of those who at different times have considered the freedom of the Indian press, European as well
as native, to be a source of danger to the State. There
are many persons who hold that the apprehensions expressed by Munro as to the effects of a free press upon the
fidelity of the native army have been borne out by the
events of 1857. To them Munro's language appears in
the light of fulfilled prophecy; * but it is extremely doubtful whether the writings of the public press, European or
native, had anything to do with the Mutiny. The pre-
ponderance of opinion is certainly opposed to this theory.
And as to the restrictions which were imposed upon the
English press in the earlier years of British rule in India,
the truth seems to be that it would have been as impossible to maintain those restrictions permanently, as it
was to maintain the Company's monopoly of the trade, or
the interdict against the free settlement of unofficial
Englishmen in the country. Anomalous as our position
in India is, and true as it may be that the tenure with
which we hold it 'never has been and never can be the
'liberties of the people,' it is now tolerably clear that the
English nation would not have been induced to tolerate,
except upon the strongest ground of proved necessity, a
permanent withholding of the liberty of the press from
their countrymen in India. That press, from the necessity
of the case, both as regards its ability and its tone, is

---

* Mr. Elphinstone, who was still living when the Indian Mutiny
occurred, took this view. The following is an extract from a letter
written by him at that time :—'The last accounts from India are
'doubtless very gloomy. The risk of fresh interests and new feelings
'arising during the interval of inaction is certainly very great, and to
'one who has just read Munro's admirable Minute, it appears that the
'full accomplishment of his prophecy is at hand.'

inferior to the press of the mother country. Its criticism is often unfair, and in its attacks there is not unfrequently an amount of personal rancour which seldom disfigures the writings of English journalists in this country. But it is never disloyal. Its attacks are directed against individual men or measures, treating them as accidental blots upon our system, and not as the types or necessary results of British rule. And notwithstanding its faults and imperfections, it cannot be denied that the English press in India has been on the whole a valuable aid to the Government, subjecting its measures to criticism which is often just and well informed, and bringing to light abuses and irregularities which might otherwise escape notice. The *Friend of India* under Marshman and Townsend, the *Madras Athenæum* under John Bruce Norton, and other Anglo-Indian newspapers in more recent times have rendered valuable services to the State, as have some of the best of the native papers, such as the *Hindu Patriot*, and one or two others conducted by educated natives and published in the English language. As regards the vernacular newspapers the case is different. The native press is a thing of very modern growth, and in the case of several of the newspapers published in the vernacular languages, liberty had so degenerated into licence, and the practice of seditious writing, of writing tending to bring the Government and its European officers into contempt and to excite antagonism between the people and the governing race, had increased to such an extent, that in 1878 it was found necessary to impose restrictions upon the vernacular press. The Act which was passed with this object was eminently successful during the few years that it remained in operation, effectually checking the licence, without interfering with the liberty of the press; but in 1882, consequent on the change of ministry which took place in this country in 1880, it was repealed, with the result that the evils against which it was aimed, are again rampant. To this section of the Indian press Munro's remarks are strictly applicable.

But the discussion of questions of the nature of those referred to in the preceding pages, applying not to the circumstances of any particular Presidency or province, but to the principles of Indian government, which, whether right or wrong, are necessarily general in their application, did not form by any means the chief occupation of Munro's official life. His main employment was the constant superintendence of the machinery of administration and the decision of questions daily arising in the several public departments. There never was a Governor who went more thoroughly into the business that came before him. On every question of any sort of importance he recorded his opinion so fully, that his note or Minute served, with but little addition or alteration, as the text of the letter or order disposing of the case. His varied knowledge of the details of business in nearly every department of the State, combined as it was with a masterly grasp of general principles, rendered Munro comparatively independent of the aid of experts. Equally at home on a question connected with the management of military bazars, or with the disposition of the troops, or with the organization of any particular branch of the army, as with the principles and details of a revenue settlement or the judicial requirements of a district, he brought to bear upon the discharge of his duties an amount of practical and varied experience such as no other Indian Governor has possessed.

His labour was incessant. Writing to a correspondent in England, he said, ' I am like an overworked horse and ' require a little rest. Ever since I came to this Govern-' ment almost every paper of any importance has been ' written by myself.' In getting through the vast quantities of work which he accomplished in this as well as in former periods of his official life, he was greatly aided by the regularity of his habits. He was an early riser, and was singularly methodical in the employment of his time.

When Munro accepted the Government, he had not intended to remain in India more than three years, and at the end of his third year of office, there being at that time, so far as he was aware, no public business of any importance, and nothing in the political outlook which seemed to require that he should prolong his stay, he sent an application to the Court of Directors to be relieved. But while this application was on its way, events were taking place which entirely altered the aspect of affairs. The failure of the usual rains in a great part of the Madras Presidency brought on a scarcity, amounting in some places to famine, which caused serious apprehension; while on the eastern frontier of Bengal complications arose, resulting in the war with Burma, in which the greater part of the troops had to be supplied from Madras. In these circumstances Munro deemed it his duty to intimate to the Home authorities that he was prepared to remain at his post, if his retention of it was considered advisable. The offer was readily accepted, and Munro's departure was indefinitely postponed.

The famine of 1824 was not the only calamity of that nature with which Munro had been called upon to deal. During the seven years that he served in the Ceded Districts there were four years of scarcity. In the first two of those years, 1803 and 1804, the failure of the crops affected the districts under Munro's charge. In 1806 and 1807 it was principally felt in the Carnatic; but in both cases prices in the Ceded Districts rose very considerably, with the inevitable result of serious distress to the poorer classes. Even at this early period Munro's views as to the proper course to be taken by the Government in dealing with famines differed but little from those which are now

M

generally accepted. The only suggestion made by him which in these days would be regarded as heterodox, but which as recently as 1874 was urged by Sir George Campbell in connection with the famine in Behár, was that under certain circumstances the exportation of grain should be prohibited; but even on this point there are expressions in his reports which show that Munro was sensible of the objections to the measure. He wrote:

Such a measure ought not to be adopted without the strongest necessity, because it hinders the farmers from making up for the loss of almost the whole of their crop by the high price of the remainder.

Writing in 1807 on the various means of mitigating a scarcity of food, he said:

The distress attending an unfavourable season may be mitigated by encouraging importation, prohibiting exportation, reducing the rents of the lower classes of ryots, and by giving employment to the poor on public works. Besides these, there is perhaps no other way in which Government can interfere with any advantage; but of all these means importation is by far the most effectual for promoting the attainment of the objects in view; for if the stock of grain in the country is supposed to be inadequate to the maintenance of the inhabitants until the next harvest, it is only by importation that it can be augmented and made to last till that period; or if the stock of grain, though equal to the subsistence of the inhabitants, be so dear as to place it beyond the reach of the lower orders, it is still only by importation that the price can be so far reduced as to enable them to purchase food. If importation could be carried to such an extent as to keep the price at a moderate rate, it would be unnecessary to take any steps for the assistance of the poor, because they would easily find employment among the other classes of the inhabitants.

Munro was in favour of employing the poor on public works, 'as near as possible to their own villages, both in

'order to save them from the expense of a distant journey
'and from the danger of perishing by pestilential disorders,
'which usually prevail wherever a crowd of poor and ill-
'fed people is drawn together from different quarters.'
He was much opposed to any system of gratuitous State
relief. He wrote :

Were Government to offer to the poor any other relief
than the wages of labour, were it to issue grain to them
gratis or at a reduced price, it would only have the effect
of increasing their number, of drawing them together
from all quarters, and of encouraging them to abandon
themselves to the protection of the public, and to neglect
the salutary means of preserving themselves by their own
exertions. In India, as well as in all other countries, the
distribution of charity will always be found to increase
the number of the poor, which will always at least keep
pace with the fund destined for their relief, whatever its
amount may be. Were grain in this country to be issued
to the poor at any particular station, the report would
soon reach the remotest corners : the relief to be afforded
would be greatly exaggerated : the poor who now procure
a livelihood from their labour, would crowd in from all
sides in the hopes of procuring it upon easier terms. It
would soon become impossible to maintain such a multi-
tude, and famine would appear among them. But this is
not the only evil which would attend their being drawn
away from their own villages ; for the loss of their labour
would be felt, and the crops now on the ground, as well
as the cultivation of the ensuing season, would suffer from
the want of hands.

In 1807 the Madras Government had so far interfered
to facilitate the importation of grain as to guarantee a
certain price for all food grains imported, with the result of
eventually overstocking the market, and unduly reducing
the price of produce in the years immediately following
the scarcity. When famine reappeared in 1824, Munro
decided to offer a bounty on all grain imported from

beyond sea within a fixed period, as being less open to objection than a guaranteed price. He also suspended certain import duties on grain which at that time formed a part of the revenue system.

The war with Burma had been threatening for some years. The ruler and the people of that country were utterly ignorant of the strength of the British Government in India. They had become an aggressive power, and had extended their territories to the borders of Bengal. In 1818 the King of Burma had addressed to the Governor-General an absurd demand for the surrender of Eastern Bengal, including Moorshedabad—a demand which Lord Hastings treated as a forgery and returned to the King. In 1823 matters were brought to a crisis by the Burmese taking possession of a small island called Shahpuri, off the coast of Chittagong, destroying the detachment in charge of it, and refusing to make any reparation for the outrage. War was declared by the Governor-General on the 24th of February, 1824. It was not until the 23rd of that month that the Madras Government received any intimation that war was inpending, and that that Presidency would be required to furnish the native branch of the force. In the mean time a disaster had occurred in the Chittagong district at a place called Rámu, where a small detachment, which had imprudently been left there in an isolated position, was attacked and put to the sword by the Burmese.

Owing to ignorance of the country on the part of most of the Governor-General's advisers at Calcutta, and to other causes, the strategic management of the war was faulty, and instead of being completed, as was expected, in a few months, two years elapsed before the Burmese were reduced to submission; nor would the operations even then have been brought to a close, if it had not been for the indefatigable exertions of Munro in furnishing

troops, ships, boats, transport, bullocks, and supplies,
taking every precaution and offering every suggestion that
could possibly be of use to secure the successful issue of
the war. In addition to the numerous official Minutes
recorded by him on every one of these subjects as the war
went on, Munro kept up a constant correspondence with
the Governor-General, placing fully and freely at the
disposal of the latter the advice which his long experience
of Indian warfare and his knowledge of the Asiatic
character enabled him to offer. These Minutes and letters
are models of the sort of co-operation which the Governor
of an Indian Presidency, possessing local and professional
experience, may render to the Governor-General, and it is
only due to Lord Amherst to say that the aid thus given
was met by him in a spirit of cordial and generous
appreciation. While the war was still in progress, Munro
was created a baronet, and at its close he received the
'thanks of the Court of Directors for the alacrity, zeal,
'perseverance, and forecast which he so signally manifested
'throughout the course of the late war in contributing all
'the available resources of the Madras Government to-
'wards bringing it to a successful termination.' The war
resulted in the Burmese being compelled to pay a crore
of rupees (at that time one million sterling) as a contribution to the expenses of the war, to cede Aracan, Assam,
and Tenasserim, and waive all claims upon Cachár. It was
not until after a second war with Burma, twenty-six years
later, that the province of Pegu became British territory.
The third Burmese war, undertaken in 1885, has brought
the whole of Burma under British rule.

Some of the opinions which Munro expressed in the
course of the correspondence on the subject of the first
Burmese war are even now by no means undeserving of
attention. We have seen that in his campaign in the
Southern Mahratta country he did not scruple to take the

field with a force which in other hands would have seemed, and probably would have been, very inadequate to the operations which had to be carried out; but in that case the circumstances were special, and the wonderful success of the campaign was as much due to Munro's extraordinary political influence over the people of the country, as to his strategy. But no general more clearly recognized than Munro did, the danger, as a general rule, of commencing a campaign with an insufficient force.

It is always dangerous, and often fatal to success, to have a force only barely sufficient to maintain themselves in a hostile country, and none to spare for detachments or distant offensive operations which it may occasionally be found advisable to undertake. It is a great advantage to begin a campaign with a commanding force, particularly in a country recently conquered. It discourages the enemy, and encourages the people of the country to join and aid us, in the hope of regaining their independence. The occupation of Rangoon ought not to make us relax in the smallest degree our preparations, or to believe that it will bring us any nearer to a peace. Our safest and our speediest way of arriving at an honourable peace, is to consider the first success as only the beginning of a general war with the Burman empire, and to engage in it with our whole disposable force.

He was equally opposed to any relaxation of the preparations for continuing the war when the time came for entertaining proposals for peace. He held that 'there is ' no time when it is more essentially requisite for an army ' to be strong than at the very moment when its com- ' mander is treating for peace.'

The following statement of the objects to be kept in view, and of the best modes of achieving them, is interesting :—

Our chief object in the present war is undoubtedly security from future aggression ; our next objects are, peace and the return of our army. There are two ways of preventing future aggression : one is by so completely breaking the power and spirit of the enemy as to deter him from ever renewing hostilities ; another is by dismembering or revolutionizing the kingdom of Ava. The means of effecting these objects are in our hands. The power of the enemy may be broken by advancing to the capital, and by showing, not only to the Burmans, but to all the tributary nations, the weakness of the military force of Ava. The kingdom may be partially dismembered by making Assam, Cachár, and all the petty states on the north-east frontier of Bengal, independent of Ava, and by retaining Aracan ; and more completely by raising up, if possible, the ancient kingdom of Pegu. Could any enterprising chief of that nation be found to assume the government, he would probably, even without any other aid than some arms, be able to maintain himself against Ava, now broken in force and fallen in character.

If the King of Ava does not seek peace before the loss of his capital, it is not likely that he would hold out long after that event. He would be deserted by his army, if we may judge from all that we have yet seen of its behaviour; he would become dispirited, and would rather offer terms than live as a vagabond. It may be said that he might fly to a distant province, and carry on a long defensive war. But Ava does not seem to be calculated, either from the nature of the country or the character of the people, for this sort of contest. An extensive country and a scanty population are usually great obstacles to invasion, and still more so to conquest; because in such countries there are seldom any places, the occupation of which can insure the command of the country. To subdue the country, troops must be spread over every part of it; and where the people are hostile, this cannot with safety be done. But Ava, though of very great extent, and very thinly populated in proportion to that extent, is from various causes more easily subjugated than such countries usually are. The population, as far as we have yet seen, are neither warlike nor hostile to us. They appear to have no particular attachment to their rulers, and to be as willing to live under our protection as theirs. The population, though thin, appear to be chiefly concentrated on the banks of the Irrawaddi, where most of their principal towns are. This river, therefore, by running like a high-road through the fertile and populous part of the kingdom, renders it perfectly vulnerable, and enables a superior army to subdue it, because the invader, by having the command of the river, has in fact the command of the country.

I do not, therefore, see much reason to apprehend that the King would attempt to protract the war long after the fall of the capital. I know of only one thing likely to induce him to hold out—the idea that we would not keep the country, but would get tired of the war, and withdraw our forces. Whatever may be intended in this respect, it will be advisable to indicate by our whole conduct a fixed design of keeping our conquests. Nothing would so soon bring the King to terms as the belief that we had such an intention, or so much encourage his holding out as a contrary opinion. The most likely means of impressing this belief would be to appoint a European officer to the charge of civil government in all the conquered territory, leaving the details in the hands of the natives under his general control; and to collect a revenue according to usage, but much lighter, in order to make it popular. This plan was adopted by Lord Cornwallis in Mysore, and was very useful in procuring supplies of grain and cattle for the army. Such an enemy as we are now engaged with, should always be made to fear the worst. If he thinks that war may terminate in the loss of his crown or of a considerable part of his dominions, he will shun it carefully. But if he thinks that there is a chance of gaining an accession of territory from success, and that there is no danger of losing any permanently from defeat, he has no sufficient motive to deter him from aggression.

If, contrary to expectation, the King should, on the advance of Sir A. Campbell, fly from his capital and refuse to treat, we cannot keep our army in Ava for ever, and must for our own safety endeavour to establish a government that will treat, and enable us to withdraw, and put an end to a war so destructive to our resources. We know from the past history of Ava that revolutions have not been unfrequent there, and that members of the royal family have often attempted to supplant the sovereign.

There is every reason to believe that this disposition is not in any degree diminished, and that the Prince of Tara-waddi or some other member of the royal family might with our assistance be encouraged to seize the government. The desertion of the capital, the disgrace attending it, the unpopularity of the King, would all favour the measure. The prince supported by us would be readily acknow-ledged. He would not have to conquer the country; he would receive possession of it from us, and he would there-fore have the strongest motive for seeking the continuance of our friendship.

As soon as peace was made, Munro renewed his appli-cation for permission to resign the government. Mean-while, owing to the serious illness of their second son, who had been born in 1823, Lady Munro was obliged to return to England before her husband. They parted in March, 1826, hoping to be reunited in the course of the following year, but they never met again. A few months after his wife's departure, Munro set out on a tour through the southern districts of the Presidency, investigating the revenue systems of Tanjore and Tinnevelly, which differed from those in force in the other ryotwár districts, and paying a brief visit to the Nilgiri Hills, then but little known, but now the most agreeable hill station in India. During the previous year, 1825, he had visited Mysore for the purpose of remonstrating with the Rájá, whom Lord Wellesley had placed upon the throne in 1799, upon his extravagance and misgovernment—a remonstrance which proved ineffectual, and was followed a few years later by the withdrawal from the Rájá of all share in the govern-ment of his kingdom. Munro expected to be able to embark for England in the spring of 1827, for his resigna-tion reached the Court of Directors in September, 1826, and it was soon afterwards settled that Mr. Stephen Rumbold Lushington, at that time one of the Political Secretaries to the Treasury, should succeed him; but, owing to causes which have not been fully explained, the formal appointment was delayed until the 4th of April, 1827, and Mr. Lushington did not embark for Madras until July. While awaiting the arrival of his successor, Munro resolved on paying a farewell visit to the Ceded Districts, his interest in which was still unabated. He left Madras for this purpose towards the end of May, and had been rather more than a month in the Ballári district when cholera appeared in his camp. On the 6th of July, shortly after reaching Pattikonda, he was attacked by the disease and died on the evening of the same day. He had attained his sixty-sixth year in the previous May, and had been upwards of forty-seven years in the service of the East India Company.

The intelligence of Munro's death was received at Madras, and in every part of the Presidency, with sentiments of the deepest regret. By all classes of the community the event was mourned as a public calamity. By the members of the civil and military services of his own Presidency Munro was regarded as a man who by his great and commanding talents, by the force of his character, by his extraordinary capacity for work, and by the justness and liberality of his views, had done more than any man in India to raise the reputation of the East India Company's service. By the natives he was venerated as the protector of their rights, familiar with their customs and tolerant of their prejudices, ever ready to redress their grievances, but firm in maintaining order and obedience to the law. On the intelligence of his death reaching Madras, Munro's late colleagues in the Government announced it in the following Gazette extraordinary : —

Madras, Monday, July 9, 1827.
With sentiments of the deepest concern the Government announces the decease of the Honourable Sir Thomas Munro, Baronet, Knight Commander of the Most Honour-

able Order of the Bath, Governor of the Presidency of Fort St. George. This event occurred at Pattikonda, near Gooty, on the evening of Friday, the 6th instant.

The eminent person whose life has been thus suddenly snatched away, was on the eve of returning to his native country, honoured with signal marks of esteem and approbation from his Sovereign, from the East India Company, which he had served for more than forty-seven years, from every authority with which he had occasion to co-operate, from the public at large, and from private friends. From the earliest period of his service he was remarkable among other men. His sound and vigorous understanding, his transcendent talents, his indefatigable application, his varied stores of knowledge, his attainments as an Oriental scholar, his intimate acquaintance with the habits and feelings of the native soldiers and inhabitants generally; his patience, temper, facility of access and kindness of manner, would have ensured him distinction in any line of employment. These qualities were admirably adapted to the duties which he had to perform in organizing the resources and establishing the tranquillity of those provinces where his latest breath has been drawn, and where he had long been known by the appellation of the *Father* of the People. In the higher stations, civil and military, which he afterwards filled, the energies of his character never failed to rise superior to the exigencies of public duty. He had been for seven years at the head of the Government under which he first served as a cadet, and afterwards became the ablest of its revenue officers, and acquired the highest distinction as a military commander. He had raised its character and fame to a higher pitch than it had ever enjoyed before. His own ambition was more than fulfilled, and he appeared to be about to reap in honourable retirement the well-earned rewards of his services and his virtues, when these have received the last stamp of value at the hand of death.

Though sensible how feeble and imperfect must be any hasty tribute to Sir Thomas Munro's merits, yet the Government cannot allow the event which they deplore to be announced to the public without some expression of their sentiments.

The Flag of Fort St. George will be immediately hoisted half-mast high, and continue so till sunset.

Minute guns, sixty-six in number, corresponding with the age of the deceased, will be fired from the ramparts of Fort St. George. Similar marks of respect will be paid to the memory of Sir Thomas Munro at all the principal military stations and posts dependent on this Presidency.

By order of Government,

D. HILL, Chief Secretary.

Shortly after the issue of the foregoing notification, public meetings were held at Madras and in the Ceded Districts, at which it was resolved to erect in honour of Munro's memory a statue at Madras and a choultry, or caravanserai, for the accommodation of travellers at Gooty, where his remains were buried.* At Pattikonda, the place of his death, the recollection of the event was perpetuated by planting a grove of trees and constructing a well with stone steps at the spot where he died.

In estimating Munro's character and career, it is natural to compare him with some of the most distinguished of his contemporaries in the Indian services, and especially with Elphinstone, Malcolm, and Metcalfe. In the greater part of India at the present day these three men are probably better known than Munro, partly because their services have been described in comparatively recent times by the pen of a popular historian and biographer, and in the case of Malcolm and Metcalfe, because much of their work lay in parts of India which now

* The body was subsequently removed to Madras, and buried in St. Mary's Church, Fort St. George, the Walhalla of the Madras Presidency. Not far from the remains of Munro lie those of Sir Barry Close, adjutant-general of the army at the taking of Seringapatam, and afterwards British Resident at Poona, and of Mr. Josiah Webbe, the able Chief Secretary to the Madras Government in the later years of the last and earlier years of the present century. Sir Samuel Hood, a distinguished naval officer, Sir Henry Ward and Lord Hobart, the two latter Governors of Madras, are also buried there.

attract far greater interest than those in which Munro was principally employed. Differing greatly in character, all these four men were endowed with remarkable capacity for administration, and all of them were men who, at any time in the world's history, and in any country, would have made their mark. Malcolm's duties took him into a somewhat wider and more varied sphere than those in which the others were employed. There were few important political transactions in India during the first quarter of the present century in which Malcolm did not play a conspicuous part. In Mysore, at Hyderabad, with Lord Lake's army in Hindustan during the second war with the Mahrattas, in the Deccan and Central India during the final struggle with that power, Malcolm rendered services, both diplomatic and military, which entitle him to a high place among the soldiers and statesmen of the time. He was a man of robust and powerful physique, animated by an enthusiasm which never flagged, genial and generous, but at times somewhat too unreserved on the subject of his services and his claims. Elphinstone and Metcalfe were civilians, but both of them proved their gallantry on more than one well-fought field. Elphinstone rode beside Wellington at Assye, and at the battle of Kirkee displayed military genius which, had he belonged to the army, must have ensured to him distinction as a commander. Metcalfe's gallant bearing at the siege of Deeg, where he took part in the assault as a volunteer, excited the admiration of the whole of Lord Lake's army, His Indian services were hardly less varied than those of Malcolm. When a very young man, he won his spurs as a diplomatist by his coolness, tact, and decision in a difficult mission to the wily and headstrong ruler of the Punjáb, Runjeet Sing; and some years later his exposure of irregularities which were disgracing the British name at Hyderabad, proved that no amount of personal incon-

venience or risk could deter him from doing what he
regarded as his duty. Of the many able men who have
served in the Council of the Governor-General, there never
was an abler than Metcalfe. It was with reference to his
conduct in that office that Lord William Bentinck wrote
the memorable words: 'He never cavilled upon a trifle,
'and he never yielded to me upon a point of importance.'
Metcalfe lived to attain a higher rank and a more prominent position than any of his contemporaries in India.
His resolute bearing in Canada at a crisis of the gravest
difficulty, and his fortitude in retaining his office there,
when he was suffering from a fatal and agonizing malady,
because he deemed that the public interests would be
injured if he left his post, have never been surpassed in
the annals of our colonial administration. But with these
high and noble qualities there was mingled a vein of self-
consciousness and over-sensitiveness, which were never
apparent either in Elphinstone or Munro. The letter
which Metcalfe wrote to the Court of Directors, when he
was passed over for the Government of Madras, could not
have been written by either of those men. Between
Elphinstone and Munro there were some strong points of
resemblance. Both were essentially single-minded men,
occupied with the work they were to do, and caring little
for the credit or promotion they might earn. Of the two,
Elphinstone was the one who probably most attracted the
affection as well as the esteem of those with whom he was
brought into contact. With much of Munro's force of
character, with a refined and cultivated intellect, he combined a gentleness of disposition and sympathy with others
which were inexpressibly attractive; but he appears to
have lacked the sustained energy, physical as well as
mental, which imparted to Munro his enormous capacity
for work, and enabled him to combine so great a mastery
of details with a firm grasp of principles. In general

society Munro was ˙probably the least popular man of the four. From very early life he was more or less affected with deafness, which at times disabled him from joining in general conversation, and increased an appearance of reserve, in some measure natural to him in his intercourse with strangers; but in the society of his intimate friends, and with all who were brought into direct communication with him on public business, he showed no lack of geniality, and by such he was regarded, not only with those sentiments of respect which his great talents, his large experience, and his broad and liberal views could not fail to inspire, but with those warmer feelings of affection which are called forth by an unselfish nature.

Reference has already been made to the opposition which some of Munro's measures encountered from the members of the civil service, and to the jealousy which at one time was felt in connection with his employment on duties considered to belong exclusively to them. No public servant ever more completely lived down antagonism and prejudice. During the seven years that he held the Government of Madras, Munro did more than any Governor had ever done to elevate the tone and raise the efficiency of the civil service, and by no body of men was his value more thoroughly appreciated than by the members of that service. When the writer of this Memoir first arrived in India, Munro had been dead upwards of fifteen years; but the memory of his work was still as fresh as if he had died but yesterday, and his name was never referred to save in terms of the greatest veneration and esteem. By the English statesmen of sixty years ago, Munro was regarded as the ablest Indian official of his time. We have seen in what estimation he was held by Mr. Canning and the Duke of Wellington, two men very different in character, by no means of one mind in politics, but cordially agreed in the high estimate which they formed of Munro. Another prominent statesman of that time, the late Lord Ellenborough, a man very unlike both to the Duke and to Canning, an unsuccessful administrator, but a remarkably shrewd critic, ranked Munro above all his Indian contemporaries. I have before me a letter written a few years ago by a distinguished civil servant who had served in India when Munro was Governor of Madras, and which contains the following remark :— 'There were giants in the days of the old Coompani Sahib, 'and amongst them Sir Thomas Munro was a head and 'shoulders taller than his brother giants.' I believe there is much truth in the judgment which these homely sentences embody; but whether this opinion be correct or not, it may confidently be affirmed that among the British statesmen and soldiers of the nineteenth century, there are not many who have rendered more valuable services to their country, few who have done more in the great work of consolidating our British Indian Empire, than Sir Thomas Munro.

THE END.

PRINTED BY WILLIAM CLOWES AND SONS, LIMITED, LONDON AND BECCLES.

A LIST OF

KEGAN PAUL, TRENCH & CO.'S

PUBLICATIONS.

3.89

1, *Paternoster Square,*

London.

A LIST OF

KEGAN PAUL, TRENCH & CO.'S

PUBLICATIONS.

CONTENTS.

	PAGE		PAGE
GENERAL LITERATURE.	2	MILITARY WORKS.	33
PARCHMENT LIBRARY	18	POETRY.	34
PULPIT COMMENTARY	20	NOVELS AND TALES	39
INTERNATIONAL SCIENTIFIC		BOOKS FOR THE YOUNG	41
SERIES	29		

GENERAL LITERATURE.

AINSWORTH, W. F.—Personal Narrative of the Euphrates Expedition. 2 vols. Demy 8vo, 32s.

A. K. H. B.—From a Quiet Place. A Volume of Sermons. Crown 8vo, 5s.

ALEXANDER, William, D.D., Bishop of Derry.—The Great Question, and other Sermons. Crown 8vo, 6s.

ALLIES, T. W., M.A.—Per Crucem ad Lucem. The Result of a Life. 2 vols. Demy 8vo, 25s.

A Life's Decision. Crown 8vo, 7s. 6d.

AMHERST, Rev. W. J.—The History of Catholic Emancipation and the Progress of the Catholic Church in the British Isles (chiefly in England) from 1771-1820. 2 vols. Demy 8vo, 24s.

AMOS, Professor Sheldon.—The History and Principles of the Civil Law of Rome. An aid to the Study of Scientific and Comparative Jurisprudence. Demy 8vo, 16s.

Are Foreign Missions doing any Good? An Enquiry into their Social Effects. Crown 8vo, 1s.

ARISTOTLE.—The Nicomachean Ethics of Aristotle. Translated by F. H. Peters, M.A. Third Edition. Crown 8vo, 6s.

AUBERTIN, J. J.—A Flight to Mexico. With 7 full-page Illustrations and a Railway Map of Mexico. Crown 8vo, 7s. 6d.

Six Months in Cape Colony and Natal. With Illustrations and Map. Crown 8vo, 6s.

A Fight with Distances. Illustrations and Maps. Crown 8vo, 7s. 6d.

Aucassin and Nicolette. Edited in Old French and rendered in Modern English by F. W. BOURDILLON. Fcap 8vo, 7s. 6d.

BADGER, George Percy, D.C.L.—An English-Arabic Lexicon. In which the equivalent for English Words and Idiomatic Sentences are rendered into literary and colloquial Arabic. Royal 4to, 80s.

BAGEHOT, Walter.—The English Constitution. Fifth Edition. Crown 8vo, 7s. 6d.

Lombard Street. A Description of the Money Market. Ninth Edition. Crown 8vo, 7s. 6d.

Essays on Parliamentary Reform. Crown 8vo, 5s.

Some Articles on the Depreciation of Silver, and Topics connected with it. Second Edition. Demy 8vo, 5s.

BAGOT, Alan, C.E.—Accidents in Mines: their Causes and Prevention. Crown 8vo, 6s.

The Principles of Colliery Ventilation. Second Edition, greatly enlarged. Crown 8vo, 5s.

The Principles of Civil Engineering as applied to Agriculture and Estate Management. Crown 8vo, 7s. 6d.

BAKER, Ella.—Kingscote Essays and Poems. Fcap 8vo. 2s. 6d.

BALDWIN, Capt. J. H.—The Large and Small Game of Bengal and the North-Western Provinces of India. With 20 Illustrations. New and Cheaper Edition. Small 4to, 10s. 6d.

BALL, John, F.R.S.—Notes of a Naturalist in South America. With Map. Crown 8vo, 8s. 6d.

BALLIN, Ada S. and F. L.—A Hebrew Grammar. With Exercises selected from the Bible. Crown 8vo, 7s. 6d.

BASU, K. P., M.A.—Students' Mathematical Companion. Containing problems in Arithmetic, Algebra, Geometry, and Mensuration, for Students of the Indian Universities. Crown 8vo, 6s.

BAUR, Ferdinand, Dr. Ph.—A Philological Introduction to Greek and Latin for Students. Translated and adapted from the German, by C. KEGAN PAUL, M.A., and E. D. STONE, M.A. Third Edition. Crown 8vo, 6s.

Becket, Thomas, Martyr Patriot. By R. A. THOMPSON, M.A. Crown 8vo. 6s.

BENSON, A. C.—William Laud, sometime Archbishop of Canterbury. A Study. With Portrait. Crown 8vo, 6s.

BLOOMFIELD, The Lady.—Reminiscences of Court and Diplomatic Life. New and Cheaper Edition. With Frontispiece. Crown 8vo, 6s.

BLUNT, The Ven. Archdeacon. — The Divine Patriot, and other Sermons. Preached in Scarborough and in Cannes. New and Cheaper Edition. Crown 8vo, 4s. 6d.

BLUNT, Wilfrid S.—The Future of Islam. Crown 8vo, 6s.

Ideas about India. Crown 8vo. Cloth, 6s.

BOWEN, H. C., M.A.—Studies in English. For the use of Modern Schools. Tenth Thousand. Small crown 8vo, 1s. 6d.

English Grammar for Beginners. Fcap. 8vo, 1s.

Simple English Poems. English Literature for Junior Classes. In four parts. Parts I., II., and III., 6d. each. Part IV., 1s. Complete, 3s.

BRADLEY, F. H.—The Principles of Logic. Demy 8vo, 16s.

Bradshaw, Henry: Memoir. By G. W. PROTHERO. With Portrait and Facsimile. Demy 8vo. 16s.

BRIDGETT, Rev. T. E.—History of the Holy Eucharist in Great Britain. 2 vols. Demy 8vo, 18s.

BROOKE, Rev. Stopford A.—The Fight of Faith. Sermons preached on various occasions. Fifth Edition. Crown 8vo, 7s. 6d.

The Spirit of the Christian Life. Third Edition. Crown 8vo, 5s.

Theology in the English Poets.—Cowper, Coleridge, Wordsworth, and Burns. Sixth Edition. Post 8vo, 5s.

Christ in Modern Life. Seventeenth Edition. Crown 8vo, 5s.

Sermons. First Series. Thirteenth Edition. Crown 8vo, 5s.

Sermons. Second Series. Sixth Edition. Crown 8vo, 5s.

BROWN, Horatio F.—Life on the Lagoons. With 2 Illustrations and Map. Crown 8vo, 6s.

Venetian Studies. Crown 8vo, 7s. 6d.

BROWN, Rev. J. Baldwin.—The Higher Life. Its Reality, Experience, and Destiny. Seventh Edition. Crown 8vo, 5s.

Doctrine of Annihilation in the Light of the Gospel of Love. Five Discourses. Fourth Edition. Crown 8vo, 2s. 6d.

The Christian Policy of Life. A Book for Young Men of Business. Third Edition. Crown 8vo, 3s. 6d.

BURKE, The Late Very Rev. T. N.—His Life. By W. J. FITZ-PATRICK. 2 vols. With Portrait. Demy 8vo, 30s.

BURTON, Lady.—The Inner Life of Syria, Palestine, and the Holy Land. Post 8vo, 6s.

BURY, Richard de.—Philobiblon. Edited by E. C. THOMAS. Crown 8vo. 10s. 6d.

CANDLER, C.—The Prevention of Consumption. A Mode of Prevention founded on a New Theory of the Nature of the Tubercle-Bacillus. Demy 8vo, 10s. 6d.

CARPENTER, W. B.—The Principles of Mental Physiology. With their Applications to the Training and Discipline of the Mind, and the Study of its Morbid Conditions. Illustrated. Sixth Edition. 8vo, 12s.

Nature and Man. With a Memorial Sketch by the Rev. J. ESTLIN CARPENTER. Portrait. Large crown 8vo, 8s. 6d.

Catholic Dictionary. Containing some Account of the Doctrine, Discipline, Rites, Ceremonies, Councils, and Religious Orders of the Catholic Church. Edited by THOMAS ARNOLD, M.A. Third Edition. Demy 8vo, 21s.

Charlemagne. A History of Charles the Great. By J. I. MOMBERT, D.D. Medium 8vo. 15s.

CHARLES, Rev. R. H.—Forgiveness, and other Sermons. Crown 8vo, 4s. 6d.

CHEYNE, Canon.—The Prophecies of Isaiah. Translated with Critical Notes and Dissertations. 2 vols. Fifth Edition. Demy 8vo, 25s.

Job and Solomon; or, the Wisdom of the Old Testament. Demy 8vo, 12s. 6d.

The Psalms; or, Book of The Praises of Israel. Translated with Commentary. Demy 8vo. 16s.

Churgress, The. By "THE PRIG." Fcap. 8vo, 3s. 6d.

CLAIRAUT.—Elements of Geometry. Translated by Dr. KAINES. With 145 Figures. Crown 8vo, 4s. 6d.

CLAPPERTON, Jane Hume.—Scientific Meliorism and the Evolution of Happiness. Large crown 8vo, 8s. 6d.

CLODD, Edward, F.R.A.S.—The Childhood of the World: a Simple Account of Man in Early Times. Eighth Edition. Crown 8vo, 3s.
A Special Edition for Schools. 1s.

The Childhood of Religions. Including a Simple Account of the Birth and Growth of Myths and Legends. Eighth Thousand. Crown 8vo, 5s.
A Special Edition for Schools. 1s. 6d.

CLODD, Edward, F.R.A.S.—continued.

Jesus of Nazareth. With a brief sketch of Jewish History to the Time of His Birth. Second Edition. Small crown 8vo, 6s.

A Special Edition for Schools. In 2 parts. Each 1s. 6d.

COGHLAN, J. Cole, D.D.—**The Modern Pharisee,** and other Sermons. Edited by the Very Rev. H. H. DICKINSON, D.D., Dean of Chapel Royal, Dublin. New and Cheaper Edition. Crown 8vo, 7s. 6d.

COLERIDGE, The Hon. Stephen.—**Demetrius.** C.own 8vo, 5s.

CONNELL, A. K.—**Discontent and Danger in India.** Small crown 8vo, 3s. 6d.

The Economic Revolution of India. Crown 8vo, 4s. 6d.

CORR, the late Rev. T. J., M.A.—**Favilla :** Tales, Essays, and Poems. Crown 8vo, 5s.

CORY, William.—**A Guide to Modern English History.** Part I.—MDCCCXV.-MDCCCXXX. Demy 8vo, 9s. Part II.—MDCCCXXX.-MDCCCXXXV., 15s.

COTTON, H. J. S.—**New India, or India in Transition.** Third Edition. Crown 8vo, 4s. 6d. ; Cheap Edition, paper covers, 1s.

COWIE, Right Rev. W. G.—**Our Last Year in New Zealand.** 1887. Crown 8vo, 7s. 6d.

COX, Rev. Sir George W., M.A., Bart.—**The Mythology of the Aryan Nations.** New Edition. Demy 8vo, 16s.

Tales of Ancient Greece. New Edition. Small crown 8vo, 6s.

A Manual of Mythology in the form of Question and Answer. New Edition. Fcap. 8vo, 3s.

An Introduction to the Science of Comparative Mythology and Folk-Lore. Second Edition. Crown 8vo. 7s. 6d.

COX, Rev. Sir G. W., M.A., Bart., and JONES, Eustace Hinton.—**Popular Romances of the Middle Ages.** Third Edition, in 1 vol. Crown 8vo, 6s.

COX, Rev. Samuel, D.D.—**A Commentary on the Book of Job.** With a Translation. Second Edition. Demy 8vo, 15s.

Salvator Mundi ; or, Is Christ the Saviour of all Men ? Twelfth Edition. Crown 8vo, 2s. 6d.

The Larger Hope. A Sequel to "Salvator Mundi." Second Edition. 16mo, 1s.

The Genesis of Evil, and other Sermons, mainly expository. Third Edition. Crown 8vo, 6s.

Balaam. An Exposition and a Study. Crown 8vo, 5s.

Miracles. An Argument and a Challenge. Crown 8vo, 2s. 6d.

CRAVEN, Mrs.—A Year's Meditations. Crown 8vo, 6s.

CRAWFURD, Oswald.—Portugal, Old and New. With Illustrations and Maps. New and Cheaper Edition. Crown 8vo, 6s.

Cross Lights. Crown 8vo. 5s.

CRUISE, Francis Richard, M.D.—Thomas à Kempis. Notes of a Visit to the Scenes in which his Life was spent. With Portraits and Illustrations. Demy 8vo, 12s.

Dante: The Banquet (Il Convito). Translated by KATHARINE HILLARD. Crown 8vo. 7s. 6d.

DARMESTETER, Arsene.—The Life of Words as the Symbols of Ideas. Crown 8vo, 4s. 6d.

DAVIDSON, Rev. Samuel, D.D., LL.D.—Canon of the Bible: Its Formation, History, and Fluctuations. Third and Revised Edition. Small crown 8vo, 5s.

The Doctrine of Last Things contained in the New Testament compared with the Notions of the Jews and the Statements of Church Creeds. Small crown 8vo, 3s. 6d.

DAWSON, Geo., M.A. Prayers, with a Discourse on Prayer. Edited by his Wife. First Series. Tenth Edition. Small Crown 8vo, 3s. 6d.

Prayers, with a Discourse on Prayer. Edited by GEORGE ST. CLAIR, F.G.S. Second Series. Small Crown 8vo, 3s. 6d.

Sermons on Disputed Points and Special Occasions. Edited by his Wife. Fourth Edition. Crown 8vo, 6s.

Sermons on Daily Life and Duty. Edited by his Wife. Fifth Edition. Small Crown 8vo, 3s. 6d.

The Authentic Gospel, and other Sermons. Edited by GEORGE ST. CLAIR, F.G.S. Third Edition. Crown 8vo, 6s.

Every-day Counsels. Edited by GEORGE ST. CLAIR, F.G.S. Crown 8vo, 6s.

Biographical Lectures. Edited by GEORGE ST. CLAIR, F.G.S. Third Edition. Large crown 8vo, 7s. 6d.

Shakespeare, and other Lectures. Edited by GEORGE ST. CLAIR, F.G.S. Large crown 8vo, 7s. 6d.

DE JONCOURT, Madame Marie.—Wholesome Cookery. Fifth Edition. Crown 8vo, cloth, 1s. 6d; paper covers, 1s.

DENT, H. C.—A Year in Brazil.. With Notes on Religion, Meteorology, Natural History, etc. Maps and Illustrations. Demy 8vo, 18s.

DOWDEN, Edward, LL.D.—Shakspere: a Critical Study of his Mind and Art. Ninth Edition. Post 8vo, 12s.

DOWDEN, Edward, LL.D.—continued.

Studies in Literature, 1789–1877. Fourth Edition. Large post 8vo, 6s.

Transcripts and Studies. Large post 8vo. 12s.

Drummond, Thomas, Under Secretary in Ireland, 1835-40. Life and Letters. By R. BARRY O'BRIEN. Demy 8vo. 14s.

Dulce Domum. Fcap. 8vo, 5s.

DU MONCEL, Count.—The Telephone, the Microphone, and the Phonograph. With 74 Illustrations. Third Edition. Small crown 8vo, 5s.

DUNN, H. Percy.—Infant Health. The Physiology and Hygiene of Early Life. Crown 8vo. 3s. 6d.

DURUY, Victor.—History of Rome and the Roman People. Edited by Prof. MAHAFFY. With nearly 3000 Illustrations. 4to. 6 vols. in 12 parts, 30s. each vol.

Education Library. Edited by Sir PHILIP MAGNUS :—

An Introduction to the History of Educational Theories. By OSCAR BROWNING, M.A. Second Edition. 3s. 6d.

Industrial Education. By Sir PHILIP MAGNUS. 6s.

Old Greek Education. By the Rev. Prof. MAHAFFY, M.A. Second Edition. 3s. 6d.

School Management. Including a general view of the work of Education, Organization, and Discipline. By JOSEPH LANDON. Seventh Edition. 6s.

EDWARDES, Major-General Sir Herbert B.—Memorials of his Life and Letters. By his Wife. With Portrait and Illustrations. 2 vols. Demy 8vo, 36s.

Eighteenth Century Essays. Selected and Edited by AUSTIN DOBSON. Cheap Edition. Cloth 1s. 6d.

ELSDALE, Henry.—Studies in Tennyson's Idylls. Crown 8vo, 5s.

Emerson's (Ralph Waldo) Life. By OLIVER WENDELL HOLMES. English Copyright Edition. With Portrait. Crown 8vo, 6s.

EYTON, Rev. Robert.—The True Life, and other Sermons. Crown 8vo, 7s. 6d.

Five o'clock Tea. Containing Receipts for Cakes, Savoury Sandwiches, etc. Seventh Thousand. Fcap. 8vo, cloth, 1s. 6d.; paper covers, 1s.

FLINN, D. Edgar.—Ireland : its Health-Resorts and Watering-Places. With Frontispiece and Maps. Demy 8vo, 5s.

Forbes, Bishop : A Memoir. By the Rev. DONALD J. MACKAY. With Portrait and Map. Crown 8vo, 7s. 6d.

FOTHERINGHAM, James.—**Studies in the Poetry of Robert Browning.** Second Edition. Crown 8vo, 6s.

Franklin (Benjamin) as a Man of Letters. By J. B. MAC-MASTER. Crown 8vo, 5s.

FREWEN, Moreton.—**The Economic Crisis.** Crown 8vo, 2s. 6d.

From World to Cloister; or, My Novitiate. By BERNARD. Crown 8vo, 5s.

FULLER, Rev. Morris.—**Pan-Anglicanism : What is it ?** or, The Church of the Reconciliation. Crown 8vo. 5s.

GARDINER, Samuel R., and J. BASS MULLINGER, M.A.—**Introduction to the Study of English History.** Second Edition. Large crown 8vo, 9s.

GEORGE, Henry.—**Progress and Poverty.** An Inquiry into the Causes of Industrial Depressions, and of Increase of Want with Increase of Wealth. The Remedy. Fifth Library Edition. Post 8vo, 7s. 6d. Cabinet Edition. Crown 8vo, 2s. 6d. Also a Cheap Edition. Limp cloth, 1s. 6d. ; paper covers, 1s.

> **Protection, or Free Trade.** An Examination of the Tariff Question, with especial regard to the Interests of Labour. Second Edition. Crown 8vo, 5s. Cheap Edition, limp cloth, 1s. 6d. ; paper covers, 1s.

> **Social Problems.** Fourth Thousand. Crown 8vo, 5s. Cheap Edition, paper covers, 1s. ; cloth, 1s. 6d.

GILBERT, Mrs. — **Autobiography, and other Memorials.** Edited by JOSIAH GILBERT. Fifth Edition. Crown 8vo, 7s. 6d.

GILLMORE, Parker.—**Days and Nights by the Desert.** Illustrated. Demy 8vo, 10s. 6d.

GLANVILL, Joseph.—**Scepsis Scientifica ;** or, Confest Ignorance, the Way to Science ; in an Essay of the Vanity of Dogmatizing and Confident Opinion. Edited, with Introductory Essay, by JOHN OWEN. Elzevir 8vo, printed on hand-made paper, 6s.

GLASS, H. A.—**The Story of the Psalters.** A History of the Metrical Versions from 1549 to 1885. Crown 8vo, 5s.

Glossary of Terms and Phrases. Edited by the Rev. H. PERCY SMITH and others. Second and Cheaper Edition. Medium 8vo, 7s. 6d.

GLOVER, F., M.A.—**Exempla Latina.** A First Construing Book, with Short Notes, Lexicon, and an Introduction to the Analysis of Sentences. Second Edition. Fcap. 8vo, 2s.

GOODCHILD, John A. **Chats at St. Ampelio.** Crown 8vo. 5s.

GOODENOUGH, Commodore J. G.—Memoir of, with Extracts from his Letters and Journals. Edited by his Widow. With Steel Engraved Portrait. Third Edition. Crown 8vo, 5*s.*

GORDON, Major-General C. G.—His Journals at Kartoum. Printed from the original MS. With Introduction and Notes by A. EGMONT HAKE. Portrait, 2 Maps, and 30 Illustrations. Two vols., demy 8vo, 21*s.* Also a Cheap Edition in 1 vol., 6*s.*

Gordon's (General) Last Journal. A Facsimile of the last Journal received in England from GENERAL GORDON. Reproduced by Photo-lithography. Imperial 4to, £3 3*s.*

Events in his Life. From the Day of his Birth to the Day of his Death. By Sir H. W. GORDON. With Maps and Illustrations. Second Edition. Demy 8vo, 7*s. 6d.*

GOSSE, Edmund.—Seventeenth Century Studies. A Contribution to the History of English Poetry. Demy 8vo, 10*s. 6d.*

GOUGH, E.—The Bible True from the Beginning. Vol. I, Demy 8vo, 16*s.*

GOULD, Rev. S. Baring, M.A.—Germany, Present and Past. New and Cheaper Edition. Large crown 8vo, 7*s. 6d.*

GOWAN, Major Walter E.—A. Ivanoff's Russian Grammar. (16th Edition.) Translated, enlarged, and arranged for use of Students of the Russian Language. Demy 8vo, 6*s.*

GOWER, Lord Ronald. My Reminiscences. MINIATURE EDITION, printed on hand-made paper, limp parchment antique, 10*s. 6d.*

Bric-à-Brac. Being some Photoprints illustrating art objects at Gower Lodge, Windsor. With descriptions. Super royal 8vo. 15*s.* ; extra binding, 21*s.*

Last Days of Mary Antoinette. An Historical Sketch. With Portrait and Facsimiles. Fcap. 4to, 10*s. 6d.*

Notes of a Tour from Brindisi to Yokohama, 1883-1884. Fcap. 8vo, 2*s. 6d.*

GRAHAM, William, M.A.—The Creed of Science, Religious, Moral, and Social. Second Edition, Revised. Crown 8vo, 6*s.*

The Social Problem, in its Economic, Moral, and Political Aspects. Demy 8vo, 14*s.*

GRIMLEY, Rev. H. N., M.A.—Tremadoc Sermons, chiefly on the Spiritual Body, the Unseen World, and the Divine Humanity. Fourth Edition. Crown 8vo, 6*s.*

The Temple of Humanity, and other Sermons. Crown 8vo, 6*s.*

GURNEY, Alfred.—Our Catholic Inheritance in the Larger Hope. Crown 8vo, 1*s. 6d.*

Wagner's Parsifal. A Study. Fcap. 8vo, 1*s. 6d.*

HADDON, Caroline.—The Larger Life, Studies in Hinton's Ethics. Crown 8vo, 5*s.*

HAECKEL, Prof. Ernst.—The History of Creation. Translation revised by Professor E. RAY LANKESTER, M.A., F.R.S. With Coloured Plates and Genealogical Trees of the various groups of both Plants and Animals. 2 vols. Third Edition. Post 8vo, 32*s.*

The History of the Evolution of Man. With numerous Illustrations. 2 vols. Post 8vo, 32*s.*

A Visit to Ceylon. Post 8vo, 7*s.* 6*d.*

Freedom in Science and Teaching. With a Prefatory Note by T. H. HUXLEY, F.R.S. Crown 8vo, 5*s.*

Hamilton, Memoirs of Arthur, B.A., of Trinity College, Cambridge. Crown 8vo, 6*s.*

Handbook of Home Rule, being Articles on the Irish Question by Various Writers. Edited by JAMES BRYCE, M.P. Second Edition. Crown 8vo, 1*s.* sewed, or 1*s.* 6*d.* cloth.

HAWEIS, Rev. H. R., M.A.—Current Coin. Materialism—The Devil—Crime—Drunkenness—Pauperism—Emotion—Recreation —The Sabbath. Fifth Edition. Crown 8vo, 5*s.*

Arrows in the Air. Fifth Edition. Crown 8vo, 5*s.*

Speech in Season. Sixth Edition. Crown 8vo, 5*s.*

Thoughts for the Times. Fourteenth Edition. Crown 8vo, 5*s.*

Unsectarian Family Prayers. New Edition. Fcap. 8vo, 1*s.* 6*d.*

HAWTHORNE, Nathaniel.—Works. Complete in Twelve Volumes. Large post 8vo, 7*s.* 6*d.* each volume.

HEIDENHAIN, Rudolph, M.D.—Hypnotism, or Animal Magnetism. With Preface by G. J. ROMANES. Second Edition. Small crown 8vo, 2*s.* 6*d.*

HENDRIKS, Dom Lawrence.—The London Charterhouse : its Monks and its Martyrs. Illustrated. Demy 8vo, 14*s.*

HINTON, J.—Life and Letters. With an Introduction by Sir W. W. GULL, Bart., and Portrait engraved on Steel by C. H. Jeens. Sixth Edition. Crown 8vo, 8*s.* 6*d.*

Philosophy and Religion. Selections from the Manuscripts of the late James Hinton. Edited by CAROLINE HADDON. Second Edition. Crown 8vo, 5*s.*

The Law Breaker, and The Coming of the Law. Edited by MARGARET HINTON. Crown 8vo, 6*s.*

The Mystery of Pain. New Edition. Fcap. 8vo, 1*s.*

Homer's Iliad. Greek text, with a Translation by J. G. CORDERY. 2 vols. Demy 8vo, 24*s.*

HOOPER, Mary.—Little Dinners: How to Serve them with Elegance and Economy. Twenty-first Edition. Crown 8vo, 2s. 6d.

Cookery for Invalids, Persons of Delicate Digestion, and Children. Fifth Edition. Crown 8vo, 2s. 6d.

Every-day Meals. Being Economical and Wholesome Recipes for Breakfast, Luncheon, and Supper. Seventh Edition. Crown 8vo, 2s. 6d.

HOPKINS, Ellice.— Work amongst Working Men. Sixth Edition. Crown 8vo, 3s. 6d.

HORNADAY, W. T.—Two Years in a Jungle. With Illustrations. Demy 8vo, 21s.

HOSPITALIER, E.—The Modern Applications of Electricity. Translated and Enlarged by JULIUS MAIER, Ph.D. 2 vols. Second Edition, Revised, with many additions and numerous Illustrations. Demy 8vo, 25s.

HOWARD, Robert, M.A.—The Church of England and other Religious Communions. A course of Lectures delivered in the Parish Church of Clapham. Crown 8vo, 7s. 6d.

HYNDMAN, H. M.—The Historical Basis of Socialism in England. Large crown 8vo, 8s. 6d.

IDDESLEIGH, Earl of.—The Pleasures, Dangers, and Uses of Desultory Reading. Fcap. 8vo, 2s. 6d.

IM THURN, Everard F.—Among the Indians of Guiana. Being Sketches, chiefly anthropologic, from the Interior of British Guiana. With 53 Illustrations and a Map. Demy 8vo, 18s.

JEAFFRESON, Herbert H.—The Divine Unity and Trinity. Demy 8vo, 12s.

JENKINS, E., and RAYMOND, J.—The Architect's Legal Handbook. Fourth Edition, revised. Crown 8vo, 6s.

JENKINS, Rev. Canon R. C.—Heraldry. English and Foreign. With a Dictionary of Heraldic Terms and 156 Illustrations. Small crown 8vo, 3s. 6d.

Jerome, St., Life. By M. J. MARTIN. Crown 8vo, 6s.

JOEL, L.—A Consul's Manual and Shipowner's and Shipmaster's Practical Guide in their Transactions Abroad. With Definitions of Nautical, Mercantile, and Legal Terms; a Glossary of Mercantile Terms in English, French, German, Italian, and Spanish; Tables of the Money, Weights, and Measures of the Principal Commercial Nations and their Equivalents in British Standards; and Forms of Consular and Notarial Acts. Demy 8vo, 12s.

JOHNSTON, H. H., F.Z.S.—The Kilima-njaro Expedition. A Record of Scientific Exploration in Eastern Equatorial Africa, and a General Description of the Natural History, Languages, and Commerce of the Kilima-njaro District. With 6 Maps, and over 80 Illustrations by the Author. Demy 8vo, 21*s.*

KAUFMANN, Rev. M., M.A.—Socialism its Nature, its Dangers, and its Remedies considered. Crown 8vo, 7*s. 6d.*

Utopias ; or, Schemes of Social Improvement, from Sir Thomas More to Karl Marx. Crown 8vo, 5*s.*

Christian Socialism. Crown 8vo, 4*s. 6d.*

KAY, David, F.R.G.S.—Education and Educators. Crown 8vo. 7*s. 6d.*

Memory : what it is and how to improve it. Crown 8vo, 6*s.*

KAY, Joseph.—Free Trade in Land. Edited by his Widow. With Preface by the Right Hon. JOHN BRIGHT, M.P. Seventh Edition. Crown 8vo, 5*s.*

*** Also a cheaper edition, without the Appendix, but with a Review of Recent Changes in the Land Laws of England, by the RIGHT HON. G. OSBORNE MORGAN, Q.C., M.P. Cloth, 1*s. 6d.* ; paper covers, 1*s.*

KELKE, W. H. H.—An Epitome of English Grammar for the Use of Students. Adapted to the London Matriculation Course and Similar Examinations. Crown 8vo, 4*s. 6d.*

KEMPIS, Thomas à.—Of the Imitation of Christ. Parchment Library Edition.—Parchment or cloth, 6*s.* ; vellum, 7*s. 6d.* The Red Line Edition, fcap. 8vo, cloth extra, 2*s. 6d.* The Cabinet Edition, small 8vo, cloth limp, 1*s.* ; cloth boards, 1*s. 6d.* The Miniature Edition, cloth limp, 32mo, 1*s.* ; or with red lines, 1*s. 6d.*

*** All the above Editions may be had in various extra bindings.

Notes of a Visit to the Scenes in which his Life was spent. With numerous Illustrations. By F. R. CRUISE, M.D. Demy 8vo, 12*s.*

KENDALL, Henry.—The Kinship of Men. An argument from Pedigrees, or Genealogy viewed as a Science. With Diagrams. Crown 8vo, 5*s.*

KENNARD, Rev. R. B.—A Manual of Confirmation. 18mo. Sewed, 3*d.* ; cloth, 1*s.* ¡

KIDD, Joseph, M.D.—The Laws of Therapeutics ; or, the Science and Art of Medicine. Second Edition. Crown 8vo, 6*s.*

KINGSFORD, Anna, M.D.—The Perfect Way in Diet. A Treatise advocating a Return to the Natural and Ancient Food of our Race. Third Edition. Small crown 8vo, 2*s.*

KINGSLEY, Charles, M.A.—**Letters and Memories of his Life.** Edited by his Wife. With two Steel Engraved Portraits, and Vignettes on Wood. Sixteenth Cabinet Edition. 2 vols. Crown 8vo, 12s.

⁎⁎* Also a People's Edition, in one volume. With Portrait. Crown 8vo, 6s.

All Saints' Day, and other Sermons. Edited by the Rev. W. HARRISON. Third Edition. Crown 8vo, 7s. 6d.

True Words for Brave Men. A Book for Soldiers' and Sailors' Libraries. Sixteenth Thousand. Crown 8vo, 2s. 6d.

KNOX, Alexander A.—**The New Playground ;** or, Wanderings in Algeria. New and Cheaper Edition. Large crown 8vo, 6s.

Lamartine, Alphonse de, Life. By Lady MARGARET DOMVILE. Large crown 8vo, 7s. 6d.

Land Concentration and Irresponsibility of Political Power, as causing the Anomaly of a Widespread State of Want by the Side of the Vast Supplies of Nature. Crown 8vo, 5s.

LANDON, Joseph.—**School Management ;** Including a General View of the Work of Education, Organization, and Discipline. Seventh Edition. Crown 8vo, 6s.

LANG, Andrew.—**Lost Leaders.** Crown 8vo, 5s.

LAURIE, S. S.—**The Rise and Early Constitution of Universities.** With a Survey of Mediæval Education. Crown 8vo, 6s.

LEFEVRE, Right Hon. G. Shaw.—**Peel and O'Connell.** Demy 8vo, 10s. 6d.

Incidents of Coercion. A Journal of visits to Ireland. Third Edition. Crown 8vo, limp cloth, 1s. 6d. ; paper covers, 1s.

Letters from an Unknown Friend. By the Author of " Charles Lowder." With a Preface by the Rev. W. H. CLEAVER. Fcap. 8vo, 1s.

LILLIE, Arthur, M.R.A.S.—**The Popular Life of Buddha.** Containing an Answer to the Hibbert Lectures of 1881. With Illustrations. Crown 8vo, 6s.

Buddhism in Christendom ; or, Jesus the Essene. With Illustrations. Demy 8vo, 15s.

LITTLE, E. A. — **Log-Book Notes** through Life. Oblong. Illustrated. 6s.

LOCHER, Carl.—**An Explanation of Organ Stops,** with Hints for Effective Combinations. Demy 8vo, 5s.

LONGFELLOW, H. Wadsworth.—**Life.** By his Brother, SAMUEL LONGFELLOW. With Portraits and Illustrations. 3 vols. Demy 8vo, 42s.

LONSDALE, Margaret.—Sister Dora : a Biography. With Portrait. Thirtieth Edition. Small crown 8vo, 2s. 6d.

George Eliot: Thoughts upon her Life, her Books, and Herself. Second Edition. Small crown 8vo, 1s. 6d.

LOUNSBURY, Thomas R.—James Fenimore Cooper. With Portrait. Crown 8vo, 5s.

LOWDER, Charles.—A Biography. By the Author of " St. Teresa." Twelfth Edition. Crown 8vo. With Portrait. 3s. 6d.

LÜCKES, Eva C. E.—Lectures on General Nursing, delivered to the Probationers of the London Hospital Training School for Nurses. Third Edition. Crown 8vo, 2s. 6d.

LYTTON, Edward Bulwer, Lord.—Life, Letters and Literary Remains. By his Son, the EARL OF LYTTON. With Portraits, Illustrations and Facsimiles. Demy 8vo. Vols. I. and II., 32s.

MACHIAVELLI, Niccolò. — Life and Times. By Prof. VILLARI. Translated by LINDA VILLARI. 4 vols. Large post 8vo, 48s.

Discourses on the First Decade of Titus Livius. Translated from the Italian by NINIAN HILL THOMSON, M.A. Large crown 8vo, 12s.

The Prince. Translated from the Italian by N. II. T. Small crown 8vo, printed on hand-made paper, bevelled boards, 6s.

MACNEILL, J. G. Swift.—How the Union was carried. Crown 8vo, cloth, 1s. 6d. ; paper covers, 1s.

MAGNUS, Lady.—About the Jews since Bible Times. From the Babylonian Exile till the English Exodus. Small crown 8vo, 6s.

MAGNUS, Sir Philip.—Industrial Education. Crown 8vo, 6s.

Maintenon, Madame de. By EMILY BOWLES. With Portrait. Large crown 8vo, 7s. 6d.

Many Voices. A volume of Extracts from the Religious Writers of Christendom from the First to the Sixteenth Century. With Biographical Sketches. Crown 8vo, cloth extra, red edges, 6s.

MARKHAM, Capt. Albert Hastings, R.N.—The Great Frozen Sea : A Personal Narrative of the Voyage of the *Alert* during the Arctic Expedition of 1875-6. With 6 full-page Illustrations, 2 Maps, and 27 Woodcuts. Sixth and Cheaper Edition. Crown 8vo, 6s.

MARTINEAU, Gertrude.—Outline Lessons on Morals. Small crown 8vo, 3s. 6d.

MASON, Charlotte M.—Home Education : a Course of Lectures to Ladies. Crown 8vo, 3s. 6d.

MASSEY, Gerald. — The Secret Drama of Shakspeare's Sonnets. 4to. 12s. 6d.

Matter and Energy: An Examination of the Fundamental Concepceptions of Physical Force. By B. L. L. Small crown 8vo, 2s.

MATUCE, H. Ogram. **A Wanderer.** Crown 8vo, 5s.

MAUDSLEY, H., M.D.—**Body and Will.** Being an Essay concerning Will, in its Metaphysical, Physiological, and Pathological Aspects. 8vo, 12s.

    Natural Causes and Supernatural Seemings. Second Edition. Crown 8vo, 6s.

McGRATH, Terence.—**Pictures from Ireland.** New and Cheaper Edition. Crown 8vo, 2s.

McKINNEY, S. B. G.—**Science and Art of Religion.** Crown 8vo, 8s. 6d.

MILLER, Edward.—**The History and Doctrines of Irvingism ;** or, The so-called Catholic and Apostolic Church. 2 vols. Large post 8vo, 15s.

MILLS, Herbert.—**Poverty and the State ;** or, Work for the Unemployed. An Inquiry into the Causes and Extent of Enforced Idleness, with a Statement of a Remedy. Crown 8vo, 6s. Cheap Edition, limp cloth, 1s. 6d. ; paper covers, 1s.

MINTON, Rev. Francis.—**Capital and Wages.** 8vo, 15s.

Mitchel, John, Life. By WILLIAM DILLON. 2 vols. 8vo. With Portrait. 21s.

MITCHELL, Lucy M.—**A History of Ancient Sculpture.** With numerous Illustrations, including 6 Plates in Phototype. Superroyal 8vo, 42s.

MIVART, St. George.—**On Truth.** Demy 8vo, 16s.

MOCKLER, E.—**A Grammar of the Baloochee Language,** as it is spoken in Makran (Ancient Gedrosia), in the Persia-Arabic and Roman characters. Fcap. 8vo, 5s.

MOHL, Julius and Mary.—**Letters and Recollections of.** By M. C. M. SIMPSON. With Portraits and Two Illustrations. Demy 8vo, 15s.

MOLESWORTH, Rev. W. Nassau, M.A.—**History of the Church of England from 1660.** Large crown 8vo, 7s. 6d.

MOORE, Aubrey L.—**Science and the Faith :** Essays on Apologetic Subjects. Crown 8vo, 6s.

MORELL, J. R.—**Euclid Simplified in Method and Language.** Being a Manual of Geometry. Compiled from the most important French Works, approved by the University of Paris and the Minister of Public Instruction. Fcap. 8vo, 2s. 6d.

MORISON, J. Cotter.—**The Service of Man ;** an Essay towards the Religion of the Future. Crown 8vo, 5s.

MORRIS, Gouverneur, U.S. Minister to France.—**Diary and Letters.** 2 vols. Demy 8vo, 30s.

MORSE, F. S., Ph.D.—First Book of Zoology. With numerous Illustrations. New and Cheaper Edition. Crown 8vo, 2s. 6d.

My Lawyer : A Concise Abridgment of the Laws of England. By a Barrister-at-Law. Crown 8vo, 6s. 6d.

Natural History. "Riverside" Edition. Edited by J. S. KINGSLEY. 6 vols. 4to. 2200 Illustrations. £6 6s.

NELSON, J. H., M.A.—A Prospectus of the Scientific Study of the Hindû Law. Demy 8vo, 9s.

> Indian Usage and Judge-made Law in Madras. Demy 8vo, 12s.

NEVILL, F.—The Service of God. Small 4to, 3s. 6d.

NEWMAN, Cardinal.—Characteristics from the Writings of. Being Selections from his various Works. Arranged with the Author's personal Approval. Eighth Edition. With Portrait. Crown 8vo, 6s.

> *** A Portrait of Cardinal Newman, mounted for framing, can be had, 2s. 6d.

NEWMAN, Francis William.—Essays on Diet. Small crown 8vo, cloth limp, 2s.

> Miscellanies. Vol. II. Essays, Tracts, and Addresses, Moral and Religious. Demy 8vo, 12s.

> Reminiscences of Two Exiles and Two Wars. Crown 8vo, 3s. 6d.

New Social Teachings. By POLITICUS. Small crown 8vo, 5s.

NICOLS, Arthur, F.G.S., F.R.G.S.—Chapters from the Physical History of the Earth : an Introduction to Geology and Palæontology. With numerous Illustrations. Crown 8vo, 5s.

NOEL, The Hon. Roden.—Essays on Poetry and Poets. Demy 8vo, 12s.

NOPS, Marianne.—Class Lessons on Euclid. Part I. containing the First Two Books of the Elements. Crown 8vo, 2s. 6d.

Nuces : EXERCISES ON THE SYNTAX OF THE PUBLIC SCHOOL LATIN PRIMER. New Edition in Three Parts. Crown 8vo, each 1s.

> *** The Three Parts can also be had bound together, 3s.

OATES, Frank, F.R.G.S.—Matabele Land and the Victoria Falls. A Naturalist's Wanderings in the Interior of South Africa. Edited by C. G. OATES, B.A. With numerous Illustrations and 4 Maps. Demy 8vo, 21s.

O'BRIEN, R. Barry.—Irish Wrongs and English Remedies, with other Essays. Crown 8vo, 5s.

OLIVER, Robert.—Unnoticed Analogies. A Talk on the Irish Question. Crown 8vo, 3s. 6d.

C

O'MEARA, Kathleen.—Henri Perreyve and his Counsels to the Sick. Small crown 8vo, 5*s*.

One and a Half in Norway. A Chronicle of Small Beer. By Either and Both. Small crown 8vo, 3*s*. 6*d*.

OTTLEY, H. Bickersteth.—The Great Dilemma. Christ His Own Witness or His Own Accuser. Six Lectures. Second Edition. Crown 8vo, 3*s*. 6*d*.

Our Priests and their Tithes. By a Priest of the Province of Canterbury. Crown 8vo, 5*s*.

Our Public Schools—Eton, Harrow, Winchester, Rugby, Westminster, Marlborough, The Charterhouse. Crown 8vo, 6*s*.

OWEN, F. M.—Across the Hills. Small crown 8vo, 1*s*. 6*d*.

PALMER, the late William.—Notes of a Visit to Russia in 1840-1841. Selected and arranged by JOHN H. CARDINAL NEWMAN, with Portrait. Crown 8vo, 8*s*. 6*d*.

Early Christian Symbolism. A Series of Compositions from Fresco Paintings, Glasses, and Sculptured Sarcophagi. Edited by the Rev. Provost NORTHCOTE, D.D., and the Rev. Canon BROWNLOW, M.A. With Coloured Plates, folio, 42*s*., or with Plain Plates, folio, 25*s*.

Parchment Library. Choicely Printed on hand-made paper, limp parchment antique or cloth, 6*s*. ; vellum, 7*s*. 6*d*. each volume.

Sartor Resartus. By THOMAS CARLYLE.

The Poetical Works of John Milton. 2 vols.

Chaucer's Canterbury Tales. Edited by A. W. POLLARD. 2 vols.

Letters and Journals of Jonathan Swift. Selected and edited, with a Commentary and Notes, by STANLEY LANE-POOLE.

De Quincey's Confessions of an English Opium Eater. Reprinted from the First Edition. Edited by RICHARD GARNETT.

The Gospel according to Matthew, Mark, and Luke.

Selections from the Prose Writings of Jonathan Swift. With a Preface and Notes by STANLEY LANE-POOLE and Portrait.

English Sacred Lyrics.

Sir Joshua Reynolds's Discourses. Edited by EDMUND GOSSE.

Selections from Milton's Prose Writings. Edited by ERNEST MYERS.

Parchment Library—*continued.*

The Book of Psalms. Translated by the Rev. Canon T. K. CHEYNE, M.A., D.D.

The Vicar of Wakefield. With Preface and Notes by AUSTIN DOBSON.

English Comic Dramatists. Edited by OSWALD CRAWFURD.

English Lyrics.

The Sonnets of John Milton. Edited by MARK PATTISON. With Portrait after Vertue.

French Lyrics. Selected and Annotated by GEORGE SAINTS-BURY. With a Miniature Frontispiece designed and etched by H. G. Glindoni.

Fables by Mr. John Gay. With Memoir by AUSTIN DOBSON, and an Etched Portrait from an unfinished Oil Sketch by Sir Godfrey Kneller.

Select Letters of Percy Bysshe Shelley. Edited, with an Introduction, by RICHARD GARNETT.

The Christian Year. Thoughts in Verse for the Sundays and Holy Days throughout the Year. With Miniature Portrait of the Rev. J. Keble, after a Drawing by G. Richmond, R.A.

Shakspere's Works. Complete in Twelve Volumes.

Eighteenth Century Essays. Selected and Edited by AUSTIN DOBSON. With a Miniature Frontispiece by R. Caldecott.

Q. Horati Flacci Opera. Edited by F. A. CORNISH, Assistant Master at Eton. With a Frontispiece after a design by L. Alma Tadema, etched by Leopold Lowenstam.

Edgar Allan Poe's Poems. With an Essay on his Poetry by ANDREW LANG, and a Frontispiece by Linley Sambourne.

Shakspere's Sonnets. Edited by EDWARD DOWDEN. With a Frontispiece etched by Leopold Lowenstam, after the Death Mask.

English Odes. Selected by EDMUND GOSSE. With Frontispiece on India paper by Hamo Thornycroft, A.R.A.

Of the Imitation of Christ. By THOMAS À KEMPIS. A revised Translation. With Frontispiece on India paper, from a Design by W. B. Richmond.

Poems: Selected from PERCY BYSSHE SHELLEY. Dedicated to Lady Shelley. With a Preface by RICHARD GARNETT and a Miniature Frontispiece.

PARSLOE, '*Joseph.*—**Our Railways.** Sketches, Historical and Descriptive. With Practical Information as to Fares and Rates, etc., and a Chapter on Railway Reform. Crown 8vo, 6s.

PASCAL, Blaise.—The Thoughts of. Translated from the Text of Auguste Molinier, by C. KEGAN PAUL. Large crown 8vo, with Frontispiece, printed on hand-made paper, parchment antique, or cloth, 12s.; vellum, 15s. New Edition. Crown 8vo, 6s.

PATON, W. A.—Down the Islands. A Voyage to the Caribbees. With Illustration. Medium 8vo, 16s.

PAUL, C. Kegan.—Biographical Sketches. Printed on hand-made paper, bound in buckram. Second Edition. Crown 8vo, 7s. 6d.

PEARSON, Rev. S.—Week-day Living. A Book for Young Men and Women. Second Edition. Crown 8vo, 5s.

PENRICE, Major J.—Arabic and English Dictionary of the Koran. 4to, 21s.

PESCHEL, Dr. Oscar.—The Races of Man and their Geographical Distribution. Second Edition. Large crown 8vo, 9s.

PIDGEON, D.—An Engineer's Holiday; or, Notes of a Round Trip from Long. 0° to 0°. New and Cheaper Edition. Large crown 8vo, 7s. 6d.

Old World Questions and New World Answers. Second Edition. Large crown 8vo, 7s. 6d.

Plain Thoughts for Men. Eight Lectures delivered at Forester's Hall, Clerkenwell, during the London Mission, 1884. Crown 8vo, cloth, 1s. 6d; paper covers, 1s.

PLOWRIGHT, C. B.—The British Uredineæ and Ustilagineæ. With Illustrations. Demy 8vo, 12s.

PRICE, Prof. Bonamy. — Chapters on Practical Political Economy. Being the Substance of Lectures delivered before the University of Oxford. New and Cheaper Edition. Crown 8vo, 5s.

Prigment, The. "The Life of a Prig," "Prig's Bede," "How to Make a Saint," "The Churgress." In 1 vol. Crown 8vo, 6s.

Prig's Bede : the Venerable Bede, Expurgated, Expounded, and Exposed. By "THE PRIG." Second Edition. Fcap. 8vo, 3s. 6d.

Pulpit Commentary, The. (*Old Testament Series.*) Edited by the Rev. J. S. EXELL, M.A., and the Very Rev. Dean H. D. M. SPENCE, M.A., D.D.

Genesis. By the Rev. T. WHITELAW, D.D. With Homilies by the Very Rev. J. F. MONTGOMERY, D.D., Rev. Prof. R. A. REDFORD, M.A., LL.B., Rev. F. HASTINGS, Rev. W. ROBERTS, M.A. An Introduction to the Study of the Old Testament by the Venerable Archdeacon FARRAR, D.D., F.R.S.; and Introductions to the Pentateuch by the Right Rev. H. COTTERILL, D.D., and Rev. T. WHITELAW, M.A. Ninth Edition. 1 vol., 15s.

Pulpit Commentary, The—*continued.*

Exodus. By the Rev. Canon RAWLINSON. With Homilies by Rev. J. ORR, D.D., Rev. D. YOUNG, B.A., Rev. C. A. GOODHART, Rev. J. URQUHART, and the Rev. H. T. ROBJOHNS. Fourth Edition. 2 vols., 9s. each.

Leviticus. By the Rev. Prebendary MEYRICK, M.A. With Introductions by the Rev. R. COLLINS, Rev. Professor A. CAVE, and Homilies by Rev. Prof. REDFORD, LL.B., Rev. J. A. MACDONALD, Rev. W. CLARKSON, B.A., Rev. S. R. ALDRIDGE, LL.B., and Rev. MCCHEYNE EDGAR. Fourth Edition. 15s.

Numbers. By the Rev. R. WINTERBOTHAM, LL.B. With Homilies by the Rev. Professor W. BINNIE, D.D., Rev. E. S. PROUT, M.A., Rev. D. YOUNG, Rev. J. WAITE, and an Introduction by the Rev. THOMAS WHITELAW, M.A. Fifth Edition. 15s.

Deuteronomy. By the Rev. W. L. ALEXANDER, D.D. With Homilies by Rev. C. CLEMANCE, D.D., Rev. J. ORR, D.D., Rev. R. M. EDGAR, M.A., Rev. D. DAVIES, M.A. Fourth edition. 15s.

Joshua. By Rev. J. J. LIAS, M.A. With Homilies by Rev. S. R. ALDRIDGE, LL.B., Rev. R. GLOVER, REV. E. DE PRESSENSÉ, D.D., Rev. J. WAITE, B.A., Rev. W. F. ADENEY, M.A. ; and an Introduction by the Rev. A. PLUMMER, M.A. Fifth Edition. 12s. 6d.

Judges and Ruth. By the Bishop of BATH and WELLS, and Rev. J. MORISON, D.D. With Homilies by Rev. A. F. MUIR, M.A., Rev. W. F. ADENEY, M.A., Rev. W. M. STATHAM, and Rev. Professor J. THOMSON, M.A. Fifth Edition. 10s. 6d.

1 and 2 Samuel. By the Very Rev. R. P. SMITH, D.D. With Homilies by Rev. DONALD FRASER, D.D., Rev. Prof. CHAPMAN, and Rev. B. DALE. Seventh Edition. 15s. each.

1 Kings. By the Rev. JOSEPH HAMMOND, LL.B. With Homilies by the Rev. E. DE PRESSENSÉ, D.D., Rev. J. WAITE, B.A., Rev. A. ROWLAND, LL.B., Rev. J. A. MACDONALD, and Rev. J. URQUHART. Fifth Edition. 15s.

1 Chronicles. By the Rev. Prof. P. C. BARKER, M.A., LL.B. With Homilies by Rev. Prof. J. R. THOMSON, M.A., Rev. R. TUCK, B.A., Rev. W. CLARKSON, B.A., Rev. F. WHITFIELD, M.A., and Rev. RICHARD GLOVER. 15s.

Ezra, Nehemiah, and Esther. By Rev. Canon G. RAWLINSON, M.A. With Homilies by Rev. Prof. J. R. THOMSON, M.A., Rev. Prof. R. A. REDFORD, LL.B., M.A., Rev. W. S. LEWIS, M.A., Rev. J. A. MACDONALD, Rev. A. MACKENNAL, B.A., Rev. W. CLARKSON, B.A., Rev. F. HASTINGS, Rev. W. DINWIDDIE, LL.B., Rev. Prof. ROWLANDS, B.A., Rev. G. WOOD, B.A., Rev. Prof. P. C. BARKER, M.A., LL.B., and the Rev. J. S. EXELL, M.A. Seventh Edition. 1 vol., 12s. 6d.

Pulpit Commentary, The—*continued.*

Isaiah. By the Rev. Canon G. RAWLINSON, M.A. With Homilies by Rev. Prof. E. JOHNSON, M.A., Rev. W. CLARKSON, B.A., Rev. W. M. STATHAM, and Rev. R. TUCK, B.A. Second Edition. 2 vols., 15*s.* each.

Jeremiah. (Vol. I.) By the Rev. Canon T. K. CHEYNE, D.D. With Homilies by the Rev. W. F. ADENEY, M.A., Rev. A. F. MUIR, M.A., Rev. S. CONWAY, B.A., Rev. J. WAITE, B.A., and Rev. D. YOUNG, B.A. Third Edition. 15*s.*

Jeremiah (Vol. II.) and Lamentations. By Rev. Canon T. K. CHEYNE, D.D. With Homilies by Rev. Prof. J. R. THOMSON, M.A., Rev. W. F. ADENEY, M.A., Rev. A. F. MUIR, M.A., Rev. S. CONWAY, B.A., Rev. D. YOUNG, B.A. 15*s.*

Hosea and Joel. By the Rev. Prof. J. J. GIVEN, Ph.D., D.D. With Homilies by the Rev. Prof. J. R. THOMSON, M.A., Rev. A. ROWLAND, B.A., LL.B., Rev. C. JERDAN, M.A., LL.B., Rev. J. ORR, D.D., and Rev. D. THOMAS, D.D. 15*s.*

Pulpit Commentary, The. (*New Testament Series.*)

St. Mark. By Very Rev. E. BICKERSTETH, D.D., Dean of Lich-field. With Homilies by Rev. Prof. THOMSON, M.A., Rev. Prof. J. J. GIVEN, Ph.D., D.D., Rev. Prof. JOHNSON, M.A., Rev. A. ROWLAND, B.A., LL.B., Rev. A. MUIR, and Rev. R. GREEN. Fifth Edition. 2 vols., 10*s.* 6*d.* each.

St. Luke. By the Very Rev. H. D. M. SPENCE. With Homilies by the Rev. J. MARSHALL LANG, D.D., Rev. W. CLARKSON, and Rev. R. M. EDGAR. Vol. I., 10*s.* 6*d.*

St. John. By Rev. Prof. H. R. REYNOLDS, D.D. With Homilies by Rev. Prof. T. CROSKERY, D.D., Rev. Prof. J. R. THOMSON, M.A., Rev. D. YOUNG, B.A., Rev. B. THOMAS, Rev. G. BROWN. Second Edition. 2 vols., 15*s.* each.

The Acts of the Apostles. By the Bishop of BATH and WELLS. With Homilies by Rev. Prof. P. C. BARKER, M.A., LL.B., Rev. Prof. E. JOHNSON, M.A., Rev. Prof. R. A. REDFORD, LL.B., Rev. R. TUCK, B.A., Rev. W. CLARKSON, B.A. Fourth Edition. 2 vols., 10*s.* 6*d.* each.

1 Corinthians. By the Ven. Archdeacon FARRAR, D.D. With Homilies by Rev. Ex-Chancellor LIPSCOMB, LL.D., Rev. DAVID THOMAS, D.D., Rev. D. FRASER, D.D., Rev. Prof. J. R. THOMSON, M.A., Rev. J. WAITE, B.A., Rev. R. TUCK, B.A., Rev. E. HURNDALL, M.A., and Rev. H. BREMNER, B.D. Fourth Edition. 15*s.*

2 Corinthians and Galatians. By the Ven. Archdeacon FARRAR, D.D., and Rev. Prebendary E. HUXTABLE. With Homilies by Rev. Ex-Chancellor LIPSCOMB, LL.D., Rev. DAVID THOMAS, D.D., Rev. DONALD FRASER, D.D., Rev. R. TUCK, B.A., Rev. E. HURNDALL, M.A., Rev. Prof. J. R. THOMSON, M.A., Rev. R. FINLAYSON, B.A., Rev. W. F. ADENEY, M.A., Rev. R. M. EDGAR, M.A., and Rev. T. CROSKERY, D.D. Second Edition. 21*s.*

Pulpit Commentary, The—*continued.*

Ephesians, Philippians, and Colossians. By the Rev. Prof. W. G. BLAIKIE, D.D., Rev. B. C. CAFFIN, M.A., and Rev. G. G. FINDLAY, B.A. With Homilies by Rev. D. THOMAS, D.D., Rev. R. M. EDGAR, M.A., Rev. R. FINLAYSON, B.A., Rev. W. F. ADENEY, M.A., Rev. Prof. T. CROSKERY, D.D., Rev. E. S. PROUT, M.A., Rev. Canon VERNON HUTTON, and Rev. U. R. THOMAS, D.D. Second Edition. 21s.

Thessalonians, Timothy, Titus, and Philemon. By the Bishop of Bath and Wells, Rev. Dr. GLOAG, and Rev. Dr. EALES. With Homilies by the Rev. B. C. CAFFIN, M.A., Rev. R. FINLAYSON, B.A., Rev. Prof. T. CROSKERY, D.D., Rev. W. F. ADENEY, M.A., Rev. W. M. STATHAM, and Rev. D. THOMAS, D.D. 15s.

Hebrews and James. By the Rev. J. BARMBY, D.D., and Rev. Prebendary E. C. S. GIBSON, M.A. With Homiletics by the Rev. C. JERDAN, M.A., LL.B., and Rev. Prebendary E. C. S. GIBSON. And Homilies by the Rev. W. JONES, Rev. C. NEW, Rev. D. YOUNG, B.A., Rev. J. S. BRIGHT, Rev. T. F. LOCKYER, B.A., and Rev. C. JERDAN, M.A., LL.B. Second Edition. 15s.

PUSEY, Dr.—**Sermons for the Church's Seasons from Advent to Trinity.** Selected from the Published Sermons of the late EDWARD BOUVERIE PUSEY, D.D. Crown 8vo, 5s.

QUEKETT, Rev. W.—**My Sayings and Doings.** With Reminiscences of my Life. With Illustrations. Demy 8vo, 18s.

RANKE, Leopold von.—**Universal History.** The oldest Historical Group of Nations and the Greeks. Edited by G. W. PROTHERO. Demy 8vo, 16s.

Remedy (The) for Landlordism ; or, Free Land Tenure. Small crown 8vo, 2s. 6d.

RENDELL, J. M.—**Concise Handbook of the Island of Madeira.** With Plan of Funchal and Map of the Island. Fcap. 8vo, 1s. 6d.

REYNOLDS, Rev. J. W.—**The Supernatural in Nature.** A Verification by Free Use of Science. Third Edition, Revised and Enlarged. Demy 8vo, 14s.

The Mystery of Miracles. Third and Enlarged Edition. Crown 8vo, 6s.

The Mystery of the Universe our Common Faith. Demy 8vo, 14s.

The World to Come: Immortality a Physical Fact. Crown 8vo, 6s.

RIBOT, Prof. Th.—**Heredity:** A Psychological Study of its Phenomena, its Laws, its Causes, and its Consequences. Second Edition. Large crown 8vo, 9s.

RICHARDSON, Austin.—"What are the Catholic Claims?" With Introduction by Rev. LUKE RIVINGTON. Crown 8vo, 3s. 6d.

RIVINGTON, Luke.—Authority, or a Plain Reason for joining the Church of Rome. Fifth Edition. Crown 8vo, 3s. 6d.

ROBERTSON, The late Rev. F. W., M.A.—Life and Letters of. Edited by the Rev. STOPFORD BROOKE, M.A.
    I. Two vols., uniform with the Sermons. With Steel Portrait. Crown 8vo, 7s. 6d.
    II. Library Edition, in Demy 8vo, with Portrait. 12s.
    III. A Popular Edition, in 1 vol. Crown 8vo, 6s.

Sermons. Five Series. Small crown 8vo, 3s. 6d. each.

Notes on Genesis. New and Cheaper Edition. Small crown 8vo, 3s. 6d.

Expository Lectures on St. Paul's Epistles to the Corinthians. A New Edition. Small crown 8vo, 5s.

Lectures and Addresses, with other Literary Remains. A New Edition. Small crown 8vo, 5s.

An Analysis of Tennyson's "In Memoriam." (Dedicated by Permission to the Poet-Laureate.) Fcap. 8vo, 2s.

The Education of the Human Race. Translated from the German of GOTTHOLD EPHRAIM LESSING. Fcap. 8vo, 2s. 6d.

*** A Portrait of the late Rev. F. W. Robertson, mounted for framing, can be had, 2s. 6d.

ROGERS, William.—Reminiscences. Compiled by R. H. HADDEN. With Portrait. Crown 8vo, 6s. Cheap Edition, 2s. 6d.

ROMANES, G. J.—Mental Evolution in Animals. With a Posthumous Essay on Instinct by CHARLES DARWIN, F.R.S. Demy 8vo, 12s.

Mental Evolution in Man : Origin of Human Faculty. Demy 8vo, 14s.

ROSMINI SERBATI, Antonio.—Life. By the REV. W. LOCKHART. 2 vols. With Portraits. Crown 8vo, 12s.

ROSS, Janet.—Italian Sketches. With 14 full-page Illustrations. Crown 8vo, 7s. 6d.

RULE, Martin, M.A.—The Life and Times of St. Anselm, Archbishop of Canterbury and Primate of the Britains. 2 vols. Demy 8vo, 32s.

SANTIAGOE, Daniel.—The Curry Cook's Assistant. Fcap. 8vo, cloth. 1s. 6d. ; paper covers, 1s.

SAVERY, C. E.—The Church of England ; an Historical Sketch. Crown 8vo, 1s. 6d.

SAYCE, Rev. Archibald Henry.—Introduction to the Science of Language. 2 vols. Second Edition. Large post 8vo, 21s.

SCOONES, W. Baptiste.—Four Centuries of English Letters: A Selection of 350 Letters by 150 Writers, from the Period of the Paston Letters to the Present Time. Third Edition. Large crown 8vo, 6s.

Selwyn, Bishop, *of New Zealand and of Lichfield.* A Sketch of his Life and Work, with Further Gleanings from his Letters, Sermons, and Speeches. By the Rev. Canon CURTEIS. Large crown 8vo, 7s. 6d.

SEYMOUR, W. Digby, Q.C.,—Home Rule and State Supremacy. Crown 8vo, 3s. 6d.

Shakspere's Macbeth. With Preface, Notes, and New Renderings. By MATTHIAS MULL. Demy 8vo, 6s.

Shakspere's Works. The Avon Edition, 12 vols., fcap. 8vo, cloth, 18s.; in cloth box, 21s.; bound in 6 vols., cloth, 15s.

Shakspere's Works, an Index to. By EVANGELINE O'CONNOR. Crown 8vo, 5s.

SHELLEY, Percy Bysshe.—Life. By EDWARD DOWDEN, LL.D. 2 vols. With Portraits. Demy 8vo, 36s.

SHILLITO, Rev. Joseph.—Womanhood: its Duties, Temptations, and Privileges. A Book for Young Women. Third Edition. Crown 8vo, 3s. 6d.

Shooting, Practical Hints on. Being a Treatise on the Shot Gun and its Management. By "20 Bore." With 55 Illustrations. Demy 8vo, 12s.

Sister Augustine, Superior of the Sisters of Charity at the St. Johannis Hospital at Bonn. Authorized Translation by HANS THARAU, from the German "Memorials of AMALIE VON LASAULX." Cheap Edition. Large crown 8vo, 4s. 6d.

SKINNER, James.—A Memoir. By the Author of "Charles Lowder." With a Preface by the Rev. Canon CARTER, and Portrait. Large crown, 7s. 6d.

** Also a cheap Edition. With Portrait. Fourth Edition. Crown 8vo, 3s. 6d.

SMITH, L, A.—The Music of the Waters: Sailor's Chanties and Working Songs of the Sea. Demy 8vo, 12s.

Spanish Mystics. By the Editor of "Many Voices." Crown 8vo, 5s.

Specimens of English Prose Style from Malory to Macaulay. Selected and Annotated, with an Introductory Essay, by GEORGE SAINTSBURY. Large crown 8vo, printed on hand-made paper, parchment antique or cloth, 12s.; vellum, 15s.

STRACHEY, Sir John, G.C.S.I.—India. With Map. Demy 8vo, 15s.

Stray Papers on **Education,** and Scenes from School Life. By B. H. Second Edition. Small crown 8vo, 3s. 6d.

STRECKER-WISLICENUS.—**Organic Chemistry.** Translated and Edited, with Extensive Additions, by W. R. HODGKINSON, Ph.D., and A. J. GREENAWAY, F.I.C. Second and cheaper Edition. Demy 8vo, 12s. 6d.

Suakin, 1885 : being a Sketch of the Campaign of this year. By an Officer who was there. Second Edition. Crown 8vo, 2s. 6d.

SULLY, James, M.A.—**Pessimism :** a History and a Criticism. Second Edition. Demy 8vo, 14s.

SWEDENBORG, Eman.—**De Cultu et Amore Dei ubi Agitur de Telluris ortu, Paradiso et Vivario, tum de Primogeniti Seu Adami Nativitate Infantia, et Amore.** Crown 8vo, 6s.

> **On the Worship and Love of God.** Treating of the Birth of the Earth, Paradise, and the Abode of Living Creatures. Translated from the original Latin. Crown 8vo, 7s. 6d.

> **Prodromus Philosophiæ Ratiocinantis de Infinito, et Causa Finali Creationis :** deque Mechanismo Operationis Animæ et Corporis. Edidit THOMAS MURRAY GORMAN, M.A. Crown 8vo, 7s. 6d.

TARRING, C. J.—**A Practical Elementary Turkish Grammar.** Crown 8vo, 6s.

TAYLOR, Rev. Canon Isaac, LL.D.—**The Alphabet.** An Account of the Origin and Development of Letters. With numerous Tables and Facsimiles. 2 vols. Demy 8vo, 36s.

Leaves from an Egyptian Note-book. Crown 8vo, 5s.

TAYLOR, Reynell, C.B., C.S.I. **A Biography.** By E. GAMBIER PARRY. With Portait and Map. Demy 8vo, 14s.

TAYLOR, Sir Henry.—**The Statesman.** Fcap. 8vo, 3s. 6d.

THOM, J. Hamilton.—**Laws of Life after the Mind of Christ.** Two Series. Crown 8vo, 7s. 6d. each.

THOMPSON, Sir H.—**Diet in Relation to Age and Activity.** Fcap. 8vo, cloth, 1s. 6d. ; paper covers, 1s.

Modern Cremation. Crown 8vo, 2s. 6d.

TODHUNTER, Dr. J.—**A Study of Shelley.** Crown 8vo, 7s.

TOLSTOI, Count Leo.—**Christ's Christianity.** Translated from the Russian. Large crown 8vo, 7s. 6d. :

TRANT, William.—**Trade Unions : Their Origin, Objects, and Efficacy.** Small crown 8vo, 1s. 6d. ; paper covers, 1s.

TRENCH, The late R. C., Archbishop.—Letters and Memorials. By the Author of "Charles Lowder." With two Portraits. 2 vols. 8vo, 21*s.*

Notes on the Parables of Our Lord. 8vo, 12*s.* Cheap Edition. Fifty-sixth Thousand. 7*s.* 6*d.*

Notes on the Miracles of Our Lord. 8vo, 12*s.* Cheap Edition. Forty-eighth Thousand. 7*s.* 6*d.*

Studies in the Gospels. Fifth Edition, Revised. 8vo, 10*s.* 6*d.*

Brief Thoughts and Meditations on Some Passages in Holy Scripture. Third Edition. Crown 8vo, 3*s.* 6*d.*

Synonyms of the New Testament. Tenth Edition, Enlarged. 8vo, 12*s.*

Sermons New and Old. Crown 8vo, 6*s.*

Westminster and other Sermons. Crown 8vo, 6*s.*

On the Authorized Version of the New Testament. Second Edition. 8vo, 7*s.*

Commentary on the Epistles to the Seven Churches in Asia. Fourth Edition, Revised. 8vo, 8*s.* 6*d.*

The Sermon on the Mount. An Exposition drawn from the Writings of St. Augustine, with an Essay on his Merits as an Interpreter of Holy Scripture. Fourth Edition, Enlarged. 8vo, 10*s.* 6*d.*

Shipwrecks of Faith. Three Sermons preached before the University of Cambridge in May, 1867. Fcap. 8vo, 2*s.* 6*d.*

Lectures on Mediæval Church History. Being the Substance of Lectures delivered at Queen's College, London. Second Edition. 8vo, 12*s.*

English, Past and Present. Thirteenth Edition, Revised and Improved. Fcap. 8vo, 5*s.*

On the Study of Words. Twentieth Edition, Revised. Fcap. 8vo, 5*s.*

Select Glossary of English Words used Formerly in Senses Different from the Present. Sixth Edition, Revised and Enlarged. Fcap. 8vo, 5*s.*

Proverbs and Their Lessons. Seventh Edition, Enlarged. Fcap. 8vo, 4*s.*

Poems. Collected and Arranged anew. Tenth Edition. Fcap. 8vo, 7*s.* 6*d.*

Poems. Library Edition. 2 vols. Small crown 8vo, 10*s.*

Sacred Latin Poetry. Chiefly Lyrical, Selected and Arranged for Use. Third Edition, Corrected and Improved. Fcap. 8vo, 7*s.*

TRENCH, The late R. C., Archbishop—continued.

A Household Book of English Poetry. Selected and Arranged, with Notes. Fourth Edition, Revised. Extra fcap. 8vo, 5s. 6d.

An Essay on the Life and Genius of Calderon. With Translations from his "Life's a Dream" and "Great Theatre of the World." Second Edition, Revised and Improved. Extra fcap. 8vo, 5s. 6d.

Gustavus Adolphus in Germany, and other Lectures on the Thirty Years' War. Third Edition, Enlarged. Fcap. 8vo, 4s.

Plutarch: his Life, his Lives, and his Morals. Second Edition, Enlarged. Fcap. 8vo, 3s. 6d.

Remains of the late Mrs. Richard Trench. Being Selections from her Journals, Letters, and other Papers. New and Cheaper Issue. With Portrait. 8vo, 6s.

TUTHILL, C. A. H.—**Origin and Development of Christian Dogma.** Crown 8vo, 3s. 6d.

Two Centuries of Irish History. By various Writers. Edited by Prof. J. BRYCE. Demy 8vo, 16s.

UMLAUFT, Prof. F.—**The Alps.** Illustrations and Maps. 8vo, 25s.

VAL d'EREMAO, Rev. J. P.—**The Serpent of Eden.** A Philological and Critical Essay. Crown 8vo, 4s. 6d.

VOLCKXSOM, E. W. v.—**Catechism of Elementary Modern Chemistry.** Small crown 8vo, 3s.

WALLER, C. B.—**Unfoldings of Christian Hope.** Second Edition. Crown 8vo, 3s. 6d.

WALPOLE, Chas. George.—**A Short History of Ireland from the Earliest Times to the Union with Great Britain.** With 5 Maps and Appendices. Third Edition. Crown 8vo, 6s.

WARD, Wilfrid.—**The Wish to Believe.** A Discussion Concerning the Temper of Mind in which a reasonable Man should undertake Religious Inquiry. Small crown 8vo, 5s.

WARD, William George, Ph.D.—**Essays on the Philosophy of Theism.** Edited, with an Introduction, by WILFRID WARD. 2 vols. Demy 8vo, 21s.

WARTER, J. W.—**An Old Shropshire Oak.** 2 vols. Demy 8vo, 28s.

WEDMORE, Frederick.—**The Masters of Genre Painting.** With Sixteen Illustrations. Post 8vo, 7s. 6d.

WHIBLEY, Charles.—**In Cap and Gown.** Crown 8vo.

WHITMAN, Sidney.—**Conventional Cant: its Results and Remedy.** Crown 8vo, 6s.

WHITNEY, Prof. William Dwight. — Essentials of English Grammar, for the Use of Schools. Second Edition. Crown 8vo, 3*s.* 6*d.*

WHITWORTH, George Clifford. — An Anglo-Indian Dictionary : a Glossary of Indian Terms used in English, and of such English or other Non-Indian Terms as have obtained special meanings in India. Demy 8vo, cloth, 12*s.*

Wilberforce, Bishop, *of Oxford and Winchester.* Life. By his Son REGINALD WILBERFORCE. Crown 8vo, 6*s.*

WILSON, Mrs. R. F. — The Christian Brothers. Their Origin and Work. With a Sketch of the Life of their Founder, the Ven. JEAN BAPTISTE, de la Salle. Crown 8vo, 6*s.*

WOLTMANN, Dr. Alfred, and WOERMANN, Dr. Karl. — History of Painting. With numerous Illustrations. Medium 8vo. Vol. I. Painting in Antiquity and the Middle Ages. 28*s.* ; bevelled boards, gilt leaves, 30*s.* Vol. II. The Painting of the Renascence. 42*s.* ; bevelled boards, gilt leaves, 45*s.*

Words of Jesus Christ taken from the Gospels. Small crown 8vo, 2*s.* 6*d.*

YOUMANS, Edward L., M.D. — A Class Book of Chemistry, on the Basis of the New System. With 200 Illustrations. Crown 8vo, 5*s.*

YOUMANS, Eliza A. — First Book of Botany. Designed to cultivate the Observing Powers of Children. With 300 Engravings. New and Cheaper Edition. Crown 8vo, 2*s.* 6*d.*

THE INTERNATIONAL SCIENTIFIC SERIES.

I. Forms of Water in Clouds and Rivers, Ice and Glaciers. By J. Tyndall, LL.D., F.R.S. With 25 Illustrations. Ninth Edition. 5*s.*

II. Physics and Politics ; or, Thoughts on the Application of the Principles of "Natural Selection" and "Inheritance" to Political Society. By Walter Bagehot. Eighth Edition. 5*s.*

III. Foods. By Edward Smith, M.D., LL.B., F.R.S. With numerous Illustrations. Ninth Edition. 5*s.*

IV. Mind and Body : the Theories of their Relation. By Alexander Bain, LL.D. With Four Illustrations. Eighth Edition. 5*s.*

V. The Study of Sociology. By Herbert Spencer. Fourteenth Edition. 5*s.*

VI. The Conservation of Energy. By Balfour Stewart, M.A., LL.D., F.R.S. With 14 Illustrations. Seventh Edition. 5*s.*

VII. Animal Locomotion ; or, Walking, Swimming, and Flying. By J. B. Pettigrew, M.D., F.R.S., etc. With 130 Illustrations. Third Edition. 5*s.*

VIII. Responsibility in Mental Disease. By Henry Maudsley, M.D. Fourth Edition. 5*s.*

IX. The New Chemistry. By Professor J. P. Cooke. With 31 Illustrations. Ninth Edition. 5*s.*

X. The Science of Law. By Professor Sheldon Amos. Sixth Edition. 5*s.*

XI. Animal Mechanism : a Treatise on Terrestrial and Aerial Locomotion. By Professor E. J. Marey. With 117 Illustrations. Third Edition. 5*s.*

XII. The Doctrine of Descent and Darwinism. By Professor Oscar Schmidt. With 26 Illustrations. Seventh Edition. 5*s.*

XIII. The History of the Conflict between Religion and Science. By J. W. Draper, M.D., LL.D. Twentieth Edition. 5*s.*

XIV. Fungi : their Nature, Influences, and Uses. By M. C. Cooke, M.A., LL.D. Edited by the Rev. M. J. Berkeley, M.A., F.L.S. With numerous Illustrations. Fourth Edition. 5*s.*

XV. The Chemistry of Light and Photography. By Dr. Hermann Vogel. With 100 Illustrations. Fifth Edition. 5*s.*

XVI. The Life and Growth of Language. By Professor William Dwight Whitney. Fifth Edition. 5*s.*

XVII. Money and the Mechanism of Exchange. By W. Stanley Jevons, M.A., F.R.S. Eighth Edition. 5*s.*

XVIII. The Nature of Light. With a General Account of Physical Optics. By Dr. Eugene Lommel. With 188 Illustrations and a Table of Spectra in Chromo-lithography. Fifth Edition. 5*s.*

XIX. Animal Parasites and Messmates. By P. J. Van Beneden. With 83 Illustrations. Third Edition. 5*s.*

XX. On Fermentation. By Professor Schützenberger. With 28 Illustrations. Fourth Edition. 5*s.*

XXI. The Five Senses of Man. By Professor Bernstein. With 91 Illustrations. Fifth Edition. 5*s.*

XXII. The Theory of Sound in its Relation to Music. By Professor Pietro Blaserna. With numerous Illustrations. Third Edition. 5*s.*

XXIII. Studies in Spectrum Analysis. By J. Norman Lockyer, F.R.S. With six photographic Illustrations of Spectra, and numerous engravings on Wood. Fourth Edition. 6*s.* 6*d.*

XXIV. **A History of the Growth of the Steam Engine.** By Professor R. II. Thurston. With numerous Illustrations. Fourth Edition. 5*s.*

XXV. **Education as a Science.** By Alexander Bain, LL.D. Seventh Edition. 5*s.*

XXVI. **The Human Species.** By Professor A. de Quatrefages. Fourth Edition. 5*s.*

XXVII. **Modern Chromatics.** With Applications to Art and Industry. By Ogden N. Rood. With 130 original Illustrations. Second Edition. 5*s.*

XXVIII. **The Crayfish :** an Introduction to the Study of Zoology. By Professor T. H. Huxley. With 82 Illustrations. Fifth Edition, 5*s.*

XXIX. **The Brain as an Organ of Mind.** By H. Charlton Bastian, M.D. With numerous Illustrations. Third Edition. 5*s.*

XXX. **The Atomic Theory.** By Prof. Wurtz. Translated by E. Cleminshaw, F.C.S. Fifth Edition. 5*s.*

XXXI. **The Natural Conditions of Existence as they affect Animal Life.** By Karl Semper. With 2 Maps and 106 Woodcuts. Third Edition. 5*s.*

XXXII. **General Physiology of Muscles and Nerves.** By Prof. J. Rosenthal. Third Edition. With 75 Illustrations. 5*s.*

XXXIII. **Sight :** an Exposition of the Principles of Monocular and Binocular Vision. By Joseph le Conte, LL.D. Second Edition. With 132 Illustrations. 5*s.*

XXXIV. **Illusions :** a Psychological Study. By James Sully. Third Edition. 5*s.*

XXXV. **Volcanoes :** what they are and what they teach. By Professor J. W. Judd, F.R.S. With 96 Illustrations on Wood. Fourth Edition. 5*s.*

XXXVI. **Suicide :** an Essay on Comparative Moral Statistics. By Prof. H. Morselli. Second Edition. With Diagrams. 5*s.*

XXXVII. **The Brain and its Functions.** By J. Luys. With Illustrations. Second Edition. 5*s.*

XXXVIII. **Myth and Science :** an Essay. By Tito Vignoli. Third Edition. With Supplementary Note. 5*s.*

XXXIX. **The Sun.** By Professor Young. With Illustrations. Third Edition. 5*s.*

XL. **Ants, Bees, and Wasps :** a Record of Observations on the Habits of the Social Hymenoptera. By Sir John Lubbock, Bart., M.P. With 5 Chromo-lithographic Illustrations. Ninth Edition. 5*s.*

XLI. **Animal Intelligence.** By G. J. Romanes, LL.D., F.R.S. Fourth Edition. 5*s.*

XLII. **The Concepts and Theories of Modern Physics.** By J. B. Stallo. Third Edition. 5*s.*

XLIII. **Diseases of Memory :** An Essay in the Positive Psychology. By Prof. Th. Ribot. Third Edition. 5*s.*

XLIV. **Man before Metals.** By N. Joly, with 148 Illustrations. Fourth Edition. 5*s.*

XLV. **The Science of Politics.** By Prof. Sheldon Amos. Third Edition. 5*s.*

XLVI. **Elementary Meteorology.** By Robert H. Scott. Fourth Edition. With Numerous Illustrations. 5*s.*

XLVII. **The Organs of Speech and their Application in the Formation of Articulate Sounds.** By Georg Hermann Von Meyer. With 47 Woodcuts. 5*s.*

XLVIII. **Fallacies.** A View of Logic from the Practical Side. By Alfred Sidgwick. Second Edition. 5*s.*

XLIX. **Origin of Cultivated Plants.** By Alphonse de Candolle. Second Edition. 5*s.*

L. **Jelly-Fish, Star-Fish, and Sea-Urchins.** Being a Research on Primitive Nervous Systems. By G. J. Romanes. With Illustrations. 5*s.*

LI. **The Common Sense of the Exact Sciences.** By the late William Kingdon Clifford. Second Edition. With 100 Figures. 5*s.*

LII. **Physical Expression : Its Modes and Principles.** By Francis Warner, M.D., F.R.C.P., Hunterian Professor of Comparative Anatomy and Physiology, R.C.S.E. With 50 Illustrations. 5*s.*

LIII. **Anthropoid Apes.** By Robert Hartmann. With 63 Illustrations. 5*s.*

LIV. **The Mammalia in their Relation to Primeval Times.** By Oscar Schmidt. With 51 Woodcuts. 5*s.*

LV. **Comparative Literature.** By H. Macaulay Posnett, LL.D. 5*s.*

LVI. **Earthquakes and other Earth Movements.** By Prof. John Milne. With 38 Figures. Second Edition. 5*s.*

LVII. **Microbes, Ferments, and Moulds.** By E. L. Trouessart. With 107 Illustrations. 5*s.*

LVIII. **Geographical and Geological Distribution of Animals.** By Professor A. Heilprin. With Frontispiece. 5*s.*

LIX. **Weather.** A Popular Exposition of the Nature of Weather Changes from Day to Day. By the Hon. Ralph Abercromby. Second Edition. With 96 Illustrations. 5*s.*

LX. **Animal Magnetism.** By Alfred Binet and Charles Féré. Second Edition. 5*s.*

LXI. **Manual of British Discomycetes,** with descriptions of all the Species of Fungi hitherto found in Britain included in the Family, and Illustrations of the Genera. By William Phillips, F.L.S. 5*s.*

LXII. **International Law.** With Materials for a Code of International Law. By Professor Leone Levi. 5*s.*

LXIII. **The Geological History of Plants.** By Sir J. William Dawson. With 80 Figures. 5*s.*

LXIV. **The Origin of Floral Structures through Insect and other Agencies.** By Rev. Prof. G. Henslow. With 88 Illustrations. 5*s.*

LXV. **On the Senses, Instincts, and Intelligence of Animals.** With special Reference to Insects. By Sir John Lubbock, Bart., M.P. 100 Illustrations. Second Edition. 5*s.*

LXVI. **The Primitive Family : Its Origin and Development.** By C. N. Starcke.

MILITARY WORKS.

BRACKENBURY, Col. C. B., R.A. — **Military Handbooks for Regimental Officers.**

I. **Military Sketching and Reconnaissance.** By Col. F. J. Hutchison and Major H. G. MacGregor. Fifth Edition. With 16 Plates. Small crown 8vo, 4*s.*

II. **The Elements of Modern Tactics Practically applied to English Formations.** By Lieut.-Col. Wilkinson Shaw. Sixth Edition. With 25 Plates and Maps. Small crown 8vo, 9*s.*

III. **Field Artillery.** Its Equipment, Organization and Tactics. By Major Sisson C. Pratt, R.A. With 12 Plates. Third Edition. Small crown 8vo, 6*s.*

IV. **The Elements of Military Administration.** First Part : Permanent System of Administration. By Major J. W. Buxton. Small crown 8vo, 7*s.* 6*d.*

V. **Military Law : Its Procedure and Practice.** By Major Sisson C. Pratt, R.A. Fourth Edition. Revised. Small crown 8vo, 4*s.* 6*d.*

VI. **Cavalry in Modern War.** By Major-General F. Chenevix Trench. Small crown 8vo, 6*s.*

D

BRACKENBURY, Col. C. B., R.A.—continued.

VII. Field Works. Their Technical Construction and Tactical Application. By the Editor, Col. C. B. Brackenbury, R.A. Small crown 8vo, in 2 parts, 12s.

BROOKE, Major, C. K.—A System of Field Training. Small crown 8vo, cloth limp, 2s.

Campaign of Fredericksburg, November—December, 1862. A Study for Officers of Volunteers. By a Line Officer. With 5 Maps and Plans. Second Edition. Crown 8vo, 5s.

CLERY, C. Francis, Col.—Minor Tactics. With 26 Maps and Plans. Eighth Edition, Revised. Crown 8vo, 9s.

COLVILE, Lieut.-Col. C. F.—Military Tribunals. Sewed, 2s. 6d.

CRAUFURD, Capt. H. J.—Suggestions for the Military Training of a Company of Infantry. Crown 8vo, 1s. 6d.

HAMILTON, Capt. Ian, A.D.C.—The Fighting of the Future. 1s.

HARRISON, Col. R.—The Officer's Memorandum Book for Peace and War. Fourth Edition, Revised throughout. Oblong 32mo, red basil, with pencil, 3s. 6d.

Notes on Cavalry Tactics, Organisation, etc. By a Cavalry Officer. With Diagrams. Demy 8vo, 12s.

PARR, Col. H. Hallam, C.M.G.—The Dress, Horses, and Equipment of Infantry and Staff Officers. Crown 8vo, 1s.

Further Training and Equipment of Mounted Infantry. Crown 8vo, 1s.

SCHAW, Col. H.—The Defence and Attack of Positions and Localities. Fourth Edition. Crown 8vo, 3s. 6d.

STONE, Capt. F. Gleadowe, R.A.—Tactical Studies from the Franco-German War of 1870-71. With 22 Lithographic Sketches and Maps. Demy 8vo, 10s. 6d.

WILKINSON, H. Spenser, Capt. 20th Lancashire R.V.—Citizen Soldiers. Essays towards the Improvement of the Volunteer Force. Crown 8vo, 2s. 6d.

POETRY.

ALEXANDER, William, D.D., Bishop of Derry.—St. Augustine's Holiday, and other Poems. Crown 8vo, 6s.

AUCHMUTY, A. C.—Poems of English Heroism : From Brunanburh to Lucknow ; from Athelstan to Albert. Small crown 8vo, 1s. 6d.

BARNES, William.—**Poems of Rural Life, in the Dorset Dialect.** New Edition, complete in one vol. Crown 8vo, 6s.

BAYNES, Rev. Canon H. R.—**Home Songs for Quiet Hours.** Fourth and Cheaper Edition. Fcap. 8vo, cloth, 2s. 6d.

BEVINGTON, L. S.—**Key Notes.** Small crown 8vo, 5s.

BLUNT, Wilfrid Scawen.—**The Wind and the Whirlwind.** Demy 8vo, 1s. 6d.

The Love Sonnets of Proteus. Fifth Edition. Elzevir 8vo, 5s.

In Vinculis. With Portrait. Elzevir 8vo, 5s.

BOWEN, H. C., M.A.—**Simple English Poems.** English Literature for Junior Classes. In Four Parts. Parts I., II., and III., 6d. each, and Part IV., 1s. Complete, 3s.

BRYANT, W. C.—**Poems.** Cheap Edition, with Frontispiece. Small crown 8vo, 3s. 6d.

Calderon's Dramas : the Wonder-Working Magician—Life is a Dream—the Purgatory of St. Patrick. Translated by DENIS FLORENCE MACCARTHY. Post 8vo, 10s.

Camoens' Lusiads. — Portuguese Text, with Translation by J. J. AUBERTIN. Second Edition. 2 vols. Crown 8vo, 12s.

CHRISTIE, Albany J.—**The End of Man.** Fourth Edition. Fcap. 8vo, 2s. 6d.

COLERIDGE, Hon. Stephen.—**Fibulæ.** Small crown 8vo, 4s. 6d.

COXHEAD, Ethel.—**Birds and Babies.** With 33 Illustrations. Imp. 16mo, 1s.

Dante's Divina Commedia. Translated in the *Terza Rima* of Original, by F. K. H. HASELFOOT. Demy 8vo, 16s.

DENNIS, J.—**English Sonnets.** Collected and Arranged by. Small crown 8vo, 2s. 6d.

DE VERE, Aubrey.—**Poetical Works.**

    I. THE SEARCH AFTER PROSERPINE, etc. 3s. 6d.
    II. THE LEGENDS OF ST. PATRICK, etc. 3s. 6d.
    III. ALEXANDER THE GREAT, etc. 3s. 6d.

The Foray of Queen Meave, and other Legends of Ireland's Heroic Age. Small crown 8vo, 3s. 6d.

Legends of the Saxon Saints. Small crown 8vo, 3s. 6d.

Legends and Records of the Church and the Empire. Small crown 8vo, 3s. 6d.

DOBSON, Austin.—**Old World Idylls,** and other Verses. Eighth Edition. Elzevir 8vo, gilt top, 6s.

DOBSON, Austin—continued.

At the Sign of the Lyre. Sixth Edition. Elzevir 8vo, gilt top, 6s.

DOWDEN, Edward, LL.D.—Shakspere's Sonnets. With Introduction and Notes. Large post 8vo, 7s. 6d.

DURANT, Héloïse.—Dante. A Dramatic Poem. Small crown 8vo, 5s.

DUTT, Toru.—A Sheaf Gleaned in French Fields. New Edition. Demy 8vo, 10s. 6d.

Ancient Ballads and Legends of Hindustan. With an Introductory Memoir by EDMUND GOSSE. Second Edition, 18mo. Cloth extra, gilt top, 5s.

ELLIOTT, Ebenezer, The Corn Law Rhymer.—Poems. Edited by his son, the Rev. EDWIN ELLIOTT, of St. John's, Antigua. 2 vols. Crown 8vo, 18s.

English Verse. Edited by W. J. LINTON and R. H. STODDARD. 5 vols. Crown 8vo, cloth, 5s. each.

    I. CHAUCER TO BURNS.
    II. TRANSLATIONS.
    III. LYRICS OF THE NINETEENTH CENTURY.
    IV. DRAMATIC SCENES AND CHARACTERS.
    V. BALLADS AND ROMANCES.

GOSSE, Edmund.—New Poems. Crown 8vo, 7s. 6d.

Firdausi in Exile, and other Poems. Second Edition. Elzevir 8vo, gilt top, 6s.

GURNEY, Rev. Alfred.—The Vision of the Eucharist, and other Poems. Crown 8vo, 5s.

A Christmas Faggot. Small crown 8vo, 5s.

HARRISON, Clifford.—In Hours of Leisure. Second Edition. Crown 8vo, 5s.

KEATS, John.—Poetical Works. Edited by W. T. ARNOLD. Large crown 8vo, choicely printed on hand-made paper, with Portrait in *eau-forte.* Parchment or cloth, 12s. ; vellum, 15s. New Edition, crown 8vo, cloth, 3s. 6d.

KING, Mrs. Hamilton.—The Disciples. Tenth Edition. Small crown 8vo, 5s. ; Elzevir Edition, cloth extra, 6s.

A Book of Dreams. Third Edition. Crown 8vo, 3s. 6d.

The Sermon in the Hospital (From "The Disciples"). Fcap. 8vo, 1s. Cheap Edition for distribution 3d., or 20s. per 100.

LANG, A.—XXXII. Ballades in Blue China. Elzevir 8vo, 5s.

Rhymes à la Mode. With Frontispiece by E. A. Abbey. Second Edition. Elzevir 8vo, cloth extra, gilt top, 5s.

LARMINIE, W. — Glanlua, and other Poems. Small crown 8vo, 3s. 6d.

Living English Poets MDCCCLXXXII. With Frontispiece by Walter Crane. Second Edition. Large crown 8vo. Printed on hand-made paper. Parchment or cloth, 12s. ; vellum, 15s.

LOCKER, F.—London Lyrics. Tenth Edition. With Portrait, Elzevir 8vo. Cloth extra, gilt top, 5s.

LUSTED, C. T.—Semblance, and other Poems. Small crown 8vo, 3s. 6d.

MAGNUSSON, Eiríkr, M.A., and PALMER, E. H., M.A.—Johan Ludvig Runeberg's Lyrical Songs, Idylls, and Epigrams. Fcap. 8vo, 5s.

MEREDITH, Owen [The Earl of Lytton].—Lucile. New Edition. With 32 Illustrations. 16mo, 3s. 6d. Cloth extra, gilt edges, 4s. 6d.

MORISON, Jeanie.—Gordon. An Our-Day Idyll. Crown 8vo, 3s. 6d.

MORRIS, Lewis.—Poetical Works of. New and Cheaper Editions, with Portrait. In 4 vols., 5s. each.

Vol. I. contains "Songs of Two Worlds." Thirteenth Edition.
Vol. II. contains "The Epic of Hades." Twenty-third Edition.
Vol. III. contains "Gwen" and "The Ode of Life." Seventh Edition.
Vol. IV. contains "Songs Unsung" and "Gycia." Fifth Edition.

Songs of Britain. Third Edition. Fcap. 8vo, 5s.

The Epic of Hades. With 16 Autotype Illustrations, after the Drawings of the late George R. Chapman. 4to, cloth extra, gilt leaves, 21s.

The Epic of Hades. Presentation Edition. 4to, cloth extra, gilt leaves, 10s. 6d.

The Lewis Morris Birthday Book. Edited by S. S. Copeman, with Frontispiece after a Design by the late George R. Chapman. 32mo, cloth extra, gilt edges, 2s. ; cloth limp, 1s. 6d,

MORSHEAD, E. D. A. — The House of Atreus. Being the Agamemnon, Libation-Bearers, and Furies of Æschylus. Translated into English Verse. Crown 8vo, 7s.

The Suppliant Maidens of Æschylus. Crown 8vo, 3s. 6d.

MULHOLLAND, Rosa.—Vagrant Verses. Small crown 8vo, 5s.

NOEL, The Hon. Roden. — A Little Child's Monument. Third Edition. Small crown 8vo, 3s. 6d.

The House of Ravensburg. New Edition. Small crown 8vo, 6s.

The Red Flag, and other Poems. New Edition. Small crown 8vo, 6s.

NOEL, The Hon. Roden—continued:
Songs of the Heights and Deeps. Crown 8vo, 6s.
A Modern Faust, and other Poems. Small crown 8vo, 5s.

O'HAGAN, John.—The Song of Roland. Translated into English Verse. New and Cheaper Edition. Crown 8vo, 5s.

Publisher's Playground. Fcap. 8vo, 3s. 6d.

Rare Poems of the 16th and 17th Centuries. Edited by W. J. LINTON. Crown 8vo, 5s.

ROBINSON, A. Mary F.—A Handful of Honeysuckle. Fcap. 8vo, 3s. 6d.

The Crowned Hippolytus. Translated from Euripides. With New Poems. Small crown 8vo, 5s.

SEAL, W. H.—Visions of the Night. Crown 8vo, 4s.

SMITH, J. W. Gilbart.—The Loves of Vandyck. A Tale of Genoa. Small crown 8vo, 2s. 6d.

The Log o' the "Norseman." Small crown 8vo, 5s.

Serbelloni. Small crown 8vo, 5s.

Sophocles: The Seven Plays in English Verse. Translated by LEWIS CAMPBELL. Crown 8vo, 7s. 6d.

SYMONDS, John Addington.—Vagabunduli Libellus. Crown 8vo, 6s.

TAYLOR, Sir H.—Works. Complete in Five Volumes. Crown 8vo, 30s.

Philip Van Artevelde. Fcap. 8vo, 3s. 6d.

The Virgin Widow, etc. Fcap. 8vo, 3s. 6d.

TODHUNTER, Dr. J.—Laurella, and other Poems. Crown 8vo, 6s. 6d.

Forest Songs. Small crown 8vo, 3s. 6d.

The True Tragedy of Rienzi: a Drama. 3s. 6d.

Alcestis: a Dramatic Poem. Extra fcap. 8vo, 5s.

Helena in Troas. Small crown 8vo, 2s. 6d.

The Banshee, and other Poems. Small crown 8vo, 3s. 6d.

TYNAN, Katherine.—Louise de la Valliere, and other Poems. Small crown 8vo, 3s. 6d.

Shamrocks. Small crown 8vo, 5s.

Twilight and Candleshades. By EXUL. With 15 Vignettes. Small crown 8vo, 5s.

Victorian Hymns: English Sacred Songs of Fifty Years. Dedicated to the Queen. Large post 8vo, 10s. 6d.

Wordsworth Birthday Book, The. Edited by ADELAIDE and VIOLET WORDSWORTH. 32mo, limp cloth, 1s. 6d.; cloth extra, 2s.

Wordsworth, Selections from. By WM. KNIGHT and other members of the Wordsworth Society. Large crown 8vo. Printed on hand-made paper. With Portrait. Parchment, 12s; vellum, 15s.

YEATS, W. B.—**The Wanderings of Oisin,** and other Poems. Small crown 8vo, 5s.

NOVELS AND TALES.

BAKER, Ella.—**Kingscote Stories.** Crown 8vo, 5s.

Bertram de Drumont. Crown 8vo, 5s.

BANKS, Mrs. G. L.—**God's Providence House.** Crown 8vo, 6s.

CRAWFURD, Oswald.—**Sylvia Arden.** With Frontispiece. Crown 8vo, 1s.

GARDINER, Linda.—**His Heritage.** With Frontispiece. Crown 8vo, 6s.

GRAY, Maxwell.—**The Silence of Dean Maitland.** Fifteenth Thousand. With Frontispiece. Crown 8vo, 6s.

GREY, Rowland.—**In Sunny Switzerland.** A Tale of Six Weeks. Second Edition. Small crown 8vo, 5s.

Lindenblumen and other Stories. Small crown 8vo, 5s.

By Virtue of his Office. Crown 8vo, 6s.

HUNTER, Hay.—**The Crime of Christmas Day.** A Tale of the Latin Quarter. By the Author of "My Ducats and my Daughter." 1s.

HUNTER, Hay, and WHYTE, Walter.—**My Ducats and My Daughter.** With Frontispiece. Crown 8vo, 6s.

INGELOW, Jean.—**Off the Skelligs.** A Novel. With Frontispiece. Crown 8vo, 6s.

LANG, Andrew.—**In the Wrong Paradise,** and other Stories. Crown 8vo, 6s.

MACDONALD, G.—**Donal Grant.** A Novel. With Frontispiece. Crown 8vo, 6s.

Home Again. With Frontispiece. Crown 8vo, 6s.

Castle Warlock. A Novel. With Frontispiece. Crown 8vo, 6s.

Malcolm. With Portrait of the Author engraved on Steel. Crown 8vo, 6s.

MACDONALD, G.—continued.

The Marquis of Lossie. With Frontispiece. Crown 8vo, 6s.

St. George and St. Michael. With Frontispiece. Crown 8vo, 6s.

What's Mine's Mine. With Frontispiece. Crown 8vo, 6s.

Annals of a Quiet Neighbourhood. With Frontispiece. Crown 8vo, 6s.

The Seaboard Parish : a Sequel to "Annals of a Quiet Neighbourhood." With Frontispiece. Crown 8vo, 6s.

Wilfred Cumbermede. An Autobiographical Story. With Frontispiece. Crown 8vo, 6s.

Thomas Wingfold, Curate. With Frontispiece. Crown 8vo, 6s.

Paul Faber, Surgeon. With Frontispiece. Crown 8vo, 6s.

The Elect Lady. With Frontispiece. Crown 8vo, 6s.

*MALET, Lucas.—***Colonel Enderby's Wife.** A Novel. With Frontispiece. Crown 8vo, 6s.

A Counsel of Perfection. With Frontispiece. Crown 8vo, 6s.

*MULHOLLAND, Rosa.—***Marcella Grace.** An Irish Novel. Crown 8vo, 6s.

A Fair Emigrant. With Frontispiece. Crown 8vo, 6s.

*OGLE, Anna C.—***A Lost Love.** Small crown 8vo, 2s. 6d.

*PALGRAVE, W. Gifford.—***Hermann Agha :** an Eastern Narrative. Crown 8vo, 6s.

Romance of the Recusants. By the Author of "Life of a Prig." Crown 8vo, 5s.

*SEVERNE, Florence.—***The Pillar House.** With Frontispiece. Crown 8vo, 6s.

*SHAW, Flora L.—***Castle Blair :** a Story of Youthful Days. Crown 8vo, 3s. 6d.

*STRETTON, Hesba.—***Through a Needle's Eye.** A Story. With Frontispiece. Crown 8vo, 6s.

*TAYLOR, Col. Meadows, C.S.I., M.R.I.A.—***Seeta.** A Novel. With Frontispiece. Crown 8vo, 6s.

Tippoo Sultaun : a Tale of the Mysore War. With Frontispiece. Crown 8vo, 6s.

Ralph Darnell. With Frontispiece. Crown 8vo, 6s.

A Noble Queen. With Frontispiece. Crown 8vo, 6s.

The Confessions of a Thug. With Frontispiece. Crown 8vo, 6s.

Tara : a Mahratta Tale. With Frontispiece. Crown 8vo, 6s.

Within Sound of the Sea. With Frontispiece. Crown 8vo, 6s.

BOOKS FOR THE YOUNG.

Brave Men's Footsteps. A Book of Example and Anecdote for Young People. By the Editor of "Men who have Risen." With 4 Illustrations by C. Doyle. Ninth Edition. Crown 8vo, 2*s.* 6*d.*

COXHEAD, Ethel.—**Birds and Babies.** With 33 Illustrations. Second Edition. Imp. 16mo, cloth, 1*s.*

DAVIES, G. Christopher.—**Rambles and Adventures of our School Field Club.** With 4 Illustrations. New and Cheaper Edition. Crown 8vo, 3*s.* 6*d.*

EDMONDS, Herbert.—**Well Spent Lives :** a Series of Modern Biographies. New and Cheaper Edition. Crown 8vo, 3*s.* 6*d.*

EVANS, Mark.—**The Story of our Father's Love,** told to Children. Sixth and Cheaper Edition of Theology for Children. With 4 Illustrations. Fcap. 8vo, 1*s.* 6*d.*

MAC KENNA, S. J.—**Plucky Fellows.** A Book for Boys. With 6 Illustrations. Fifth Edition. Crown 8vo, 3*s.* 6*d.*

MALET, Lucas.—**Little Peter.** A Christmas Morality for Children of any Age. With numerous Illustrations. Fourth Thousand. 5*s.*

REANEY, Mrs. G. S.—**Waking and Working ;** or, From Girlhood to Womanhood. New and Cheaper Edition. With a Frontispiece. Crown 8vo, 3*s.* 6*d.*

Blessing and Blessed : a Sketch of Girl Life. New and Cheaper Edition. Crown 8vo, 3*s.* 6*d.*

Rose Gurney's Discovery. A Story for Girls. Dedicated to their Mothers. Crown 8vo, 3*s.* 6*d.*

English Girls : their Place and Power. With Preface by the Rev. R. W. Dale. Fifth Edition. Fcap. 8vo, 2*s.* 6*d.*

Just Anyone, and other Stories. Three Illustrations. Royal 16mo, 1*s.* 6*d.*

Sunbeam Willie, and other Stories. Three Illustrations. Royal 16mo, 1*s.* 6*d.*

Sunshine Jenny, and other Stories. Three Illustrations. Royal 16mo, 1*s.* 6*d.*

STORR, Francis, and TURNER, Hawes.—**Canterbury Chimes ;** or, Chaucer Tales re-told to Children. With 6 Illustrations from the Ellesmere Manuscript. Third Edition. Fcap. 8vo, 3*s.* 6*d.*

STRETTON, Hesba.—**David Lloyd's Last Will.** With 4 Illustrations. New Edition. Royal 16mo, 2*s.* 6*d.*

WHITTAKER, Florence.—**Christy's Inheritance.** A London Story. Illustrated. Royal 16mo, 1*s.* 6*d.*

PRINTED BY WILLIAM CLOWES AND SONS, LIMITED,
LONDON AND BECCLES.

MESSRS.

KEGAN PAUL, TRENCH & CO.'S

EDITIONS OF

SHAKSPERE'S WORKS.

THE PARCHMENT LIBRARY EDITION.

THE AVON EDITION.

*The Text of these Editions is mainly that of Delius. Wher-
ever a variant reading is adopted, some good and recognized
Shaksperian Critic has been followed. In no case is a new
rendering of the text proposed; nor has it been thought necessary to distract the reader's attention by notes or comments*

1, PATERNOSTER SQUARE.

[P. T. O.

SHAKSPERE'S WORKS.

THE AVON EDITION.

Printed on thin opaque paper, and forming 12 handy volumes, cloth, 18s., or bound in 6 volumes, 15s.

The set of 12 volumes may also be had in a cloth box, price 21s., or bound in Roan, Persian, Crushed Persian Levant, Calf, or Morocco, and enclosed in an attractive leather box at prices from 31s. 6d. upwards.

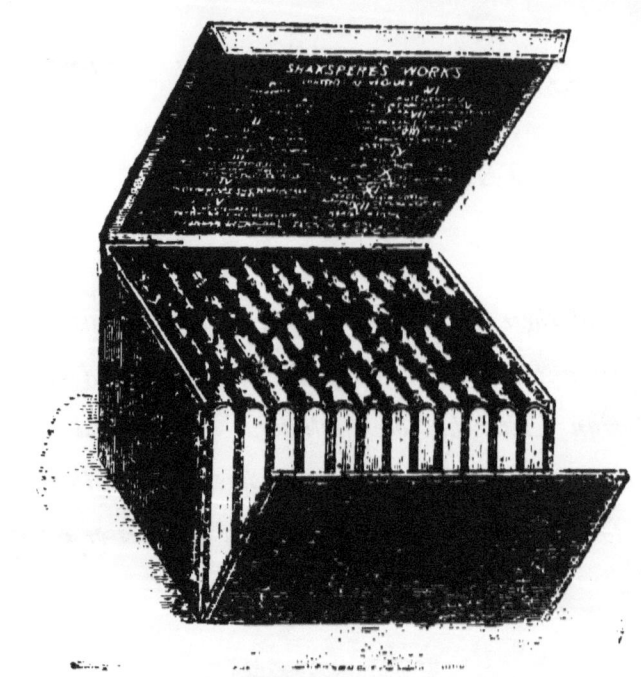

SOME PRESS NOTICES.

"This edition will be useful to those who want a good text, well and clearly printed, in convenient little volumes that will slip easily into an overcoat pocket or a travelling-bag."—*St. James's Gazette.*

"We know no prettier edition of Shakspere for the price."—*Academy.*

"It is refreshing to meet with an edition of Shakspere of convenient size and low price, without either notes or introductions of any sort to distract the attention of the reader."—*Saturday Review.*

"It is exquisite. Each volume is handy, is beautifully printed, and in every way lends itself to the taste of the cultivated student of Shakspere."—*Scotsman.*

LONDON: KEGAN PAUL, TRENCH & CO., 1, PATERNOSTER SQUARE.

SHAKSPERE'S WORKS.

SPECIMEN OF TYPE.

Salar.   My wind, cooling my broth,
Would blow me to an ague, when I thought
What harm a wind too great might do at sea.
I should not see the sandy hour-glass run
But I should think of shallows and of flats,
And see my wealthy Andrew, dock'd in sand,
Vailing her high-top lower than her ribs
To kiss her burial. Should I go to church
And see the holy edifice of stone,
And not bethink me straight of dangerous rocks,
Which touching but my gentle vessel's side,
Would scatter all her spices on the stream,
Enrobe the roaring waters with my silks,
And, in a word, but even now worth this,
And now worth nothing? Shall I have the thought
To think on this, and shall I lack the thought
That such a thing bechanc'd would make me sad?
But tell not me : I know Antonio
Is sad to think upon his merchandise.
    Ant. Believe me, no : I thank my fortune for it,
My ventures are not in one bottom trusted,
Nor to one place ; nor is my whole estate
Upon the fortune of this present year :
Therefore my merchandise makes me not sad.
    Salar. Why, then you are in love.
    Ant.   Fie, fie !
    Salar. Not in love neither? Then let us say you
    are sad,
Because you are not merry ; and 'twere as easy
For you to laugh, and leap, and say you are merry,
Because you are not sad. Now, by two-headed
    Janus,
Nature hath fram'd strange fellows in her time :
Some that will evermore peep through their eyes
And laugh like parrots at a bag-piper ;
And other of such vinegar aspect

www.ingramcontent.com/pod-product-compliance
Lightning Source LLC
Chambersburg PA
CBHW030108030726
47498CB00007B/2295